Deb Stratas

Producer & International Distributor
eBookPro Publishing
www.ebook-pro.com

A BURNING LONDON SKY
Deb Stratas

Website: debstratas.com

ISBN 9798866860944

A Burning London Sky

A WWII Historical Fiction Novel

DEB STRATAS

ReadMore Press

DISCOVERING THE NEXT BESTSELLER

Sign up for Readmore Press' monthly newsletter and get a FREE audiobook!

For instant access, scan the QR code

Where you will be able to register and receive your sign–up gift, a free audiobook of

Beneath the Winds of War
by **Pola Wawer,**

which you can listen to right away

Our newsletter will let you know about new releases of our World War II historical fiction books, as well as discount deals and exclusive freebies for subscribed members.

A Burning London Sky is dedicated to my
Grandma **Wirth**, who was a loving presence
in my life. She lived far away, so unfortunately,
I didn't see her often. But she always showed me
great love and kindness. The character of Alice
is named and modeled after her.

I miss you, Grandma!

Glossary

- **A spot of** – a small amount of something.
- **Ack-ack guns** – British World War II jargon for anti-aircraft guns.
- **Anderson shelter** – a temporary air raid shelter erected outside UK households during World War II.
- **ARP** – Air Raid Precautions, organizations dedicated to protecting civilians from air raids.
- **ATS** – Auxiliary Territorial Service.
- **Barrage balloon** – a large, tethered balloon used to defend ground targets against aircraft attacks.
- **Biscuit / bikkie** – unlike an American biscuit, a British biscuit is a hard or crisp cookie.
- **Bits and bobs** – an assortment of random items.
- **Blighty** – Britain (informal).
- **Brolly** – umbrella (shortened).
- **Chuffed** – pleased or proud.
- **Chum** – friend.
- **Civvies** – civilian clothing.
- **Clotted cream** – a thick, heavy cream usually served on cakes and desserts such as English scones.
- **Cuppa** – a cup of tea (shortened).
- **Daft** – silly or stupid.
- **Dogfight** – an aerial battle between aircraft.
- **Fringe** – bangs.
- **Jerry** – an Allied nickname given to Germans and Germany.
- **Kip** – sleep or rest.
- **Layette** – a collection of clothing and accessories for a newborn child.
- **Lippy** – lipstick (shortened).

- **NAAFI** – Navy, Army, and Air Force Institutes.
- **Natter** – chat, talk conversationally.
- **Nippy** – a waitress who worked for the J. Lyons & Co tea shops and cafés in London.
- **Peaky** – pale or sick
- **RAF** – Royal Air Force, the British air force.
- **Scone** – a traditional British round baked good much like an American biscuit.
- **Smashing** – amazing, excellent.
- **Ta** – thank you (informal).
- **Ta ra** – goodbye (informal).
- **Tea** – besides its use to describe a hot drink infused with leaves, in the UK "tea" also refers to a light afternoon meal or snack.
- **The Tube / Underground** – the London underground transportation system (equivalent to the New York Subway).
- **WAAF** – Women's Auxiliary Air Force
- **WRNS** – Women's Royal Navy Services.
- **WVS** – Women's Voluntary Services.

CHAPTER ONE

The railcar screeched its tires as it pulled into Earl's Court station. Maggie rose tiredly to her feet and exited with the throng through the narrow doors. Ignoring the evening Londoners staking their shelter spots for the night, Maggie climbed the stairs into the June night. Gulping the fresh air, she shifted her gas mask from one shoulder to the other as she rooted around in her handbag. Bloody hell, she'd forgotten her torch. She'd have to use her instincts to find her way home in the blackout. Setting her slim shoulders, she combed a hand through her blonde hair and set off on the short walk home.

Although the London Blitz had ended, the war that was supposed to be over by Christmas 1939 waged on. Beginning on Black Saturday, London was attacked on fifty-seven straight nights. At different times, as many as 300 to 400 German aircraft flew over the coast by day, intent upon bombing London into ruin. One of every six Londoners was made homeless at some point during the Blitz, and at least 1.1 million houses and apartments were damaged or destroyed. Over 40,000 civilians had been killed, and almost every household had experienced the heartbreaking loss of a family member, either during the bombings or in active service. The Kingston household was no exception. But everyone carried on – what choice did they have?

Maggie had spent another day at the WVS mobile canteen, and couldn't even count the number of cups of tea she'd poured or buns she'd passed out.

The canteen was now parked back at Paddington Station, since it wasn't as needed to refresh the firefighters, ARP wardens, police, and other first-aid workers at live bomb sites.

Now, in June 1941, the makeup of the clientele had changed. New military recruits still rushed to the station with teary loved ones as they headed off to training camps across the country. It wasn't just men. Women in all branches of the military – ATS, WRNS, and WAAFs-hoisted their kitbags, kissed their boyfriends goodbye, and clambered up train steps as impatient whistles blew. It was a sea of khaki, blue, and green.

Returning in equal numbers were injured men, on crutches, with arms in casts, in bandages, and some with serious burns or missing limbs. Many had the dazed look of soldiers who had seen horrific things in combat that could never be unseen. They were welcomed home by hospital staff, eager mothers, and joyful wives with new babies.

But the alighting passengers that captured Maggie's attention were the refugees from European countries, huddling together. Clutching their meager belongings, they sought safety from Hitler's relentless oppression. Maggie scanned each tiny family for Micah, his parents, and sister. The Goldbachs had left London to help Micah's ailing grandfather in Paris, and had been forced to flee to the south of France when Hitler had invaded. She hadn't heard from him in months, but still held her breath each time she saw a tall, lean young man appear on the train platform. But it was never him.

Maggie's heels clicked on the pavement as she slowly made her way home. Micah. She had trouble conjuring his image after a year, but could still picture his kindly brown eyes and slow smile. The two had been friends and neighbors since childhood, and in the summer before the war had their friendship deepened. Both were shy, so they'd not spoken any love words. But they took long walks, shared poetry, and played music together as their feelings grew. Micah had asked her to write to him in France, and they had exchanged warm letters. Maggie checked the post eagerly, devouring any piece of news from him. The thin airmail papers were worn thin from constant re-reading.

Oh Micah, where are you? Are you safe? Are you thinking of me?

Micah and his family had escaped to the family farm in Toulouse. His ailing grandfather kept them in France, trying to reconstruct their jewelry business whilst trying to make something of the farm. Micah didn't share their troubles but Maggie knew times were harsh, and food scarce in occupied France.

She picked her way along familiar streets, automatically avoiding debris or broken glass from bombs. Like all Londoners, her other senses were heightened without the benefit of sight. She smelled lingering cordite from a fire in a nearby street. Clouds sailed across a sky periodically lit by a half-moon and Maggie was grateful for the intermittent light to guide her way. Although there was a chill in the air, she could smell the dampness of an earlier spring rain. Surely, this hopeful feeling meant that Micah was still alive. But when would she hear from him again?

As she turned onto Longridge Road, she heard a small squeak. She stopped and waited. She heard it again, but now it sounded more like a weak meow. She stilled again to determine where the sound was coming from. Peering into the darkness, she made out the remains of a row of townhouses that had recently sustained bomb damage. Most of the rubble had been removed but broken brick piles poked up here and there amongst burnt timbers and shards of window glass.

The meow seemed to come from one of the piles of bricks. She moved towards it, praying for some moonlight to shine the way.

"Here kitty, kitty. Here kitty, kitty," Maggie called in a low voice punctuated by kissing noises. She didn't want to frighten the little guy. She paused again, listening to see if she was headed in the right direction. Nothing.

"Here kitty, kitty. Come on, I won't hurt you. Where are you, little one?" Maggie cooed. The kitten must have been left behind after its owners were killed, injured, or evacuated.

She was rewarded with a tiny cry.

Scrabbling towards the sound, Maggie felt around the pile of bricks in front of her, heedless of the scratches to her hands and forearms. The mound was about two feet high and she pulled the bricks down seeking the kitten. Feeling nothing, she moved left and began throwing bricks and mortar off the next pile.

"Ouch," she cried aloud. A sharp pain in her right arm made her stop and straighten up. She felt blood spurting from a wound just above her elbow. Damn, some piece of steel or frame had punctured her arm. She whipped her scarf from around her neck and wrapped it tightly around the injury. The blood was already lessening although she could feel the arm pulsing. Having been trained in First Aid, she hoped she wasn't in shock.

"Meow," called the kitten, redirecting Maggie's attention. The sound was closer.

"Where are you, little chap? Can you hear me? Meow a tad louder." Maggie resumed her brick-pulling and throwing.

A cloud passed in front of the moon, leaving the sky momentarily clear. The moon cast just enough light for Maggie to scan the wreckage. Just beyond the fingertips of her left hand, she spotted two large blue eyes fixed upon her and bent to pull away the bricks and debris around the tiny face.

"It's alright, little one. I'm here to help you. Just a moment more and I'll have you free. Shhh now," Maggie soothed as she fought to rescue the trapped animal.

The clouds covered the moon again and Maggie worked in the dark, talking to the kitten the whole time. Within a few minutes, she'd freed the last rocks and rubble covering the small cat. She gently pulled out the kitten who was shaking and shivering – from cold or fear – or both.

The little kitten was barely larger than Maggie's hand. He was gray with soot, but his blue eyes looked adoringly at his rescuer.

"We need to get you home, kitty. I wonder how long you've been trapped in there."

She carefully felt the kitten's limbs and was satisfied that nothing was broken. It seemed the poor thing had been wedged into a wall of bricks and was too weak to push them away. He was probably starving too.

Maggie used her good arm to tuck the kitten inside her coat to warm him as she backed away from the bomb site. She was out of breath and rather sweaty. She was sure she looked a mess with soot and dust in her hair and on her coat. She hoped she hadn't ruined one of her last pair of stockings.

Cooing to her new friend, Maggie made it home in less than five minutes and by the time she had made it to the top of the front steps of the townhouse, she was exhausted.

"Hello, is anyone home? I have a little surprise." Maggie sat down on the bottom step of the stairs to the first floor, carefully taking out the kitten from her coat. He was purring!

"Mags, whatever is it? What's the surprise?" Maggie's identical twin sister, Tillie bounced into the foyer from the hallway. Her shoulder-length blonde hair hung in loose curls. Her brown eyes widened at the sight of her sister.

"Love, whatever has happened to you? Were you caught in a raid? You're covered in dust. Is that blood?" She rushed forward, her face a picture of concern.

"It's worse than it looks, Tils. I've rescued a kitten, and got a trifle dirty in the process."

"Let's see the little love," she knelt before her sister and reached for the dusty piece of fluff. "Aren't you adorable?"

"I heard him in the pile of rubble around the corner and I dug him out. I don't think he's injured," Maggie explained.

Tillie checked for broken bones. She was an ambulance driver in Central London and her examination was fast and thorough.

"He seems fine, but rather filthy. I wonder what color he is under all this grime. He has the loveliest blue eyes." She handed him back to Maggie and turned her keen eye on her sister.

"Now you seem a little worse for wear. Pale, in fact." She unraveled the scarf. "What happened to your arm, love?" Her voice was calm and soothing. "This cut may need stitches." She called over her shoulder. "Trev, can you come? Maggie has hurt herself."

Trevor Drummond was Tillie's new fiancé, a handsome London firefighter.

"Yes, darling, what is it?"

Trevor was tall with black hair, blue eyes, and a devastating smile. He adored Tillie and had become a firm favorite with the family. His smile turned to a serious look as he saw Tillie bent over her twin.

"It's nothing, Trev. I cut my arm rescuing this little fellow. It bled a bit, but I tied it off. I'm sure it will be fine." Maggie protested, hating all this attention.

"I think she needs stitches, Trev. Can you have a look?" Tillie gazed at her fiancé, concern clouding her brown eyes.

Trevor immediately squatted down to Maggie's level, and gently took her arm, keeping up a light banter the whole while.

"You did well to apply pressure straightaway, Maggie. You stopped the bleeding and actually, Tils – I shouldn't think she needs stitches. It's a nasty gash, to be sure, but not that deep. I say we get this girl to the morning room for a restoring cup of tea, and get her cleaned up to ensure there's nothing caught in the wound. And whoa! Who is this scrawny kitty?"

"I think I'm going to call him Robbie," Maggie replied, visibly relieved that her injury wasn't more severe. She stood up, feeling rather wobbly. "And a cup of tea would go down a treat. Is Mum in the morning room?"

Trevor and Tillie helped Maggie down the hall, where Alice Kingston sat with her customary knitting in her lap. She jumped to her feet in alarm when she saw her disheveled daughter. Explanations were swiftly made as Maggie sat on the sofa, relieved to be more comfortable.

In no time, tea and biscuits appeared. Tillie brought her first-aid kit, washed Maggie's cut, and bandaged it deftly. A bowl of warm water and a towel were produced, and little Robbie was washed and dried.

"He's gray," exclaimed Maggie with delight. And indeed, he was an adorable smoky color. "My, he can't be over six weeks old. Are you hungry, darling?" She nuzzled him.

"I've brought him a saucer of milk, Mags." Tillie placed a dish on the floor.

Maggie set him down, and Robbie took an unsteady step to lightly lap at the milk. Everyone oohed over the cute kitten.

"I guess we're keeping him, then," said Alice, only partly joking.

"Is that alright, Mum? We can put up leaflets and ask the neighbors but I doubt he has an owner. I'd love to have him," Maggie snuggled him in her lap, gently patting him.

"He's certainly making himself at home," laughed Tillie. "He's fast asleep in your lap."

"So, he is. Well, Maggie, you'll need to ask your father when he's home from his ARP duties in the morning. But I doubt he'll object to a small scrap of a kitten, love," Mum smiled.

"Thanks, Mum," Maggie stifled a yawn. "I think I need to get him sorted for the night and have a wash-up. Tillie, will you help me? I hope you don't mind another roommate?" Maggie stood up.

"Not at all," Tillie replied. "I'll see Trevor out and then rummage in the basement kitchen for a box or case for him."

Maggie threw her a grateful smile.

"Thanks everyone for your help. I hope I haven't spoiled your evening."

"On the contrary, Maggie. You've given us a spot of fun," Trevor replied gallantly. He walked hand-in-hand with Tillie to the front door, where they lingered to say their goodbyes.

Maggie climbed the stairs with little Robbie cradled in her arms. She laid him on the bed as she shed her dusty clothes, slipped on her nightdress and washed the dust and dirt from her face and hands. She couldn't do much with her hair, but she did give it a good brush as she sat at the twins' dressing table. Robbie mewed and stared at her through the mirror.

As she climbed into bed, Tillie arrived with a wooden crate filled with shredded newspaper.

"This should do him for the night, love," Tillie said with a grin. "Tomorrow you can decide where to keep the box. I just hope he doesn't cry too much tonight for his mother."

"He'll be fine with me, won't you Robbie?" Maggie murmured, as she crawled under the covers.

"So, give over, Mags. Why are you calling him Robbie?" Tillie started her own nighttime rituals.

"I just like the name, that's all," Maggie replied sleepily.

"I don't believe you for a second, Margaret Kingston." Tillie picked up the hairbrush and turned to her sister. "I bet it has something to do with Micah, doesn't it?"

But her twin was fast asleep with Robbie contentedly curled in her left arm.

Tillie stifled a yawn and finished her nightly one hundred strokes. There was never a dull moment around the Kingston household. She slid into the narrow bed next to her sister and promptly fell asleep.

CHAPTER TWO

"I suppose that's meant as an early birthday gift for you then, Maggie," her father joked over the breakfast table. His flat voice revealed the hearing injury he'd suffered in the Great War, and which kept him out of this one. To his unceasing regret. Calmly, he poured his tea from under the warm pink-and-white flowered tea cozy.

"Give over, Pops. I found the kitten, proper. You're not that easily off the hook for a gift. With a war on, I'm not expecting loads," Maggie teased with a wry grin.

"Speak for yourself, Mags," Tillie raised an eyebrow. "It's my birthday tomorrow, too. Albeit celebrating does seem rather hollow this year."

She gazed at her sister, searching for the ever-present sadness and blue smudges under Maggie's eyes.

"Have you had any word from France?" She asked hopefully.

Her parents and younger sister Katie all turned to Maggie.

"None," she replied shortly. "Micah's last letter was weeks ago. And bleak it was. He and his family are struggling to survive in Toulouse." She looked around the table with tears in her eyes. "I'm just that worried about Micah. And all of them."

The Goldbachs had left London early in the war for their native France. Micah's father had insisted on returning to help his ailing father with his small jewelry business. Samuel, Ruth, Micah, and his sister Hannah had gone to Paris, and found both the grandfather and business in poorer condition than expected. Sorting the muddle, the family were forced to flee to Toulouse in the unoccupied area of France, once the Germans had seized Paris. Antisemitism ran high, and the Jewish family believed it would be safer to stay on their grandfather's small farm in the south.

"It must be so difficult for them, love. Struggling to work a small farm, and then the grandfather slipping away. I wish there was something we could do to help," Alice spoke gently, and touched Maggie's hand.

"Thank you, Mum. Please don't feel sorry for me – or them. Micah and his family are strong. And with Grandfather's weak heart, his death was sad, but not unexpected." Maggie paused and sat up a little straighter.

"And you *can* help. Albeit English-born, Micah can't, or won't, leave his parents in such a dangerous place so isolated and alone. Hannah is almost thirteen, and she was also born here in London. Has Uncle Thomas made any inroads towards bringing her back to England?" Maggie looked hopefully toward her father.

"It's near impossible to get anyone out of France right now, poppet," Pops answered directly. "But if anyone can help, it's Thomas. We shall ask him tomorrow at supper."

Thomas was Shirley Fowler's husband, Alice's dear older sister. The couple lived at 12 Longridge Road – just down the street - since they'd been bombed out of their house during the Blitz. Thomas held a senior position in the government, so was exempt from military service. He couldn't speak of his role, but from time to time he gave the family bits of inside information that spoke of his high standing. And he seemed to have connections that could prove invaluable for Micah and his family.

"Thanks Pops," Maggie replied in a slightly raised tone so her father could hear her properly. "I'm sure he's doing his…" Maggie's voice trailed off as she wrinkled her nose. "What's that smell?"

"Oh, good gracious!" squealed Alice as she leaped to her feet. "I've gone and burnt the toast again."

"Not again, Mum. I suppose it is oatmeal then," Katie sighed. "I miss Faye's cooking."

Tillie glanced sharply at her younger sister.

"Mum's doing her best, Katie. And you understand Faye is doing her bit for the war."

Their housekeeper, Faye, had left early in 1940 to become a nurse. The family sorely missed her cooking and her steady management of their busy household. Their daily maid, Jessie, had also signed on to become a land girl, doing the heavy farm work needed as farmers signed on for active service. Judging by their letters, they were both adapting well to their new war lives. The women of the Kingston household cheerfully – mostly - took on the extra household duties besides their war work.

As the fighting continued, British tempers flared and emotions ran high. Thankfully, the Blitz had finally ended, but rationing and standing in line was still a daily hassle, with new items added to the ration as time passed. Everyone yearned for their loved ones, either in service, missing in action, or killed. It seemed no end was in sight.

"Rally on, girls. It's a beautiful June day and no bombs overhead. No oatmeal for me, Mum. I'm off to my shift. And I shan't be home for supper – Trevor and I are having an early meal and then the cinema – I'm keen to see *That Hamilton Woman*." Tillie kissed her Mum and Dad on the cheeks and bounced up the stairs. "Ta ra, everyone."

"Pops, are you about ready? I'll just pop upstairs for my things, and we can be off." Katie worked in Walter's accounting firm and they traveled together daily. She leaned over her mum and gave her a quick hug. "Sorry, Mum, for what I said about Faye. Your cooking is smashing, you make a big effort."

"It's alright, love. It's not my strong suit, but I hope I am improving – at least a tad. See you tonight." Alice smiled at her youngest daughter, a mirror of her own looks. Where the twins were tall and fair, Katie and her Mum were short with dark curls, albeit Alice's bun was streaked with gray. She'd passed on her large brown eyes and wide smile to all her children. Katie didn't have the glamorous looks of her sisters, but was cute and bubbly.

Within moments, the kitchen had been cleared by all but Maggie and her mother.

"Another cup of tea, love?" Alice held up the teapot.

"Lovely, Mum. It doesn't taste the same without sugar, but it still goes down a treat."

Alice poured them both a fresh cup and added a few precious drops of milk.

"I'm going to collect Shirl for the shopping. It always seems to go faster when you have someone to natter with." She peeked out the window. "Albeit I dare say we may be queuing in the rain today. At least it's warm." She sighed.

"Poor Shirl. She hasn't had a good war." Alice clucked. "Losing Geoffrey so early on at Dunkirk. Shirley doted on that boy. She hasn't really sprung back from that. And then getting their house bombed and wiped out during the worst of the strafing. I can't imagine losing all my precious things. My poor sister."

"It was dreadful them losing their only child," Maggie breathed. "I miss my cousin, too. Geoffrey was always a load of fun. It seems every family has been affected by this wretched war, Mum. We see it all around us, every day."

Maggie sipped her tea thoughtfully. They both thought of Kenny, the youngest of their own family – reported MIA from his naval ship, and not a word in months. But they didn't speak of him. It hurt too much.

"Mum, I'll get on with the washing up. I'm not due at the WVS for a couple of hours. You set off to Aunt Shirley's, and give her a kiss for me. You always make her laugh – or at least smile."

"Ta, love. We've got a birthday supper to get on for tomorrow, haven't we?"

"And I've a kitten to see to. Poor Robbie must be looking for his breakfast." Maggie finished the last of her tea, took the cup and saucer to the sink, and ran lightly up the steps with a small saucer of milk.

They left Alice pondering whatever she was going to do about ingredients for a birthday cake, let alone bake it herself. Shopping list in hand, she collected her brolly, shopping basket, and set off purposefully to meet up with her sister.

In the event, it was a jolly birthday meal. Alice and Shirley had combined ration coupons, and Trevor's mum, Isla had also joined in. Isla was an excellent cook, and even brought the cake, a lemon drizzle, the t wins' favorite.

Isla Drummond had become such a frequent visitor to the Kingston house she was almost family. She lived alone in the apartment where she had raised Trevor alone. Her husband had been killed in the Great War, and the mother-son duo had been inseparable since. Alice suspected she was lonelier than she let on, and welcomed her company and cooking any time.

"Aunt Shirley, this pie is lovely. What's in it?" Katie asked as they were all sitting around the dining room table. She gave her aunt an encouraging smile. They'd grown close over the years.

Everyone laughed. It was risky to inquire too deeply about wartime cooking. Housewives everywhere despaired of making normal recipes with so many shortages. They turned to the radio programs and government leaflets to try to turn dodgy ingredients into an appetizing meal.

"It's called Beef and Prune Hotpot, Tillie. We scraped together the beef, and our veg allotment of potatoes and leeks, mixed all together with the stewed prunes to make the pie. There wasn't an onion to be found, so I'm that pleased it's not too awful."

"It's more than fine, Shirl," chipped in Walter, as he spooned in Brussel sprouts alongside a mouthful of pie.

"We have masses of food, even if plain fare. For that we should be grateful," Isla smiled. She was an older version of her son with the same piercing blue eyes and tall, slender frame. Where his hair was jet-black, hers was a fading blonde, streaked with gray. She was a painter and had an artistic elegance in all she did.

Maggie glanced at her sister. Tillie nodded.

"Uncle Thomas, is there is any news concerning bringing Micah's sister Hannah from France? I'm ever so worried about her, and she is English born." Maggie chewed her lower lip.

Thomas put down his fork. He was a serious man, in his late forties, of middle height, slightly stout with brownish-gray hair, and inquisitive brown eyes.

"I have made inquiries, Maggie. That she is British and underage is an excellent start. Assuming her papers are in order as you've verified previously, and she has her parents' written permission, that should all be satisfactory." Thomas ticked down the list on his fingers.

"Walter and I are prepared to provide room and board – and love – to that sweet girl." interrupted Alice.

"Just so, Alice." Walter gave her a small smile. Maggie felt a sliver of hope.

"What gets problematic are two matters. Firstly, getting her released into our care – even temporarily – is a delicate matter." He paused. "And she's Jewish. I believe I can arrange transport for her with my French contacts. But she may be turned away when she reaches British shores."

Tillie gasped and reached for her sister's hand.

"Surely not," she objected.

"Shh, Tils. Just let Uncle Thomas finish." Maggie squeezed her sister's hand and turned back to her uncle.

"You need to understand there are a number of steps in this endeavor, Maggie. I'm fairly certain we'll manage to get Hannah released to us, but it's going to take time. And patience. I'll keep you informed as much as possible, but most probably not as often as you would like. Have faith, Maggie." He smiled his precise smile again.

"Thank you, Uncle Thomas. I seem to have developed heaps of patience, thanks to this war. Sometimes all we seem to do is wait. And queue. Just please tell me what I need to do. Micah and his parents will be proper reassured to hear we are working to get Hannah safe."

"The news from France – even unoccupied France – is disquieting. Jewish people have been forced to register with the government. Their businesses are being shut down, and they are being persecuted at alarming rates. It would be most advantageous for all of them to come back to England – as soon as possible. I cannot underscore this more strongly, Maggie. The whole family needs to escape back to England. At once." Thomas sat back.

The fall of France had been swift, unexpected, and nothing short of staggering. It began in the spring of 1940 when German forces invaded Denmark and Norway. Both fell alarmingly quickly – Denmark almost straightaway, and Norway within a matter of weeks.

Then Germany turned its sights on The Netherlands and Belgium. Drawing Allied forces in defense, Germany pressed hard against French forces, which caused massive chaos and confusion. With no Allied reserve to mount a counterattack, the German offensive trampled and overran the country, almost all the way to the English Channel, near Abbeville in record time.

Britons watched in horror, never believing Hitler could conquer

France and occupy the country less than two hundred miles across the channel.

All of this raced through Maggie's mind. The situation in France was more appalling than she could have imagined. She turned pale.

"Don't scare the poor girl, Thomas. It can't be all that bad," Shirley tried to smooth over the situation.

Thomas said nothing, but held Maggie's gaze. She nodded soberly.

"Any chance of birthday cake at this gloomy celebration?" Katie tried to lighten the mood.

The older women moved to stand, but Thomas held up a hand.

"Just one more point. This is not common knowledge yet – but I have it on reliable authority that by the end of the year, mandatory conscription will begin for women. All unmarried women and childless widows between the ages of twenty and thirty will be liable for call-up. Either that or factory work. Tillie, you'll be reserved because of your ambulance work. But Maggie and Katie – you will be called up. It's best you know now, so you may choose what branch of service in which to enlist – sooner rather than later."

The assembled party was speechless.

"So, my WVS service doesn't count," Maggie asked tentatively.

Maggie had volunteered to work with the Women's Voluntary Service early in the war. Besides knitting circles with Mum and Aunt Shirley, the WVS carried out vital war work – accompanying minor children to lodgings in the country, re-homing families who lost their homes during the bombing, sorting and handing out mountains of donated clothing, and much more.

It had been a natural fit for Maggie to work in a WVS canteen. Before the war, she and Tillie had loved their jobs as Nippies – the friendly and efficient waitresses as the ever-busy Lyons Corner House restaurants. It seemed a lifetime ago.

Maggie worked with a team of two to three other women aboard mobile WVS canteens – serving tea, sandwiches, and biscuits to firefighters, medical staff, light and heavy removal men, ARP wardens, and anyone in the thick of fighting the Blitz.

Maggie had gone to work when others ran for shelters. She never got used to it, though she spent many shifts with screaming bombers overhead, incendiaries falling on and around the van, blazing heat and roaring flames inches from the little van.

Day after day, and night after night, she had seen death, destruction and bone-crushing weariness. She had also seen the Blitz spirit – a steely determination to carry on, and to help others in life and death situations. Often at great personal risk. Surely, this was as essential to the British war effort as any enlistment to the army, navy or air force?

"To be honest, I'm uncertain how WVS work will be classified. It's quite possible that it may qualify as a reserved occupation," Thomas shrugged. "I'm forewarning you that if it doesn't, the time is now to choose which service appeals to you – before the British government decides on your behalf."

"I understand, Uncle Thomas. Thank you," Maggie stole a glance at her twin. This would require a serious conversation. Somehow the evening got warmer.

"Cake anyone?" Isla asked from the doorway. "It's still meant to be a birthday, isn't it?"

CHAPTER THREE

"That was quite the twenty-fifth birthday, sis," squealed Tillie as she plopped onto Maggie's bed. "A twin talk is sorely needed." In her pale-yellow wrapper, pin curls framed her freshly scrubbed face. She reached for the Ponds cream, applying it liberally to her cheeks, nose, chin, and forehead.

"Too right," murmured Maggie, her nose deep in Robbie's furry neck. "The meal was lovely, and Mrs. Drummond's cake was heavenly. Light as air, and so fluffy." She too was ready for bed, in well-worn flowered cotton pajamas. "So much to consider, though."

"What a bolt from Uncle Thomas. Women in uniform. What are we to do? Do you reckon we'll actually be called up to fire guns?" Tillie's eyes were wide.

"I shouldn't think so. The government has been proper resolved that women will never be in combat zones. Albeit the war must really not be going our way if women are needed to fight."

"My goodness. I didn't even take that into account," Tillie shivered despite the warm night.

"It seems like you are classified in a reserved occupation with your ambulance work. You're not considering leaving, are you?" Maggie snuggled Robbie in her lap, as she sat cross-legged on the bed.

"I don't know what to think, love. I assumed that Trevor and I would both continue in our jobs for the duration – him as a firefighter, and me driving ambulance. Or at least until we get married. Then, I'd make our home together." She blushed a little. "But now that the Blitz has finished – we hope – the work has slowed. We still get call-outs, of course, and there are ongoing air raids, but it's much quieter. And now that I'm here to look out for his mum, Trev is itching to join the Services and do his bit for England." She chewed her fingernail.

Maggie looked up at her sister.

"He wants to join the RAF as a firefighter. They need trained firefighters to help with aircraft rescues and breakout fires at the bases. It's very dangerous, Mags," her voice trembled. "You see how Jerry has targeted our airfields from the outset of the war."

Maggie sighed. Hearing a far-away siren through the open window brought home that danger lurked in every corner.

"Too right, Tils, but we've all gotten so much better at coping with air attacks, haven't we? Our defenses are improved. I should hope we've learned a thing or two since 1939. Would Trevor be stationed in England? You'd still manage to see him on leave, wouldn't you?" She thought of Micah, somewhere in France, impossibly out of touch. A stab pierced her heart.

"Presumably, yes, but with the RAF, you never know. He could be posted anywhere the Royal Air Force flies."

Maggie handed the kitten to her sister.

"I realize what you're thinking, Tillie. Colin was in the RAF, and he didn't make it. But he was a flyer. Trevor will be on the ground, and he's awfully well-trained. It's not the same."

Tillie absently patted Robbie until he purred contentedly.

"A rear gunner. Colin was a rear gunner, and he was shot down. I loved him, Mags. We were meant to be married. You know how devastated I was when I heard the news. My heart broke. You saw firsthand – you helped mend the pieces." She gulped. "And now, Trevor and I are engaged. I can't lose him, I just can't." Tears misted her eyes.

"Shh, love. I saw how much you cared for Colin. He was a lovely man and he adored you. You'll never forget him. But have faith in Trevor. He will be careful. And he is at his best helping others. He's in top form. It's not the same. He's going to be alright."

She climbed onto her twin's bed and hugged her, both of them aware there were no assurances in war.

"With Trevor all but signed up, what should I do, Mags? Should I stay put driving ambulance, or am I more useful as a driver for the Army, or in another service? I don't know what to do. Should I put off any decision until we hear more about Trevor's post?" Her words tumbled over each other.

"Maybe. What about nursing? It seems a likely next step for you with all your ambulance experience?"

"I've thought of that, Mags. But there are masses of training, and testing, and so on. Perhaps I'm naïve, but I like to think the war will end before I'm fully trained. Or Trev and I may start a baby – once we're married, naturally." Tillie sputtered a little. "All that to say, I'm baffled about which way to turn at the moment."

"You don't need to decide anything as yet, Tils. Like Uncle Thomas said, you probably have a few months until conscription and the rules are declared. And once you're married, the regulations may change. Let things settle."

She paused for a moment to think, staring out into the dark night.

"But I must decide sooner rather than later. I doubt my WVS work will be sufficient to keep me out of active service. It's quieted loads since the end of the Blitz. To be honest, serving tea and buns doesn't seem enough anymore. When the bombs were dropping every night, it felt like vital work supporting the rescue workers, police, and firefighters. Now, I need to do more."

"My, that's quite a speech for you, Mags. What branch of service are you weighing up? Surely not a factory job? As critical as that work is, I just can't see you on a line assembling airplane parts or munitions."

Maggie shuddered.

"Me neither. Maybe the ATS? You've seen the posters – *You are wanted, too! Join the ATS.* I don't want to be a cook, but perhaps office work? I have some experience in Pop's business, and I like numbers and organizing." She shrugged. "I expect they will match my skills with the jobs needed."

"My goodness. You have given this some thought, Mags. The army. With that drab khaki uniform? What's appealing about that?" Tillie's laugh filled the room.

"I'm not quite sure, really. It seems grounded somehow. Practical, useful. The WRNs and WAAFs sound more intimidating. Being in the women's navy or auxiliary air force somehow seem out of my grasp. The uniforms are more striking – especially the blue and fitted WRN kit, but I'm not joining up to look smart, am I?" Maggie tried to remain serious whilst Tillie was still giggling.

"Go on, then," Tillie replied, dumping the lump of gray kitten into her sister's lap. "I suppose I'll have to look into the ATS myself. I can't let you wear that dreadful khaki uniform on your own. Or perhaps Katie will join up with you? She'll need to settle on something before long too."

Maggie slipped under the cover, placing Robbie at the foot of the bed.

"We ought to chat to her about this soon," yawned Maggie. "But I'm done in. Happy Birthday, Tils."

Tillie turned off the light and climbed into her own bed.

"Goodnight, darling. Happy Birthday to you, too."

Tillie was soon asleep, but Maggie was restless. The constant worry of Micah and fears for Hannah never left her mind. But the talk of the ATS had stirred up old, but never-long-buried feelings of inadequacy. What she hadn't told Tillie was that the reason she chose the army was partly her belief that she wasn't good enough for the more elite services. The glamorous air force and the dangerous navy seemed out of her reach. The army felt solid, and more suitable for her. She finally fell asleep, troubled about her place in the world and worthiness to hold it.

* * *

"I've got it. It's Trev for me," Tillie called as she dashed down the stairs. He was taking her for dinner and an afternoon walk. The hall was empty, and the house was silent.

Tillie had dressed in a red and white flowered shirtwaist dress with short, puffed sleeves and a white collar. Her honey-blond hair hung in loose curls to her shoulders, and she wore her Victory Red lipstick and matching nail varnish. Her white clutch handbag complimented her small white straw hat adorned with a red ribbon. She was fresh and summery.

She answered his second knock with a smile. He was dressed casually in a light blue linen sports coat, white shirt, navy-blue pants, and casual shoes. Eyes twinkling, dimple flashing, his wicked smile made Tillie's heart flutter a mile a minute. How she loved this man!

"Hello sweetheart," he kissed her. "You look beautiful."

"Thanks, Trev. You look smashing yourself." She picked up her handbag. "Shall we go?"

"Is no one at home? I wanted to say hello to your mum." He knew the townhouse well, and started down the hallway towards the morning room.

Tillie put a hand on his sleeve to stop him. "I don't think so. No one answered when I called out. Mum may be at the shops."

He raised an eyebrow and stopped mid-stride.

"Perhaps we should just stay in then, Tils." He took her in his arms, and gave her a proper kiss.

"Now darling, someone is bound to turn up at any moment around here." Tillie broke away reluctantly.

"All right, Tils. I'm fair starving for dinner, in the event. Off we go." He gallantly opened the door, and they went out into the June sunshine.

Walking along the London streets, they were immune to the signs and ravages of war all around them. Sandbags piled against buildings, windows crisscrossed with tape to avoid glass breaking inward, craters gaping in the pavement and roads, left by bombs and shelling, and damaged buildings and apartments, either abandoned or completely burnt to the ground, everywhere. Most Londoners didn't even bother with their gas masks anymore.

Trevor and Tillie had seen it all and more. As a London firefighter and ambulance driver, both had been in the thick of the danger. Like Maggie, their work started when the air raid alarm sounded, and finished long after the all-clear. Both had seen enough death and destruction to make them sick. Rescuing burning and injured Londoners trapped in fiery buildings and under the rubble of bombed-out houses was rewarding but draining – physically, mentally, and emotionally. They both loved their work, and were a wholehearted support to each other, providing a comforting presence to confide in after horrific shifts.

Settling in a local restaurant, they swiftly ordered corned beef on toast and cold drinks. There wasn't much more on the menu, so they were content with even that. It was busy, but the couple only had eyes for each other.

"How is Maggie bearing up after what Uncle Thomas said last night? Is she hopeful about Hannah?" Trevor was concerned for his future sister-in-law.

Tillie nodded.

"She's determined to bring her here. And once Maggie has made up her mind, that's it. She will follow any lead and chase down any path to make it so. Believe it or not, she's more bothered about signing up for active service. Her mind is proper set on the ATS."

Trevor took a long gulp of his beer and gave a low whistle.

"The Auxiliary Territorial Services. That is serious. Is she thinking she might be stationed in France, and somehow find Micah and his family?"

"She didn't say, Trev, but perhaps. I should think she wants to do her bit, and perhaps it will also be a distraction. I shouldn't wonder if she wants to stay close to home for when Hannah comes. She'll be feeling protective towards Micah's little sister. I can't help thinking I should do the same. She's my twin, and we've always stuck together." She smiled nervously.

"Tillie, we've talked about this. You are already doing essential and dangerous work driving ambulance and administering first aid. And we're getting married soon if I'm not mistaken? In fact, it's way beyond time to set a date. We don't know when this war will end, but we deserve to start our life together. We shan't be able to have a big wedding, but surely, we can have a proper celebration – especially if both our mothers have their say."

Tillie laughed and sipped her lemon squash.

"I can't wait to be Mrs. Trevor Drummond. It's so hard to plan anything in these uncertain times. How about next May? I'd love a spring wedding, and maybe Micah will be home. And Kenny." She bit her lower lip.

"May 1942 has a smashing ring to it. You decide the date, sweetheart. I'm not hopeful the war will yet be over, but perhaps Kenny will be home safe, and Hannah, too. It's a large family I'm joining." He covered her hand with his larger one. "I love you, Tillie. That's a long time to wait, but with me signing on to the RAF as a firefighter, the time will fly by. Get it?" He teased as he saw the smile on her face freeze.

"Have you done it, Trevor? Come clean. Did you sign on already?"

"No, sweetheart. I wouldn't do that to you. But my aim is to tell my mum that I've decided, and sign on before the end of the month. She'll be crushed, Tils. I'll need you to cheer her up and keep her company. I'm all she's ever had." His forehead furrowed. "But I am that relieved you are here. That eases my mind so much."

Tillie's thoughts crashed around her head. Trevor gone from her day-to-day life, in danger somewhere in England, counting purely on letters and short leaves. Worrying when she didn't hear from him for weeks on end. It would be a trying time, but nothing more than millions of other women faced across the country. She straightened her shoulders and gave Trevor a reassuring smile.

"It is time, my love. Shall we go and see your mum together? I want her to know she can lean on me whilst you're away. I'm proud of you, Trev."

"You are the strongest woman I know, Mathilda Kingston. We'll get through this together. Let's finish up here and pop round Mum's flat. It makes it so much easier for me knowing you'll be here looking after her."

Tillie nodded, leaving the rest of her meal untouched. She'd lost her appetite, a ball of fear forming in her stomach.

"How brilliant to see you both," Isla was all smiles when the pair came by a short time later. "Come through," she ushered them into the warm kitchen. "Would you like tea? Have you had a lovely afternoon walk?"

"Ta, Mum. Tea would go down nicely. We've worked up a thirst walking through the park," Trevor dropped into a worn kitchen chair as Tillie sat opposite him. A warm breeze fluttered the white curtains in the small window over the sink.

"Can I help, Mrs. Drummond," Tillie offered.

"No, I've just stuck on the kettle. I've made some honey and ginger biscuits. Not the most rousing, to be sure, but with the war..." Her voice trailed off, as she shrugged.

"Mum, your baking is always tops. I may have to stuff a few in my pocket," her son reassured her.

As she fussed with the tea things, Tillie gave Trevor an encouraging smile. As Isla poured boiling water over the tea leaves in her brown teapot, Trevor took a deep breath.

"Mum, we've something to tell you." He began.

"You've set a wedding date. How marvelous. A summer wedding, I hope?" She beamed from ear to ear. She adored Tillie and couldn't wait for her to join their tiny family.

"Well, actually we were thinking May, but we haven't settled on a precise date, yet. I've left that to Tillie." Trevor sidestepped the real reason for their social call.

"May is brilliant," Isla clapped her hands. "The spring flowers will be out, and Tillie – you will be a charming bride."

"Mum, that's not what we wanted to tell you." He cleared his throat.

"You're joining up, aren't you?" She asked dully, as her smile disappeared.

"Yes, Mum, and don't fuss – please. You understood I'd been thinking about it. The RAF needs trained firefighters. We don't know when and where the Germans will attack by air again – but they will. I'm needed to help fight fires at air force bases. It's my duty, Mum. I can't stay here and fight simple fires when I'm able-bodied and ready to do more. Dad wouldn't be proud of me."

Isla stood, a trifle unsteadily.

"Excuse me. I just need a minute." She rushed to her bedroom.

Tillie looked at Trevor in alarm, as she half-stood.

Trevor shook his head.

"Just leave her for a moment."

Ten minutes later, Isla bustled back into the kitchen, tears in her eyes. But resolve was there, too.

"It's alright, Trevor. Of course, I understand. Remember what Prime Minister Churchill said:

'We shall fight on the beaches, we shall fight on the landing grounds, we shall fight in the fields and in the streets, we shall fight in the hills; we shall never surrender.'

I shall bear it, darling Trevor. You will make both me and your father proud."

Trevor jumped up to hug his mother.

"Mum, you're a brick. I'm chuffed that you see I must do this. I couldn't face myself as a man if I didn't go where I'm most needed. And our Tillie will be here to keep you company. You two can natter away making wedding plans."

Tillie smiled at her future mother-in-law.

"Trev is right. We'll stick together, won't we?"

Isla felt shaky, and fought back the lump in her throat.

"We surely will, dear. Now, who would like another cuppa? I want to hear all about this upcoming wedding."

CHAPTER FOUR

August 1941

"I'm that nervous, I hope I get it right." A young woman in an ill-fitting gray suit whispered to Maggie.

"I'm sure you'll be fine," Maggie smiled at her. She gazed around the bare waiting room at the group of young women in various stages of document completion and fidgeting. Brave-looking women in uniform peered out from posters labeled *YOU are wanted too! JOIN THE A.T.S.*

After much deliberation and discussion with her father, she'd decided to sign on with the ATS, and today was the interview.

"My name is Philippa Murley, but everyone calls me Pip. What are you hoping for?" The young woman addressed Maggie again.

Pip had curly black hair, warm green eyes, and perhaps a tad too much makeup. Her cheerful smile matched her sparkly eyes and her bust strained against her blouse.

"Hello. I'm Maggie Kingston. I'll be content with anything, but hopefully not cook. Perhaps something clerical. And you?" Maggie couldn't help but admire Pip's bubbly nature.

"I'm on cloud nine just to be getting out of the house. I'm the eldest of six kids. As long as there are no nappies, I'll be chuffed anywhere they plonk me. I work in a local shop. Where are you from? My family's in Woking."

"Nice to meet you, Pip. We're from Earl's Court. Six children – my goodness that's heaps."

An official-sounding voice interrupted them.

"Kingston. Margaret Kingston. I'm Sgt. Lockridge. Please follow me."

Maggie stood up, her heart dropping. She felt tense, her palms were clammy, and she resisted the urge to wipe them on her smart blue skirt. As she followed the stern-looking woman in uniform through to an office, Pip mouthed good luck.

Maggie nodded and disappeared behind the closed door.

A thorough medical, detailed questionnaire, interview, and ninety minutes later, Maggie was led to a side room and told to wait. She was surprised to see Pip sitting there, along with an auburn-haired girl that Maggie didn't recognize.

"Hello, Maggie. Are we in trouble?" Pip reapplied a bright coral lipstick and adjusted her hat.

Maggie took a seat next to her new friend, crossed her legs, placed her handbag neatly in her lap, and shrugged.

"I expect I did alright. I told them about my experience in the WVS and my father's office business. I suppose we'll find out soon enough."

"I'm Evelyn Chase. From Essex. Nice to meet you both. How did you get on?" The auburn-haired girl joined the conversation.

The women had just finished introducing themselves when the door opened. Sgt. Lockridge came into the room, exuding authority and competence.

"Right then. Chase, Kingston, Murley. You've all passed the entrance requirements with an A1 rating for your medicals and done well on the basic testing. I'll speak to each of you individually now. Chase?"

It was a statement, not a question. Evelyn scrambled to her feet and followed the brisk footsteps of the imposing sergeant.

"Are we allowed to speak?" Pip whispered.

"I'm not sure, but there's no one here," Maggie whispered back. "It seems we're up to scratch so far."

A quarter of an hour passed with no sign of Evelyn. Maggie and Pip waited, one sitting calmly, the other fidgeting.

At last, the door opened, and Sgt. Lockridge swept in again, calling for Maggie. Pip gave her an encouraging smile as Maggie rushed to follow.

"Sit down, Miss Kingston." Sgt. Lockridge sat behind a tidy oak desk in a small office, which smelled slightly of burnt coffee. It was a hot, August day, and the room was oppressive, despite an open window letting in a listless breeze. It didn't seem to affect Sgt. Lockridge – she looked crisp and immaculate in her khaki green ATS uniform. Black hair was pulled back into a tight bun at the nape of her neck, and she sat ramrod straight. Glancing at the papers before her, she had just a hint of a smile as she gave regarded Maggie directly.

I suppose I'll be trained to look just like this, Maggie's thought was fleeting as she sat up a little straighter.

"I'll get straight to the point. The Auxiliary Territorial Services is looking for more women to work with the anti-aircraft equipment. Our fit young soldiers are needed in combat zones, and we've been experimenting with mixed batteries on the AA sites. So far, the results have been excellent." Her smile widened a bit. "Women have performed brilliantly and done as good a job as the men. Some say even better. So, we are expanding to bring on even more women into these roles.

It is a dangerous job. If you make the grade, you will be assigned to a squadron somewhere in England. You'll receive intensive training and testing. At any stage, you may be eliminated, then re-assigned to another function within the ATS. This does not mean you've failed. It shows you don't have the requisite skills or aptitude for this demanding position.

You have a fitting background and exceptional results on the aptitude tests so far – particularly mechanical and optical problem-solving. You appear to be a suitable candidate for range-finding, predicting or spotting."

Maggie struggled to make sense of the unfamiliar terms.

"If you're interested in being considered, there are several more rigorous tests to pass. You'll be retested at a higher standard for your eyesight, hearing, and overall fitness. The most grueling tests will be to gauge your nerves. You'll be placed in an anti-aircraft simulator under attack, and will have to operate the specialized equipment whilst battling intense conditions. If you can handle the strain and pressure, you'll be passed through.

Miss Kingston, I must stress again that this is a much more dangerous position than clerk. Your AA bunker will be attacked by enemy planes. Injuries and fatalities will occur. But you will perform a vital service to the ATS and contributing significantly to the Allied war effort." She took a breath. "Do you have any questions, Miss Kingston?"

Maggie's head was spinning. Could she operate those big guns that she'd seen in the parks around London? Did she have the courage and stamina for such a demanding job? Could she do it? The old insecurities came rushing back, and she felt slightly faint. Tillie would be so much better at this. Tillie was much braver. She herself only wanted a sheltered role as a clerk.

"I wouldn't actually be firing the guns, would I, Sgt. Lockridge?" Her voice sounded tinny and small.

"No, I should have made that clear. By royal command, it is illegal for women to operate guns of any sort in wartime. You'll be on mixed teams with the men who will operate the guns, based on the vital information you provide, should you qualify."

Maggie gulped, at a loss for words. Tillie would know what to say. Maggie needed more time to think.

"This is a considerable undertaking, Miss Kingston. You have forty-eight hours to come back to us with a decision about your willingness to take this on. Then we'll test you and proceed from there. You are a bright young woman, Miss Kingston. You will do well in any ATS position. That's all. You may leave through there." She pointed to a door on the opposite wall that Maggie hadn't noticed when she sat down.

"Thank you, Sgt. Lockridge. I'm honored to be considered and will give you my answer within the allotted time." Maggie shook her hand. She felt a mad urge to salute, but merely nodded. She wasn't enlisted – yet.

Leaving the room in a daze, she didn't know what to do or think. She'd never needed a twin talk more!

But her news would have to wait.

As she got back home, she spotted Tillie sitting on the front steps - with Mum! She hurried along, willing it not to be bad news. The day seemed to get even hotter.

"Maggie, we've been waiting for you. You've a letter – from France!"

Maggie froze on the spot. Please let it be from Micah.

Tillie waved the familiar grayish airmail envelope with blue-lined framing aloft. Maggie fought not to seize it.

"News of Hannah coming to London, do you reckon?" Tillie probed, as she stood up and handed the letter to her sister. She looked fresh in a blue cotton blouse and brightly patterned dirndl skirt. Her hair was pulled back into Kirby grips.

"Hello Mum, Tillie. Would you mind dreadfully if I read this alone? I promise I'll share the contents straightaway. It's just so long since I've heard from him." Maggie's hand shook as she took the letter from Tillie. Micah's well-known handwriting scrawled across the envelope. He was alive! Or at least he was when he wrote this letter.

"Certainly, love. We understand, don't we Tillie? We are just ever so curious if he's heard anything from the local government since Uncle Thomas began his inquiries."

"Take your time, Mags. Mum and I will stick the kettle on." Tillie gave her sister an encouraging smile as they both went down to the kitchen.

Maggie nodded gratefully, and turned the letter over slowly in her hands, before climbing the steps, hanging on to the polished oak banister with trembling fingers.

Reaching her room, Maggie absently took Robbie onto her lap, as she carefully allowed herself to feel all her senses as she handled the letter. #56. She and Micah had started numbering their letters, as they often turned up out of order. The last letter she'd received was #51. She'd missed five letters! After smelling it, and running her fingers over Micah's handwriting, she slowly opened the envelope and began to read.

"Dearest Maggie,

I don't know if any of my letters are reaching you. The situation here is rather dire. More and more restrictions are placed upon us daily. It's almost impossible to find any work other than meager farming, which at least is providing us with some food for ourselves and any Jews that pass through and need shelter.

We were astonished and grateful when Papa was contacted by the local authorities to arrange Hannah's safe passage to London and into your family's loving care. As a family, we are forever in your debt. We understand she needs to be prepared to leave on a moment's notice, and we've triple-checked her documents for accuracy.

Maggie, I'm not certain if my parents will be able to leave France, even from the unoccupied zone. You'll understand that I cannot abandon them. Mama has become frail and fearful. Both my parents have lost weight, and I am sleepless worrying for their health under this persecution. I keep hope that once Hannah is safely in England, we can somehow follow shortly. I am apprehensive for our future if we don't.

My little one, I long to share more words of love and hope for you and us, but what's most urgent is to get you word of our family's total agreement and gratitude for the Kingstons taking in our little Hannah. You'll find her quieter and somewhat changed. I'm sure life home life will soon put the bloom back in her cheeks. She is highly intelligent and will prosper in school once she's settled. Take care of my little sister. Believe that you are in my heart and mind each day.

Love, Micah x"

Tears coursed freely down Maggie's cheeks as she read and re-read Micah's words. She wouldn't let him or his family down. None of them would.

Maggie placed the letter on top on the growing pile in her chocolate tin, closed it and slid it under her bed. She felt instantly cooler after washing her face and changing into a cotton shirtwaist dress decorated with sunflowers.

Did she wish Micah had expressed more words of love in this last letter? Of course, she did. She longed for a promise from him, some plans for their future. But she understood. He was serious-minded and would never give his word on a vow that he couldn't fulfill. Once he committed to her, she knew it would be forever. She must hold fast to this.

Life for him and his parents certainly sounded precarious. He had surely diminished the actual conditions under which they were straining to survive. She felt this in her bones. He didn't want to worry her and her family. It must be simply dreadful. She didn't even try to imagine how they were living. She conjured an image of their time at Brighton Beach, just before the war. They had swum in the cold sea, walked along the pebbled beach, and spoken tentatively about their feelings for each other. She sighed and put Robbie down. Patience, girl, she told herself, patience.

Running down the stairs, she pasted a smile on her face.

Tillie and Alice were sitting at the long kitchen table and had just been joined by Katie. The trio chatted casually, teacups clattering. The conversation stopped when Maggie appeared in the doorway.

"Are you alright, love," Alice was quick to ask. "Please tell us it's not bad news."

"Mum, stop," Katie interjected. "Every letter doesn't mean bad news."

Tillie had been staring steadily at her twin during this exchange.

"Have a cuppa, darling. Take your time."

Maggie sat, gathering strength to share the news. She felt exhausted.

"It's not bad news. It's good news. Micah said his parents were touched and moved by our surprising offer to help Hannah escape France and live with us. They agree wholeheartedly and await further instructions."

"That's smashing, Mags," Katie burst out exuberantly.

"Was there anything else?" Tillie asked, sensing there was more.

"Conditions are severe in France, even in the unoccupied zone. Just as Uncle Thomas forewarned us. Micah doesn't say much, but it sounds grim." She struggled with a catch in her throat.

"Oh darling, I'm so sorry," Tillie said softly. "Somehow, we'll have to get him and his parents out, once Hannah is safely here. We must." Tillie was concerned for her sister.

Maggie nodded and gulped her tea to soothe her aching throat.

"Let's keep our eyes on what's next, Maggie. We will do whatever it takes to evacuate Hannah from France, and go on from there." Alice didn't like the glum faces around the table.

Katie helped herself to a cinnamon biscuit, her dark curls drooping in the August heat.

"What about your ATS interview, Mags? I almost forgot all about it." Katie slapped her forehead.

"I nearly did, too," Maggie responded, giggling. "You won't believe it. They want me to test for working on the anti-aircraft equipment."

Maggie dropped her news and waited for the explosive response.

Which came straightaway.

"You. An ack-ack girl? That's smashing, love," Tillie enthused as she thumped her on the back.

"Well done, you," echoed her mother, albeit she looked slightly aghast. "An ack-ack-girl. My goodness. But won't that be dangerous?"

"Yes, Mum. Extremely. But they need more women for mixed batteries on the guns. I suppose women can do the job as well as men."

"Shooting guns at Nazi planes," gasped Alice. "Surely not."

"No, not shooting – but spotting and working the predictor machines, whatever that all is. I have two days to decide if I want to be considered. There's loads more testing so I may not even pass through."

"And what will you do, darling?" Tillie asked. "Are you for it?"

"I'm not certain yet. I need to…"

"Think about it," Tillie finished with a laugh. "Well do give it a proper think. You'll get it right after a time."

Maggie threw her twin a grateful look. Tillie always knew the right thing to say.

"You'll fix on the right decision, love. You always do," Mum put in the last word.

CHAPTER FIVE

" The arrangement is to meet the boat from France on a Friday. Micah will have to transport Hannah from Toulouse to the departure point at Manche, most probably by farm cart. That will consume several days, but the train is far too dangerous for Jews, especially leaving from the unoccupied territory. Supposing they arrive safely, Hannah will be smuggled aboard a fishing boat that makes the weekly journey to Bournemouth. She'll be safe once she lands and we collect her." Uncle Thomas had joined them for supper the next evening, and carefully explained the plan.

"The most perilous aspect of the journey is reaching the northern part of France undetected. And then, slipping aboard the boat. Finally, not being discovered and sent back. It won't be easy for any of them, particularly Hannah." He looked around the table at the serious faces of the Kingstons.

"When do we go to Bournemouth, Uncle Thomas?" Maggie asked, her face white as a sheet.

"My contacts in France should be able to notify me once Micah and young Hannah have reached the departure point. From there, it's a matter of waiting until the next Friday, and all being well, discovering Hannah aboard. It may take several attempts, so we must be patient."

"How will we sort it, Thomas?" Alice asked worriedly. This all sounded exceedingly dangerous.

The little group barely noticed what they were eating – corned beef, cabbage, and cauliflower – as they sat around the long walnut table in the dining room, all eyes on Thomas.

"I have business in Bournemouth, so I'll make the journey there for the next few Fridays." He turned to Maggie, who had opened her mouth to speak. "I'm sorry, young lady, but I must do this alone. I can travel faster and lighter on my own. I'll be able to collect her and bring her swiftly to London." He finally allowed himself a small smile. "And you can then welcome her Kingston-style." He sat back, the high-backed chair creaking.

"What a raft to take on board, Uncle Thomas. I didn't dream the escape would be so fraught with danger, but we trust you and your arrangements. And thank you so much." Maggie gazed intently at her uncle. "And so do Micah and his family. They realize they are asking you to undertake an enormous task."

"She's an English girl, and we need to take care of our own. I'll say no more until I have proper news to share."

"That poor girl will be frightened to death," Alice tutted. "We must make her warm and welcome when she arrives." She absently offered the cauliflower around.

"Is there a chance that she won't make it, Uncle Thomas?" Tillie asked the question which was on everyone's mind.

"Yes, there are several aspects that all need to align impeccably to secure her safe arrival. She and Micah may never make it to the departure point. They could be arrested, in point of fact."

Maggie took a deep breath to steady herself.

"As Jews, they will be in peril outside of the unoccupied zone. They must abide by extremist laws – businesses taken away, curfews, being banned from cinemas, public parks, museums, restaurants, markets, and so much more." He took a deep breath.

"But I have faith in your young man, Maggie," he continued seriously. "He'll not put his sister under needless threat. It will be a rough journey for them – likely sleeping outdoors some nights, or at the mercy of farmers along the route."

As usual under stress, Maggie turned white, whilst Tillie turned many shades of red.

"Boarding the fishing vessel is another significant risk for Hannah. The preparations have been made, but we won't see if it all runs to plan until I see her safely on English soil. The channel crossing can be trying

42

if the sea is stormy, but let's not borrow trouble. A calm night will be for the best, all around." He picked up his fork to tuck into his chilled meal.

There was a poignant silence as everyone considered the looming undertaking. Maggie was the first to break it.

"Since this is a moment for news, I have some to share," she said quietly. "As it happens, I shan't be able to accompany you to fetch Hannah. I've signed on to the Women's Auxiliary Territorial Services. And they've asked me to test for the special forces. I'm not to say more than that."

"Special forces?" Thomas' head whipped around to study his niece. "Are you talking about the Anti-Aircraft Command of the Royal Artillery?"

Shirley gasped much like her sister had done two days prior.

"The ack-ack guns? Surely not, love?" She cried.

"Aunt Shirley, I'm not meant to say, but it would be operating the equipment, not shooting. Women are prohibited by royal proclamation. But you mustn't tell a soul."

"Thank heavens for the sense of His Majesty. Women firing guns, my word," Shirley fluttered.

"Maggie, that's brilliant. Well done, you." Walter nodded at his daughter.

"Smashing, Mags, I'm ever so pleased you settled on it," Tillie winked at her twin. The two had chatted for hours about it the night before. Tillie had been the one to suggest that Maggie might be closer to Micah as the ack-ack guns were mainly stationed in London or in coastal locations facing France. As a cook or clerk, she would likely be shipped overseas to who knew where.

"I expect if the army has faith in me, I should just get on with it," Maggie replied simply.

"I don't know what to say except who would like a cuppa?" Alice fussed, pride battling with worry.

"Dear, I should think something a little stronger is in order. Do we have any brandy left in the cellar?" Walter stood.

"I believe so," Alice furrowed her brow.

"Just so," Walter lumbered out of the room, while the others got up and retired to the drawing room.

Over brandy and tea, the talk turned to Trevor.

"How is he getting on with his basic training then, Tillie?" Aunt Shirley asked.

"Pretty well, so far. The RAF base for firefighters is Weeton Barracks – north of Liverpool."

"Bit of a distance from London, but at least he's on British soil. I understand that qualifying RAF pilots are now training overseas – in America and Canada." Katie stopped short, thinking she'd put her foot in her mouth again. She had a habit of speaking before thinking.

There was a brief pause as they all thought of Colin Redwood – Tillie's RAF fiancé who had died in the Battle of Britain.

Tillie glided over her sister's remark.

"Too right. He's only a train away, albeit they are never on schedule these days." Tillie brought them back to the present. "He's not keen on early morning marches and cold wash-ups, but he's dead eager to learn new mechanical skills and methods to put out airplane fires. Apparently, it's quite a bit more complicated than routine house firefighting. Having already learned the basics during the London Blitz, he's a bit ahead of the other lads. They call him the old man. Many of them are just eighteen or nineteen."

"How long is the training?" Maggie asked.

"I should think about ten weeks, but I'm not quite sure. Then he's likely to be posted at an RAF base here in England."

"Besides putting out aircraft fires, he'll be involved with rescues, as well, I suppose?" Shirley asked, her head bent over her ever-present knitting, another pair of woolen socks for distant British soldiers.

"I expect so, Aunt Shirl. It will definitely be risky work, but he loves helping people. I've cautioned him not to take too many chances, but you know Trev. Wherever someone needs a helping hand – that's where you'll find him." Tillie put on a brave face.

"Will he get any leave before being assigned to an RAF base?" Mum asked. "We must give him a proper send-off."

"Mum, you're always looking for a pretext for a Kingston get-together," laughed Tillie.

"Well, why not?" Alice said with a shrug. "We have had little to celebrate lately."

"Perhaps when Hannah comes, we could do both," Maggie offered.

"Smashing idea," Katie agreed.

"Anyone for more tea?"

Just then the air raid signal started blaring.

"Bloody hell," Katie cried, as they all scrambled to their feet. "I supposed we were done with these nightly attacks.

"Katie, language," admonished Alice, but she was already in action, gathering her knitting, and bustling everyone out of the room.

They moved quickly, collecting torches, blankets, and assorted bits and bobs to keep them occupied in the Anderson shelter.

"It's going to be a squash with seven of us, but needs must. Everyone down the stairs, and out through the kitchen. It's a warm night, in the event." Mum rushed them, as the familiar sound of Moaning Minnie followed the little group out the back door and down into the shelter.

Two bunks had been built opposite the narrow bench, and the family and Robbie squeezed together in the tight space. The sun was still shining outside, but it was gloomy indoors – both by light and mood.

"We all thought we were done with air raids, attacks, and sheltering – especially with Hitler turning his attention towards the Soviet Union. But the war is still on, and we must fight until victory is ours, just as Mr. Churchill says. So steady on, everyone. None of us wanted our evening to end in this way, but…" Walter tried to rally their spirits.

"There's a war on," the others added miserably.

"There is indeed. Perhaps this will be a brief raid tonight."

"We must take our example from our King and Queen," Alice said, knitting needles clicking. "Just look at what happened to them in Plymouth. It was a near thing."

In March, King George VI and his consort, Queen Elizabeth, had visited the Plymouth dockyards to inspect the extensive bomb damage inflicted by Nazi warplanes. Hitler had known before the planned royal visit. However, luckily his timing had been off. Their Majesties had concluded their inspection, raising morale as they expressed their sympathy by visiting bombed-out St. Andrews Parish Church.

A fierce air attack missed the royals by mere hours as the city was attacked again.

"Just imagine if they'd only been delayed. Or stayed longer giving comfort, and then been caught out in the raid," Tillie observed gravely, shaking her head in the gloomy shelter. "It doesn't bear thinking about – we might have lost our beloved King and Queen."

"And yet, they still carry on. Staying in London with the rest of us, the Queen is a bright spot in her cheery outfits as she and the King visit newly homeless families and shattered communities. It's proper inspiring," Maggie added in her quiet way.

"And the young princesses, too," Katie chimed in. "Remember that sweet broadcast on the wireless last year. Princess Elizabeth and Princess Margaret encouraged the young evacuated children to be brave and strong?"

"Oh, that was lovely, dear," cooed her mum. "Remember how adorable they sounded saying goodnight to all the children?

'My sister is by my side and we are both going to say good night to you. Come on, Margaret.'" Katie perfectly mimicked the high-pitched voice of the fourteen-year-old princess.

"'Good night, children.'" Tillie joined in squeakily mimicking the ten-year-old Princess Margaret Rose.

"'Good night, and good luck to you all.'" Katie finished the quote before breaking into a fit of giggles.

"Katie, you're incorrigible," Aunt Shirley sighed as the shelter erupted with laughter.

"And so funny. You were spot on with that impression. You lightened the mood, thank you, love," Maggie smiled in the darkness.

"I shouldn't wonder if it wasn't the Queen herself who arranged that broadcast on the *Children's Hour*. She recognized it would boost morale no end," Tillie mused.

"I've heard tell that even Herr Hitler is afraid of her," Uncle Thomas chuckled. "It's been reported that he called her the most dangerous woman in Europe."

"That sweet lady?" Alice exclaimed.

"Make no mistake," Thomas continued. "She may appear sweet and gentle on the outside, but she has a core of iron. It's marvelous the way she supports the King. She never puts a foot wrong."

46

"No doubt," his wife agreed.

"Now that Herr Hitler has turned his sights towards the Soviet Union, perhaps these nights in the shelter will be fewer and fewer," Walter offered hopefully, in his flat voice.

"I should hope so," Alice agreed.

The British had been shocked when Germany had violated the 1939 non-aggression pact with Stalin and mounted a massive attack further east. Stalin had been frozen in disbelief, and the Germans took advantage by bringing over three million soldiers – decimating the Soviet air force and causing some initial capitulation of the Soviet front line with surprise attacks. There were even rumors now – unthinkable – of mass killings of Jews, communists, and Roma peoples. The British newspapers emphasized the Soviet resistance and skirted around the reports of persecuted shootings. It was becoming evident that Hitler was a bloodthirsty monster. It was believed that he coveted the vast expanses of the Soviet empire as future expansion land for the Aryan nation. This after conquering Yugoslavia, Bulgaria and Greece. It was almost impossible to grasp.

Thomas kept his thoughts to himself.

Everyone lapsed into their own thoughts as the evening wore on. The silence was calm but strained. Alice, in particular, had been badly affected by the nightly Blitz bombing in 1940 and 1941. She tended to startle easily, and loud noises made her jumpy. She knitted furiously, trying to push away the memories of the smells, sounds, and the appalling sights of those many nights, and worse mornings. After their own house had been hit with ear-splitting explosives, the family had timidly emerged from the shelter to find the house intact, but all the windows and doors blown off, and many of their belongings outlandishly and curiously rearranged by the sideways force of the blasts. It had taken weeks to clear away, the plaster dust settling almost as soon as it was wiped up. Please let that not happen again, she told herself over and over again.

Has Micah left the little farm with Hannah, and are they making their way across treacherous roads to the coast? Was it a wretched goodbye between Mr. and Mrs. Goldbach and their only daughter? Did they cling to each other, vowing to reunite someday? Oh Micah, if anyone could will a loved one safe, it's me sending you my most fervent desire for a journey that leaves you both unscathed. Maggie's thoughts raced around and around her head.

How can I decide which branch of the armed forces best suits me when I can hardly choose what to have for breakfast? Katie chewed the inside of her lip, fussing in silence. Tillie and Maggie were wonderful big sisters, but hard to live up to. Beautiful, accomplished, kind, and brave – Katie felt every inch the smaller and weaker sister. She'd sort out the service question another day. She couldn't cope with such a big decision on her own.

Oh Geoffrey, I miss you, Shirley turned over in her mind for the thousandth time. Being in the shelter brought back the dark days after she and Thomas had received the ghastly news that their son had died on Dunkirk Beach. My poor boy, dying whilst the German fighters and bombers attacked and shelled the stranded British Expeditionary Forces for days. Did you call for me at the end, my dear boy? I would gladly give up the remainder of my life to see you for just one day. Shirley swallowed the tears that threatened to overtake her as Thomas reached for her hand.

Just think about the wedding, Tillie told herself. Maybe early May. She couldn't wait to be Trevor's wife in every way. The love she felt for him scared her at times. It was so much more intense and overwhelming than anything she had ever felt for Colin. A stab of guilt halted her reverie. She had to stop feeling bad about her ex-fiancé. He would want her to be happy. She believed she deserved it. She wanted more than anything the time to bask in it, with her dashing soon-to-be-husband.

Lost in thoughts mingled with fear, Maggie and Tillie clutched hands, tensing the buzzing planes overhead, crashes, thumps and the searing sounds of incendiary bombs dropping over London.

The all-clear sounded about one a.m. They had heard no overhead action, so assumed it was somewhere far from them. The exhausted little group climbed out of the shelter and into the house for a few hours of precious sleep before embarking on another busy day.

CHAPTER SIX

"I will miss you so much, Mags. It shan't be the same at home without you," Tillie struggled to hold back tears as she clung to her sister.

Train whistles blew all around them at Euston Station, the grimy smell gritty and familiar. Neither of them noticed the looks people cast at the striking identical twins. It happened everywhere they went together, and they were used to it.

Maggie was determined to make this a calm farewell. The last thing she could bear was an emotional scene.

"Me too, Tils. But twins are never really separated, are they?"

"You'll write and tell me how you get on? I may just join up to find you," Tillie joked.

"I'm counting on you to help out Mum, and look after my Robbie. I'm that wretched about leaving him."

"Mags, you never told me. Why did you name that cute little kitten Robbie?"

Maggie checked her watch and picked up her bag.

"Micah sent me a Robbie Burns poem – *O My Love is Like a Red, Red Rose*. It was proper romantic, Tils. I named Robbie after him. Do take good care of him." Maggie kept to herself what a comfort little Robbie had been, keeping Micah somehow close to her.

Maggie's train pulled into the station, metal screeching against metal on the tracks.

"I will, darling and I'll write you straightaway when we hear anything more about Hannah. Do you think you'll get compassionate leave to come and settle her in?"

"I don't know Tils, but I doubt it. I'll give it a crack when the time comes. I must go, Tillie. Look after Mum and Dad and Katie," her voice broke, "and most of all that handsome fiancé of yours. We have a wedding to plan, don't we?"

As with so many hard farewells, it seemed as if Maggie were there one minute, and gone the next. Tillie gazed around the station, thinking of all the tearful goodbyes and joyous hellos experienced here every day.

She sighed, adjusted the strap of her gas mask, and determined to be cheerful. Her sister was counting on her, after all.

* * *

"Blimey, is it you, Maggie?"

Maggie heard a familiar voice as she stowed her kit bag overhead. She looked over her shoulder and was gobsmacked to see – Pip!

"Oh, how lovely - a friendly face. Are we both headed to the same destination?" Maggie didn't dare say more, mindful of the war posters cautioning against loose talk in public places.

"Here. Have a seat next to me. I'm bound for Northampton, are you?" This last was said in a whisper.

Maggie nodded and sank thankfully down, grateful not to be standing for the long journey ahead.

Pip babbled for most of the three-hour trip, requiring mostly nods and smiles from her new companion. This suited Maggie. She was not adept at small talk and wasn't keen to share her innermost secrets with a stranger – particularly on a train.

Several soldiers smoked, chatted and laughed in the crowded car. The air was blue with all the smoke. Pip struck up a conversation with one of them, giving Maggie a moment to breathe, look out the window and collect her thoughts.

"Do you reckon Evelyn will be here?" Pip asked, as they pulled into the station several hours later.

"I suppose we'll find out soon enough," Maggie smiled, as she picked up her bag and alighted from the train with the crowd.

They were efficiently rounded up by an army sergeant, who assigned them to an ancient truck for the final, bumpy leg of the journey to the training camp.

Once there, the jumbled group of men and women was greeted by Sergeant Mundy, a tall, gray-haired woman with a no-nonsense air.

"Form a queue, quickly please. Men to the right, women to the left. Right, when I call your name, step forward. I will tick you off my list and assign you to your barracks. Form a separate queue and move smartly across the field to your assigned accommodation." She waved her hand in the general direction of a row of barracks.

By the time Sgt. Mundy got to her, Maggie was a bundle of nerves. She stepped forward on wobbly legs as her name was called, and barely heard that she was assigned to Barracks A. She managed to join the proper line and found herself in a large tent alongside a half-dozen other young women, including Pip.

"Hello, I'm Joan Liddell, Hut A Leader. Drop your gear by an empty cot, and I'll take you around the camp. Upon our return, I'll show you how to make up your biscuit. Then you'll have your medical, be issued temporary kit, supper, downtime, lights out."

Maggie looked around the canvas hut. There were twelve cots, a stove in the middle of the tent, and little else. She chose the closest empty cot, which happened to be nearest the door. Pip threw her bag on the one next to hers, and the two hurried after Joan, who was fast disappearing through the wooden door.

Maggie noted the women's shower, dining hall, hospital, and what Joan called a situation tent – where the new recruits were to be tested for fitness, eyesight, and hearing.

She saw where she was meant to collect her temporary uniform, which would be swapped for a permanent one at the end of their training period, should she be accepted as an anti-aircraft operator.

She learned that a biscuit was a three-square pieces of straw-stuffed bedding, which was to be her mattress. They all watched a demonstration of how to make up their small iron cot with the biscuit, gray blankets, and a pillow.

"Crikey, they are not messing around, are they?" Pip groaned as she sunk on her cot. "I'm worn out already."

"Murley, on your feet. No talking. Over to the medical hut."

Pip jumped up straightaway.

"Yes, Ma'am," she shot back.

Further to the standard medical tests, the girls were vaccinated against typhoid and tetanus. Much to their mortification, they were then subjected to humiliating examinations for VD, parasites, rashes and lice, and declared FFI – Free from Infection.

"That was bloody degrading," Pip hissed as they stood in line to get their temporary kit. "They were that fierce were those jabs." She rubbed her arm.

Maggie was also dejected going through such a personal invasion of her body, head, and armpits. It was excruciating. She nodded, keeping her head up, hoping that it was a once-in-a-lifetime humiliation. She was later to learn that it was a monthly exercise.

Next up were haircuts. Maggie realized her shoulder-length golden hair wouldn't be permitted in the service, so bravely offered to go first. They only chopped off about four inches, but the recruits were sternly told to keep it pinned up under their caps at all times.

"Not the smartest look, but in for a penny, in for a pound," Pip shrugged philosophically, fluffing her short curls. Some of the other new recruits took it much harder, and there were more than a few tears.

"I suppose now we get kitted out," Maggie commented, as they seemed to move at lightning speed from station to station throughout the afternoon.

The standard issue included the basic ATS khaki uniform, underwear which the girls affectionately called passion killers, heavy lace-up shoes, boots and socks, tops and shorts for physical exercise, a gas mask, personal items, eating utensils, and kits for polishing shoes and buttons. And much more. Specific ack-ack kit would be provided once they passed the training. If they did.

"What's a hussif?" Pip asked as they dragged themselves back to their barrack. Their arms overflowed with their kit which they would still need to organize and neatly fold. They'd been dismissed and were off duty until the next morning.

"It's a sewing kit, silly. It's a nickname for a 'housewife.' We have to mend our own uniforms, everything really. In order to pass inspection every day. We're meant to keep a keen eye out for missing buttons, or tears of any kind." Maggie grinned at her new friend. She missed Tillie, but was happy that Pip was bunking in with her. It was always good to experience new things together with a friendly face.

"We must stick together, Kingston. You're all I've got, you daft girl." They giggled and entered the hut.

"That's me, done and dusted," declared Pip as they unpacked. They had each been assigned a small two-drawer stand next to their cots, so it took no time to unpack. Maggie could tell that tidiness was not one of Pip's strengths. Her cot and blankets were a mess, and the top of her small chest of drawers was already cluttered.

"What do you reckon so far, Maggie? Or I suppose I should call you Kingston?" Pip's smile revealed a dimple on her left cheek and even white teeth.

"I expect it's too soon to say, really. And please do call me Maggie. At least here in private. I have never worn trousers before. That will take some getting used to. And these biscuits don't have a patch on my comfortable bed at home, but I suppose we'll be that tired at night that it won't matter. Getting on alright?" She turned to her new friend.

"Well, I'm not sharing a bed with any of my brothers or sisters, so I should think it's brilliant. Ready for supper? Maybe we'll find Ev."

Maggie nodded, and the pair headed straight to the mess.

Standing in line for supper, Maggie was pleased at the portion sizes. It looked like the ATS soldiers would be well fed after what would undoubtedly be long training days. She piled her tray with fried offal, cauliflower, and spinach. A blackberry crumble and watery tea completed the meal. The women chose an empty table and quickly met Agnes, Maisie, and Barbara, and Evelyn! Pip was happy to see their London acquaintance, who had also been selected for ack-ack training by the look of it.

The tall auburn-haired woman looked to be in her early twenties. She seemed a bit shy – more timid than outgoing Pip.

"Bloody hell, Evelyn. You've got two different colored eyes."

Indeed, she had. Everyone at the table turned to examine the now-blushing woman with one green eye and one brown one.

"Give over, Pip. It's not that uncommon. My aunt is just the same – albeit it switched the other way around. Her left eye is green, and the right is brown."

"Well, I never," Pip shook her head. Maggie shuddered. She would have to get used to Pip's blunt outbursts.

Maggie sat back, sipping her tea and letting the sounds of the mess float around her. It was a mix of accents, cockney, high class, Scots, Welsh, and so many more all blended together. She supposed this was the way it was in the army, or any of the services, for that matter. It took all kinds to serve, and everyone was equal in the King's armed forces.

"Shall we take a turn around the camp before lights out? It's sure to be an early morning tomorrow," Pip suggested. "I fancy one more look-round to ensure I don't put a foot wrong tomorrow."

Maggie raised an eyebrow. This seemed uncharacteristically dutiful of her fun-loving friend.

"And to scout out the men on the base. We'll be spending masses of time together. I may just as well see what, or rather who, is on offer." She winked at Maggie.

Three quarters of an hour later, they returned to their barrack, their home for the next few weeks, and got ready for bed.

Maggie was feeling rather overwhelmed, and needed some private time to think on her first day in the army. She lay on her bed letting the buzz of chatter float around her.

Pip chattered to their nearest cot neighbor, Ada, an East End girl.

"Right, attention privates. It's lights out at half past, so nip smartly to wash up, and change into your pajamas, so you're not caught short. Pack your civilian clothes in the cases and labels provided. They'll be posted to your homes in the morning," Joan Liddell barked at the new recruits.

"At first light, no dilly dallying. Up at once, ablutions, dress in uniform, and present yourselves for inspection and drill." She gave the orders for the rest of the short evening and day ahead.

The room buzzed with the women chatting about what was about to happen to them next.

"And no talking after lights out. That's all."

The women hurried to obey the orders.

Maggie took out her sketch pad and pencil to draw a picture of the inside of the hut, as the others headed to wash holding their sponge bags, while a few were unpacking, and others chatting with their new friends.

After a quick wash, Maggie put on her crisp new khaki pajamas, and scrambled into bed. She hoped to scribble a note to Tillie, but didn't have the time. A more important letter needed to be penned.

"Dear Micah,

I'm writing this from an ATS training camp 'somewhere in England.' I hope I'm allowed to say even that. It's been a feverish day, from my last farewell to Tillie at the rail station, which seems an age ago, to the camp initiation all day. It's all rather difficult to take on board.

I'm on an iron cot, resting on my new biscuit – which is rather less comfortable than my bed at home with Robbie. I expect it will be a breeze to make up in the morning, which is a good thing, as it will be an early start.

You won't believe it, but the shopgirl I met at my first interview is also training for the same special job. Her name is Pip Murley. She is from London, and cheerful as can be. She will keep me on my toes, I'm certain of it.

I have a full set of kit, which will take me some time to sort and fig-ure what goes with what, and how it all fits together.

They've cut our hair, which isn't too awful, at least for me. Some of the girls are quite distraught.

I should think having these women all on top of each other is going to be a challenge. I'm not sure how much time I'll have on my own, but I suppose we'll be kept rather hard at it. It's noisy as can be, and some girls have stuffed cotton balls in their ears so they can sleep – it's that loud.

Tomorrow is an early start with inspection and drill, which sound ominous. Then perhaps some testing and special training – I dare not say more.

I have heard no word about Hannah's arriving as of yet. At night, I can't stop imagining the pair of you trudging in dangerous conditions to arrive at your embarkation port. Dear Micah, I so hope you are both safe. I can't help wishing you'd be arriving alongside little Hannah, yet I realize this isn't possible. I long to see you.

Please trust we will all take proper care of her. I'm sorry I won't be there to take charge of her myself, but Mum, Tillie and even Aunt Shirley will fuss over her, no doubt.

I know not when this letter will reach you, or under what circumstances, but I will never stop writing.

I must go now, the lights will be out any minute, and I'll be plunged into darkness in a strange room.

I promise to send you a sketch or two in my next post.

All my love,
Maggie xx"

CHAPTER SEVEN

It seemed as if Maggie had just closed her eyes when bright lights and the loud voice of their hut team leader abruptly woke her from a deep sleep.

"On your feet, girls. Drill practice in twenty minutes."

Groggy recruits rubbed their eyes in the dark and struggled to orient themselves.

As Joan repeated her commands, Maggie rolled back the thin blankets, and sat up, blinking. Realizing where she was, she jumped out of bed, arranging her blanket and bedclothes into three neat piles; she put on her new uniform, and took her place with the other girls in line for a quick wash.

The sun was barely up when the recruits from Huts A and B assembled on the field. Sgt. Mundy was already there; ready to put them through their paces. For the next ninety minutes, Maggie snapped to attention when ordered, standing ramrod straight. Learning to march was practiced for quite some time, as some girls got their hands and feet jumbled, and knocked into each other. Maggie soon learned to raise her left hand, and lead with her right foot when commanded *right turn* and the opposite for a *left turn*, both at a ninety-degree angle. This was called either a left or right march. They drilled repeatedly until it became almost automatic to turn and march on command, alternate arms swinging in the air. Maggie perspired in the warm khaki uniform and longed for a cup of tea and some breakfast.

"Who knew left and right would be such a trial?" Ev puffed as they were dismissed from drill and sent to the mess hall. "I dare say I learned how to walk eighteen years ago, but it seems I didn't know what I was doing."

"And we have to do it again every day whilst in training," Pip whined. "And physical training as well."

"I suppose it's to instill a sense of military discipline in all of us. So that we can perform by instinct when necessary. I take heart that we are receiving the same basic training as all the forces – with the same aim of victory."

"Blimey, Maggie. It's a bit early for such a patriotic speech, isn't it?" Pip teased.

"Sod off, Murley," Maggie scolded. "We're all here for the same purpose, aren't we? For now, I'm so hungry I could eat almost anything, including rations."

Maggie and her friends waited in the long mess tent line for watery tea, powdered eggs, and toast. She was scarcely halfway through, when Sgt. Mundy burst into the mess and ordered the girls from Huts A and B outside for vision and hearing tests.

"They don't give us half a chance, do they?" Pip moaned, as she gulped the last of her tea.

Maggie decided silence was safest, so she merely nodded.

Two long tables had been set up outside.

"Sound off in threes and form queues," Sgt. Mundy ordered. The girls quickly complied.

"Today, you'll be tested for vision and hearing. Some of you will be eliminated straightaway, and the ATS will find other duties for you. As the training progresses, it will get harsher, and more of you will fail. By the end of the training, only a few of you will still stand with me. Do your best and good luck."

Maggie and Pip exchanged worried looks.

The hearing test was simple. Maggie had to pinpoint the locations of various pings coming at her on a round target.

The vision test had three parts. Besides a standard eye test, Maggie was tested for color-blindness and lastly, had to identify various objects while military doctors recorded her accuracy and speed. She was uncomfortable being watched, but tried to concentrate. She kept thinking of her brother Kenny, who had been reported MIA from the Navy in 1941. I'm doing this for you, Kenny, she told herself.

After her tests, Maggie and her group of eight were ordered to another tent for their first lecture with the other trainees, all looking slightly depleted as the day wore on. A musty smell invaded her nostrils, as she sat on a hard wooden bench. She was slightly surprised to see men, but then remembered she might qualify for a mixed battery, so the gunners needed training too.

Sgt. Mundy stood facing the group, next to a blackboard. IT ISN'T EASY TO SHOOT DOWN A PLANE was written in large block letters.

Using a wooden stick, she read the statement aloud, pointing at each word on the board, clearly relishing her repeated introduction.

"With a field gun whilst sitting still, shooting at a fixed target, mathematically you can only expect to hit once in a hundred rounds." She paused for effect, as the men and women scribbled in their army-issue notebooks.

"Atmospheric conditions and changes in how the charge burns cause this rather low hit rate. But it's even more difficult with anti-aircraft fire. The target is not sitting still. It could move anywhere up to 300 mph, and will constantly alter its course. If the target – a plane – is flying high, it may take twenty to thirty seconds for the shell to reach it, so the gun must be laid a corresponding distance ahead. Add to this that the range must be determined so that the fuse can be set, AND all of this must be done continuously so that the gun is always laid in the correct direction.

When you are ready to fire, the plane is actually two miles away – even if the engine roar sounds as if it's directly overhead. And, the gunners may have to aim at a point two miles even further to hit it with a shell. If the plane does not alter course or height – and it probably will – the shell may hit the plane." She paused, her audience rapt.

"To put this into a perspective that some of you may understand, it's like hitting a pheasant with a rifle in the dark. And, perfectly coordinated teamwork is essential. Anyone man – or woman – can ruin the shot, albeit inadvertently."

"Seems rather a merry chase," muttered a young man in the back.

"Did you have something to say, soldier?" Sgt. Mundy snapped, turning to the offending interrupter.

"Sorry, Ma'am. I just wondered how often the AA guns hit their targets," a short soldier with reddish hair stood to attention. A giggle rippled through the group.

"At ease. In fact, I was just coming to that. Would it surprise you to learn that during the entirety of 1940 – just last year – AA batteries shot down 444 enemy aircraft? This sum doesn't include the probables – airplanes that were shot and then limped out over the coast and crashed into the sea."

The young soldier gave a low whistle.

"Sorry, Ma'am," he repeated. "That's smashing."

"On behalf of all our anti-aircraft batteries, I thank you. May I continue?" Sgt. Mundy retorted sarcastically.

The tent rumbled in suppressed laughter, as the private nodded, and sat down, blushing to the roots of his red hair.

"During the first two years of the war, AA batteries shot down just on 600 enemy planes over English skies. In contrast, in the same time period, fighters destroyed 3,900. That means that guns bring down one plane for every six brought down by fighters. The numbers range month to month of course, but that's still an impressive figure, wouldn't you agree?"

A sea of faces nodded. Pip elbowed Maggie, who ignored her.

"You may be questioning how does our record stand up to the Germans? This is difficult to pinpoint. Particularly because our planes tend to fly lower to ensure better accuracy, thereby making themselves easier targets. What I can say is that our *known* bomber losses are lesser than the enemy's *known* losses, taking proportion into account.

What I can also tell you is that the German respect and fear for our AA fire has grown. And the number of planes shot down is not the only measure of the effectiveness of anti-aircraft success."

She moved to the blackboard and wrote another statement; TO DISTURB THE AIM, AND DETER THE FAINT-HEARTED. Again, she punctuated each word by tapping on it with her stick.

"This is why you are here. To make it as difficult as possible for the enemy to fire on us. To rattle their concentration and instill a loud commotion to distract them. We don't know – and we'll never know – how many enemy bombers have turned tail because of the muscle and force of our AA fire and presence.

All of this may sound exciting, even thrilling. And yes, at times it can be. But it's also exceptionally dull. You may wait months, even years before encountering enemy bombers and actually shoot the guns. Yet, you'll be expected to be on high alert and readiness at all times, in anticipation of an attack at any moment. Finally, when a target appears, it may only be for a few seconds. Or it may be too high and out of range. Or if our own aircraft are too close, you won't be permitted to fire at all.

The conditions are grueling – being at instant readiness at all times – day or night, maintaining the equipment to a high standard, all in addition to daily drills, PT, training, and any other duties the King's army sees fit to assign to you," Sgt. Mundy paced and stared intently at her audience.

"I should hope by now, you realize the seriousness of the responsibility that may be handed down to you – if you meet the mark. You've been identified as having the potential to perform this vital role. Don't let me, the ATS or His Majesty down." She paused again for effect.

"Now, you are dismissed for dinner, after which we will delve into the specifics of the equipment and how to operate it."

The girls quietly headed to another hearty meal, chatting about the serious job they'd been tasked with.

The sun burned down as the day progressed and Maggie wiped her brow. Her woolen uniform felt itchy.

Her group of eight was marched to a field where concrete bunkers were dug about four feet into the ground.

"We'll start with spotting. I'm going to explain how it works. Pay attention. Ask questions. You must understand exactly how this equipment operates. Lives depend on it. Understand?" Sgt. Mundy was in her element.

"Yes, ma'am," the girls yelled loudly.

On a tripod stood a piece of equipment about three feet long. It had an eyepiece on one end and a thick pair of binoculars attached to the middle. Another pair of binoculars sat on a nearby table.

"This is called an identification telescope. You'll work in teams of three. One of you will use the standard binoculars for the initial aircraft spotting. The second will spot using a searchlight. Number three will use the eyepiece to identify the type of plane, and then work the heavy-duty binoculars, following the target along a horizontal line." She stopped for a moment, seeing confused faces.

"You'll be attending daily lectures – and one of the key topics is aircraft identification – both ours and theirs. You'll soon recognize by sight and sound which aircraft are approaching. Now, to continue – the third spotter will call out the plane's position on the line to the women working the next post. Questions?"

"Will we always be on the same post?" A short, blonde soldier tentatively asked.

"It depends," responded Sgt. Mundy crisply. "At first, it's vital that you all learn every station. During an air attack, you will be assigned posts as needed. Depending on your skills, you may be designated to one piece of equipment more than another." She nodded at the recruit.

"Next is the predictor machine. Two of you will work this piece of equipment, which means monitoring the gauges which track height and speed of incoming aircraft, factoring in atmospheric conditions. Then you'll compile the figures and calibrate the plane's position as it flies toward a target spot. This tells the shooting crew the length of fuse required on the anti-aircraft gun."

"Will we be shooting the guns, ma'am?" another girl from the back asked.

"No, that's illegal. Only the men will operate the actual guns. You will work in mixed teams, and your roles are just as critical to the entire operation. Now, as I was saying, once you've made the calculation, you will notify the fifth team member who will call it out to the men."

She clapped her hands.

"Now, each of you get familiar with all aspects of both machines. Turn on the spotlight, look through the binoculars and familiarize yourself with all the gauges on the predictor. I'll start testing you in fifteen minutes." She smiled wickedly. "And then we'll commence with timed testing."

Maggie wanted to groan, but wiped a bead of sweat from her brow, and re-adjusted her helmet.

For the next three hours, the recruits sprinted from post to post, spotting and predicting to timed testing. Sweat poured down Maggie's face, neck and back as she worked the circuit with the rest of the girls.

Finally, it all ended and Maggie dragged herself, placing one foot in front of the other as she and Pip made their slow way back to their hut.

"I can't even think straight, I'm that tired," Pip tucked a limp strand of hair behind her ear.

"Too right, Pip," Maggie agreed, trying to muster up a smile. "I had the best of intentions to write letters home tonight, but I'm not sure I can even pick up a pen."

But after a speedy wash-up, she wrote a brief letter to Tillie for the morning post. She shared her training experience and urged her sister to write back with news of home and little Robbie. She was too weary to be homesick, but she missed her little soft bundle of gray fur purring next to her.

The same training continued for a week, with the new recruits gaining speed and confidence. Maggie started to believe she wouldn't be half-bad at the job and particularly liked the maths calculations and mental challenge of working the predictor machine.

A letter from Tillie turned up just when Maggie was feeling homesick.

"Darling Mags,

I miss you dreadfully, but am ever so proud of what you're doing. Our bedroom is lonely without you, but Robbie has taken to sleeping with me, which is brilliant for me and him.

Trevor and I have begun to make wedding plans. It will have to be a small do with the war and all, but I still want it to be special. Of course, you'll be my chief bridesmaid, darling. I'm not sure how we'll sort it, but I would love for you and Katie to wear pink frocks. As for my dress, it's going to have to be a borrow from somewhere, with Mum doing her best mending to make it into something proper. Thank heavens we can get a cake from Lyons.

Do write back and tell me how you are getting on with the training.

63

I should think you will be the finest ack-ack girl in the whole of Britain. We are all hoping you'll be stationed close by — isn't that selfish of us?

Sorry to tell you that Uncle Thomas has made two unsuccessful trips to the coast, and returned without Hannah. He doesn't say much, but we are all trusting she'll be with us for Christmas. I realize that's your fervent wish as well.

Katie is still uncertain about which branch of the forces she fancies. You know she can be a ditherer! She'll have to decide soon, if Uncle Thomas is right about the women's conscription coming before Christmas.

Goodbye for now, dear sister. I'm sure you'll be at the top of your group. Write soon.

Love always,
Tillie xx"

Maggie dropped the letter on her lap, wiping away a tear. Tillie's warmth jumped off the page, and Maggie felt a wave of homesickness. Poor Hannah. Where was the young girl? Stranded on the road? Turned back? She was on tenterhooks, thinking of Micah's sister in danger. Penning a quick response, she turned in early. She wasn't ready for any girl talk tonight.

For the next five days, the recruits trained extensively. Six women were already released, including several that Maggie and Pip had met the first night.

CHAPTER EIGHT

"You'll see that we've made the first cut," Sgt. Mundy hollered in her booming voice. "You lot are showing the most potential – so far. Now, on to the next level. You'll be tested with proper pilots dropping smoke grenades to simulate a more realistic combat situation."

It was a warm day, but a light drizzle sprinkled down steadily.

"Cor, won't that be a barrel of laughs," Lizzie, assigned to their team that day, muttered. "Jus like ter bloody Blitz comin down on us."

"Not quite, Private," the sergeant brusquely corrected. "There are no bombs being dispatched from these aircraft. But we will see how you operate under the more realistic sounds you'll be hearing nightly."

Maggie was assigned to the Predictor team. As the planes were signaled, three spitfires approached, and dropped their smoke grenades within fifty yards.

Lizzie, on the spotter team, called out the plane's locations. Maggie and three other women fed the information into the machine, and shouted the results to Evelyn, who had joined her team. Then Ev called them out to the gun team about fifteen yards away.

It was loud, smoky, and frightening, all at the same time. But Maggie was proud of herself for keeping calm. She found she really enjoyed working the Predictor machine, and was determined to keep at it, doing her best.

Again and again, the planes barrelled in, dropping their white smoke, simulating German bombers attacking an Anti-Aircraft site.

This went on for a few days, and Maggie was starting to feel confident on the Predictor. Eventually, Sgt. Mundy announced that their team had performed well which was high praise from their demanding leader. The girls were dismissed for supper, and happily strolled to the mess tent.

"Those simulations brought home how dangerous our role is, good and proper," Pip exclaimed over corned beef, cabbage, and potatoes. "It's going to take all our concentration to run hard like that – particularly at night."

"I suppose that's what basic training is all about. Train us until everything becomes utterly mechanical, and we act without thinking," Barbara added. She had survived the first week, but Maisie hadn't.

"My throat is throbbing from all the shouting. I suppose we'll get used that too," Ev shoved in another mouthful of cabbage.

"I just 'ope I don't panic and let down me other teammates," Lizzie added. "I can see 'ow we will get proper chummy – livin and workin tergether."

Maggie thought of Tillie, and how they often thought alike. Perhaps her ack-ack squad

friends would also read each other's minds in a similar manner. It would come in handy when on duty.

"We have to stick together, girls. Our lives, and many others, depend on it," Pip said soberly. The others nodded thoughtfully.

Maggie found her work fascinating; other aspects of army life were not as much fun. PE, for example. Thinking herself fit, the marching, push-ups, sit-ups, jumping, running, and other physical training were still exhausting and dreary. Daily inspections, and polishing boots and buttons until they shone, soon lost their charm. But Maggie cheerfully took on all her army duties and attempted to do her best. She found she liked the rules, and felt self-assured without forever being compared to her twin.

Before the final assessments, the remaining soldiers had to sit through one last lecture by Sgt. Mundy. By now, the note-taking had become somewhat boring while rather benefiting from the actual experience they had all gone through in the last weeks. The group was much smaller, and lifelong friendships had been formed.

Once again, a message on the blackboard greeted them.

PREVENT ACCURATE ENEMY BOMBING.

"I should hope by now that you realize the crucial role that Anti-Aircraft plays in winning the war. The ATS knows it, the entire British army acknowledges it, Their Majesties King George VI and Queen Elizabeth appreciate it, and all the British people will one day celebrate it."

Maggie's heart almost burst with pride hearing this. She vehemently hoped she'd made the grade, and would be selected to do her bit for King and country. She squeezed Pip's hand and gave her an encouraging smile.

"At its core, the impact of AA gunfire is to keep all enemy aircraft at a high altitude, and to deter or prevent them from flying a straight course and hitting their targets. If a plane cannot fly low or straight, it's prevented from bombing accurately. And, its chances of doing serious damage are reduced.

In London alone, at least 50% of enemy raiders have been turned back before entering the defended zones. And many of the bombers retreated almost straightaway. Take this to heart.

I appreciate some of you have ambitions to shoot down loads of enemy planes. Remember, for AA fire to actually destroy a plane, the shell must burst within 50-100 feet of the target. That's almost unachievable. Even if the shot is perfectly timed and the fuse is accurately set to burst the shell at exactly the precise place and moment, the aircraft has only to deviate slightly or jinks from its course to escape unharmed.

And lastly, never forget that a central function of AA guns is to pinpoint the exact position of the aircraft to our own fighters. Our guns can fire a round to two to draw the fighter's attention to the enemy – even when the plane is out of range.

You may believe we play second fiddle to the bombers and fighters. But the AA teams – your teams – play a fundamental role in allowing our flyers to achieve their aims, which is all for the common good.

If there are no questions, company dismissed." Sgt. Mundy laid down her stick. The tent was strangely silent, before applause started rumbling somewhere in the back. Within seconds, the soldiers stood and showed their pride and appreciation with loud clapping. For the first time, Sgt. Mundy gave a broad smile. Maggie had to hold back tears. It was a touching moment.

"That was smashing," Pip declared as they left the tent. "I never thought old Mundy had it in her to inspire us like that."

"It made me ever so proud," Maggie admitted. "I just hope all the work, lack of privacy, marching, and AA practice has been enough. I do so want to serve on the Predictor machine."

Pip hugged her.

"Have faith, love. I don't suppose they'll chuck us out at this late date."

In no time, six weeks had flown by. Maggie and the other girls were already used to the early hours, parade marching, relentless training, and mess food. Friendships were cemented, some for life, and a sense of camaraderie pervaded the group.

Of the original twenty-two girls, only fourteen made it to the end of the training. Maggie, Pip, Ev, Lizzie, and Barbara had all made it, and today they discovered where they'd be assigned after a short leave. Maggie was hoping for a London post. But if assigned to a coastal station, she'd at least be closer to Micah. There were stations in Liverpool, Dover, Southampton, Leeds, and Cornwall. She wished she'd be posted together with one of the other girls, which would make it so much easier.

Sgt. Mundy called in the trainees one-by-one. Maggie was one of the last to be summoned.

"Kingston, you've done well in your basic training. You have a steady bearing, and a head for maths. Congratulations. You'll be posted to a London base – South Thames division. Do the ATS proud. You are an official member of the Royal Artillery, and you are no longer a Private. You've been promoted to rank of Lance-Bombardier. This is the equivalent of Lance Corporal in the ATS system. You'll be given two stripes to stitch to your tunic."

She shook Maggie's hand. Maggie felt rather dazed. A Lance-Bombardier!

She thanked her CO, and rushed to compare notes with the other girls. As feared, they were scattered to different bases. Except Pip!

"I'll be with you in London, Mags," her friend cried. "I'm praying we'll have to live on base. I joined the army to get away from all the little blighters in my family." The two girls hugged close.

The next day, they were assigned their uniforms. Transport was arranged, and the girls split up, with promises to stay in touch.

Maggie and Pip both traveled on the Euston to Northampton line, but in reverse. They were both eager for a little time at home before the war became alarmingly real.

* * *

Maggie alighted from the train, feeling smart in her ATS uniform, a khaki shirt and belted tunic over a lighter khaki skirt. She was now entitled to wear the white anti-aircraft defense badge designating her as a gunner girl. She didn't think the khaki lace-up brown service shoes and thick beige stockings were becoming, but that was part of her uniform, which would prove practical. Even her underwear was khaki. She was afraid she'd be dreaming in khaki green for years to come.

"Mags!" Tillie cried. Without warning, Maggie was enveloped in a tight hug. "You've cut your beautiful hair."

Maggie pulled back and grinned at her twin.

"Darling, I didn't know you were coming. And yes, I had to get it bobbed. No hair touching the shoulders in the army." Maggie was thrilled to reunite with her cherished sister.

Linking arms, the young women made a striking pair as they strode to the tube. Honey blonde hair, large brown eyes, and warm smiles had always drawn attention to them. Now, fit and strong, they exuded youth and confidence and an unassuming glamour.

"I'm just off to my ambulance shift, but I couldn't let you be unmet at the train. Besides, I have a surprise for you outside."

Maggie's heart jumped to her throat – could it be Micah? Of course not, she chided herself. He was far away in France. She shook her head, resolved to be just as happy to see Mum and Dad, or dear Katie. She hoisted her kit over her shoulder, feeling slightly odd in these familiar surroundings with her dear sister, compared to the overwhelming intensity of the last six weeks.

They pushed through the hectic station amongst a sea of uniforms in all colors, shapes, and sizes. Injured soldiers were met by tearful families, and embarking young men and women bade farewell to loved ones.

"And here we are, ducks. Look who's come to meet you." With a dramatic flair, Tillie waved her arm at a young girl sitting on a bench. Hannah!

"Oh Maggie," the young girl sobbed, overwhelmed. She threw herself at Maggie and the two clutched each other tightly. Maggie patted Hannah's braids and gently soothed her.

"But when? How?" Maggie sputtered over the young girl's head to meet Tillie's eyes. Her sister nodded.

"All of that can wait," she replied. "Let's get home and you can tell me all about it. Are you alright?" Maggie was shocked to see how thin Hannah had become. And her face looked older than her years with a wary expression and haunted eyes.

Tillie had to get to work, so Maggie rode home with Hannah on the underground. The younger girl clung to Maggie, and they babbled about the weather and other unimportant things until they reached home.

"You look that official in your uniform, I hardly recognized you," Hannah said with awe.

"It's just me, you silly old thing," Maggie teased, desperate to keep things light.

"You can't know how glad I am to see you, Maggie. Everyone has been more than kind, but I really needed to see you."

"Of course, love. You're safe now. And I'm gasping for Mum's tea and scones. Any chance of jam, do you think?"

Hannah shook her head.

"Likely not, since jam is now on the ration. But with Aunt Alice, you never know. She's got a few treats put by, I'm quite certain."

Only Mum was home, waiting with a big smile and a fresh pot of tea.

"Oh Mum, how good it is to see you. And to drink a proper cup of tea." Maggie kissed her mother on the cheek, as they all seated themselves in the morning room.

"Darling, how long have you been in London? What can you disclose about your travels?" Maggie blissfully sipped her tea and nibbled a biscuit. She loosened her tie and kicked off her sturdy shoes.

Hannah squirmed slightly in her chair, seeming to make herself smaller.

"Take your time, love," Maggie encouraged kindly, nodding at the young girl.

"I was collected by Uncle Thomas just three days ago. It was a stormy crossing from France, but I was that relieved to be coming home, it didn't matter," Hannah began in a voice so low that Maggie strained to hear.

"I'd been waiting in Bournemouth for several weeks." She bit her thumbnail, and Maggie noticed all her fingernails were chewed to the quick. "Micah brought me from Toulouse. Papa had arranged for us to stay with friends of Grandfather. It was a squash with their entire family, but we were that grateful to have a place to stay. They had a one-year-old baby girl named Rachel. When we first got there, she ran behind her Mama's skirts and screamed when she saw me. But as we stayed so long, she came to know me. By the end, she even sat on my lap for a cuddle. I hope she doesn't miss me too much." She stopped and looked out the window.

"Go on, Hannah," Alice urged. "And remember, you're safe now."

"Before that, it took us almost a fortnight to make the road trip. We rode part of the way with a kind couple who picked us up in a cart, but we had to walk a good bit of the rest. Papa and Micah did what they could to sort safe places for us to stay, and some were brilliant. But one night, we stayed at a farm. As we neared it, a young boy ran to the road and told us that Nazis had been doing sweeps in the area, and his father, the farmer, couldn't take us in. He was afraid for us and his own family. It was too far for us to get to the next place at night. The farmer suggested we sleep in his brother's deserted barn about five miles away. We walked, staying as close to the road as possible, and used moonlight to guide us. We were so exhausted by the time we found it, we just huddled under our bundles of clothes under the hay and fell asleep. I woke up, hearing the rustle of animals in the hay – rats. I hardly slept. You know how afraid I am of mice and rats, Maggie?" She attempted a weak smile. Maggie nodded and held her hand.

"That's about it," Hannah seemed to run out of steam. "It was such a wrench to leave Micah there, but he had to look after Mama and Papa, you understand?" She put her head in her hands, and tears splashed down her face. "Saying goodbye at the dock was the second hardest thing I've ever done."

No one spoke but they all understood how hard parting from her parents had to have been.

Maggie jumped up and rushed to soothe the child.

"There, there. It's going to be alright," she crooned over and over again until Hannah's tears subsided.

After a while, Hannah dried her tears and reached into her pocket.

"I have a letter for you," she said in a shaky voice. "From Micah."

CHAPTER NINE

Hannah handed a well-worn envelope to Maggie, who almost gasped when she saw Micah's achingly familiar handwriting. She placed it in the pocket of her uniform.

"Thank you, love. Did Micah say anything else – for me? Any message?" Maggie held her breath.

"He wanted me to assure you he is well, and not to worry about him. And that the red, red rose is still alive. I asked him what he meant by that. He just smiled and said you would understand."

Maggie chuckled, a shiver running up her spine.

"I do," she replied simply, her heart brimming with love. "Now, has Mum got you settled in yet?" Maggie quickly changed the subject. Later, she would reflect on Micah's words, by herself.

The letter burned a hole in Maggie's pocket, but she resolutely waited until she was alone so she could savor every word.

The rest of the day was spent ensuring Hannah was cozy in a spare box room upstairs on the top floor, reuniting with Robbie, and helping Mum scrape together a welcome home supper.

"Darling, please help yourself to any of my clothes that fit, or Mum can mend to make fit. You're near as tall as Tillie and me, albeit you are more slender. I won't have use for any of my civvies for some time to come, so I'd be delighted if you would wear whatever suits you."

"Thank you, Maggie. That's ever so generous of you. I did bring a few things with me from France, but the dresses are well-worn and too short. Yours are most welcome."

Maggie took Hannah's hands and the two of them sat down on the narrow bed in the box room.

"Love, this is a trying time for you. I'm sure you miss your family dreadfully. And it's far from ideal that I can't be here to help you. I'm so very sorry about that." She felt inadequate to help this lovely young girl whilst away at a live ack-ack site.

"It's okay, Maggie. There's naught you can do about that. I wish you could be here more too, but there's a war on." Her face turned up in a tiny lopsided smile.

"Aha, making jokes. I suppose that's a good sign."

"Honest, Maggie. I'll be alright. Your family has been more than kind. But I'd like to write to you if that's alright?" She asked shyly.

"I should hope so. You're my sister now. I expect full school reports, and who else is going to tell me about sweet Robbie?" Maggie wished she could do more. But writing letters – that she was good at.

Maggie was happy that Hannah seemed to have bonded with Robbie. It lessened her guilt for leaving them both. Hannah's bubbly, outgoing nature would return, but it would take time. Until then, the family would support her in every way possible, to let her heal at her own pace. They'd held a small party to celebrate Hannah's thirteenth birthday. The young girl had been so moved by the homemade gifts and makeshift birthday cake. It warmed all their hearts.

After regaling the family with amusing stories of ack-ack basic training and her new friends, Maggie excused herself for an early night with a leisurely bath, comfortable soft bed, and her own blessedly quiet solitude.

Tucked up with Robbie, she at last opened Micah's letter.

"Dearest Maggie,

If you are reading this, it means that Hannah is safe with you, and for that I am eternally grateful. She has seen too much for a girl of thirteen. Your calming presence will soothe her troubled spirit.

I can't see what lies ahead for Papa, Mama and me. I grapple with the unsolvable problem of how to return to you and protect my parents at the same time. I've tried and failed to procure English papers for them. They are virtual prisoners here in France. I can't leave them, but I crave the sight of you, the scent of you, and to be with you for always.

I won't frighten you with a description of life here. It is callous and unkind, and only getting worse.

Trust that I will find the means to come to you, my little one. Somehow. Be patient. I care for you like no other. I dare not say more.

Look after Hannah. She is clever and will prosper in school. Write when you can, and please do send me a drawing or two. Post is scarce, but it may get through.

I will leave you with this beautiful poem, which can speak to my feelings for you far better than this poor writer's attempts.

One Day I Wrote her Name
By Edmund Spenser

One day I wrote her name upon the strand,
But came the waves and washed it away:
Again I wrote it with a second hand,
But came the tide, and made my pains his prey.
"Vain man," said she, "that dost in vain assay,
A mortal thing so to immortalize;
For I myself shall like to this decay,
And eke my name be wiped out likewise."
"Not so," (quod I) "let baser things devise
To die in dust, but you shall live by fame:
My verse your vertues rare shall eternize,
And in the heavens write your glorious name:
Where whenas death shall all the world subdue,
Our love shall live, and later life renew."

With my love,
Micah xx"

Maggie dropped the letter to her lap, fighting back tears. She stroked the ruby pendant necklace Micah had given her before he left for France, so long ago.

Maggie and Micah had known each other since childhood. The Goldbachs and Kingstons had been neighbors, and the children had spent holidays together with the two families. Micah and Maggie had shared their love of music and poetry. Micah played the piano beautifully, and Maggie had a beautiful singing voice. Their love budded just as the war began when they realized they had feelings deeper than friendship for each other. Separation had deepened their love through letters that had gotten more romantic. Would it survive the war? And would Micah love the real her, or did he have an idealized view that would crumble when they reunited? Was she enough for him? Maggie's insecurities bubbled up, making her annoyed with herself for not believing herself good enough and not trusting him enough.

Her heart swelled as a painful lump grew in her throat. Wistful and angry all at once, she cursed the war that kept her apart from her true love and answering these important questions.

"Bloody hell. When will this wretched war ever end?"

"And just who are you shouting at, love?" Tillie burst into their bedroom, smelling of smoke and cordite, with dirt smudges on her cheeks and in her hair.

"Oh, just myself, Tillie. I've gotten a letter from Micah, and I miss him so much." She bit her lower lip, trying to regain control.

The sisters hugged, and talked well into the night, both sharing pent-up feelings and fears about their beloved men.

But the war intruded yet again. Within twenty-four hours, Maggie was expected to report to her new ack-ack team. Mum and Pops saw her to the station.

"Mum, I'll have every other Sunday afternoon off, so I shall see you soon. And I'm here in London. Not far away at all. Please don't cry." How she hated tearful farewells.

"Yes, Maggie, love. Best foot forward, now." Alice stuck out her chin and willed her tears to stop. It was just so grim seeing off another child to war service. She hugged her tight and let her go.

Walter kissed her on the cheek.

"Start as you mean to go on, poppet, and you won't go far wrong. You'll be splendid. Goodbye."

He put an arm lightly on his wife's back as Maggie smiled one last time and boarded her train.

* * *

She reported to her new post at Thames South. Wearing her service dress, she put on her khaki uniform of cotton shirt, collar, tie, jacket, skirt, belt, stockings, cap, and sturdy tie-up shoes. As an ack-ack gunner, she had also been issued battle dress, which consisted of pants instead of the skirt. She also got a khaki denim uniform of long-sleeved shirt and pants. Between the pants, long underwear, and heavy boots that had to be polished every night, Maggie felt her femininity slip away.

Unsure, she opted for the standard ATS uniform and hoped she'd gotten it right. She'd managed the rest of the large kit (over forty items, some rather unfamiliar), including something called a teddy bear coat, which she was certain would be useful in the upcoming wintry nights out of doors. With a pang, she wondered when she'd be wearing frilly dresses and nylons again. She supposed that was the way of the army, to turn them into soldiers, stripping away their identity – male or female.

She spied Pip's friendly face, and the two chatted and linked arms as they waited for orders. Several men and women milled about and Maggie was relieved to see they were all in different uniforms.

She looked around the gun site. A command center was located behind the two guns, which pointed south. The center looked similar to the one in training – an oblong enclosure that housed the predictor, spotters' telescopes, and the height finder.

She was delighted to be assigned to an eight-person crew with Pip, two other girls and four men.

"Right then," announced a tall man in his forties. "I'm Sgt. Griffiths, your GPO – Gun Position Officer. This is my assistant Sgt. Morrow. I am in control of gun firing, observing the subsequent effects, and identifying any suspicious planes in the area. Sgt. Morrow will relay my orders to the guns, and is responsible for fire discipline." A stout, middle-aged balding man nodded at the GPO.

"Fire discipline? What's that when it's at home?" Pip whispered to Maggie. Maggie shushed and elbowed her.

"There are two units assigned to Thames South. Squadron-A has been here throughout the blitz and has seen a great deal of active service." Sgt. Griffiths nodded to a group of four men and women standing together, some smoking, others chatting casually. "They are chuffed to have you on relief.

You new lot will be Squadron-B. You'll be organized in exactly the same manner – four women as spotters and predictors, with four men firing the guns. There will also be floaters assigned to relieve you for breaks and off-duty days.

You'll be on duty for twelve hours, and off for twelve. 0700 to 1900 and 1900 to 0700. Squadron B – you'll start tonight at 1900 hours. Dismissed."

Pip and Maggie exchanged an agitated look. This war was becoming real very quickly.

The girls dropped their kit in the women's barracks, selecting adjoining metal cots. It all seemed familiar.

"I hope that stove blasts out some heat. The last one just bilged out black smoke. We're going to need it – the nights are getting cooler." Pip surveyed their new digs. "Why do these tents all smell like wet socks?" She wrinkled her nose in disgust.

"Nothing ever properly dries out from the sweat and rain, I expect. And I hope we get some real heat. It's the only warmth we've got in here. Except for piling on our coats, I suppose. But let's not bother about that until it happens. Shall we unpack a few things before dinner? We've a busy afternoon before starting our first shift tonight. And then, could we review the German aircraft identification one more time?" Maggie asked worriedly. "I want to be able to recognize enemy aircraft within seconds. Last night, I dreamt of Henkels and Messerschmidts."

Pip laughed out loud.

"You are too much, Maggie. You have memorized them all brilliantly. You can pinpoint an enemy plane in seconds. I'm the one who needs drilling."

"Give over, Pip. You have an incredible memory. I am that nervous about our first night on the guns. I don't think I can eat a thing – my stomach is doing somersaults." Maggie dropped down on her cot, chewing on her bottom lip.

"Well, the chances are mighty slim we'll even see active service tonight, love. You heard Sgt. Mundy – it's a real possibility we won't see German bombers or fighters for weeks, or even longer."

"I suppose you're right. I just want to do my job properly. I can't be the one to let down the side."

"You fuss too much, Maggie. Let's go suss out the mess and use our spotting skills to see if we can find a man under the age of forty."

Maggie pealed with laughter.

"Onward soldier," she motioned as she pulled down her skirt to straighten it, and smoothed her hair.

Their search for promising young men bore no fruit, but the girls met a few more ack-ack personnel. Maggie noticed the men's rations were bigger than theirs. Were the gunner girls meant to work less than their male counterparts did? She wondered.

After the meal, it was time for parade and drill practice. No PT today because of their late arrival to camp, but Maggie didn't miss it one bit.

At supper, Maggie and Pip wasted no time in getting acquainted with the Mixed Battery #677 personnel. Working so closely with the squadron for weeks or maybe months to come, Maggie needed to get to know them. They'd be relying on each other in life and death situations daily. She didn't realize it yet, but she'd be working with these seven soldiers for the best part of the war.

The four men were all middle-aged, and veterans of WW1 – Alfred, Gordon, Morris, and Simon. Alfred Brownlee looked to be the father of the group. He was in his mid-fifties, and had been a truck driver in Essex before the war. A family man, Alfred had three daughters, all of them in the ATS. He looked a bit gruff, but seemed calm. Maggie had a good feeling he could be counted on in an emergency.

Gordon Waltham was slightly younger, with dark bushy eyebrows and twinkling gray eyes. He had worked as a security guard in a bank in Lincolnshire. He'd lost a son in the Battle of Britain, and doted on his daughter, who was married and had two little boys. Calling himself Gordo, he would likely be the joker of the squad.

Morris Sharp was quiet but friendly. Born and raised in London, he was a second-generation baker. His shop had burnt down during the Blitz, and he'd decided to join up to get his revenge on the enemy. His wife had moved to stay with her mother in Surrey. Short, and with a large mole next to his left eye that Maggie studiously avoided staring at, he nodded and smiled at everything.

Simon Quimby was a married clerk in a law office. He proudly showed the girls a picture of his wife and son. His boy was a naval rating stationed overseas, and had played an active part in the Dunkirk rescue.

Rounding out the team were two other women – Louise Greenwood and Adeline Speck. Lou was very young, and a tiny thing. Maggie hoped she'd be up to the task. And Adeline, who swiftly asked them to call her Addy, was a cockney girl, who looked to be able to give as well as she got.

Maggie took her first shift with Squad-B that night. It was quiet, and so she got acquainted with the team a little better, which gave them all the opportunity to practice more with the equipment. She was still nervous, but she'd improve with time and repetition, wouldn't she?

CHAPTER TEN

December 1941

Walter stood up, reached over to turn off the radio, and sunk back into his easy chair.

"That's it then. America is now in our war," he said solemnly as he scanned the drawing room. Alice had put down her knitting while she listened to the BBC's Alvar Lidell. She shook her head, her grayish-brown bun shaking at the nape of her neck.

"It's awful to imagine them being bombed at Pearl Harbor. It doesn't bear thinking about, particularly those innocent civilians," she tsked. "What will happen next, I wonder?"

"It also seems the Soviets have life yet in them. Driving the Germans back from Moscow in a chaotic scramble is satisfying news as well. I daresay Hitler's forces aren't well prepared for the harsh Soviet winters." Walter couldn't contain a small smile.

"I'm that thankful the Americans are finally joining in. We've needed them for so long," Tillie's tone was intense. "Now, we will end this war soon, and all our men can come home." She tossed her blonde hair.

The little group grew silent thinking of Kenny, Maggie, Micah, and Trevor; and all the other soldiers, airmen, and sailors fighting for freedom against Hitler and the Nazis. Hannah kept her eyes on her lap, lost in her own thoughts.

Katie cleared her throat.

"It seems like the right time for me to make my own trifling declaration."

All eyes turned to the Kingston's youngest daughter.

Petite, brown-haired with freckles, Katie was a youthful version of her mother.

"I've settled on the WRNs, the navy," she announced proudly.

Alice gasped.

"Mum, I'm meant to sign up before I'm conscripted. I'm almost at the deadline, as it is. I've put it off long enough."

"You've done tremendous work volunteering with the WVS over the last two years, love. You wouldn't consider doing full days?" Alice asked, fearfully. Could she not keep even one of her children out of this wretched war?

"Mum, that won't do," Katie replied gently. "I've thrashed it out in my mind. And Pops and I have talked it over, haven't we?" She looked to her father for support.

Walter nodded.

"I considered the ATS, but I'm nothing as clever as Maggie, so I'd never make the grade for ack-ack. I never learned how to drive before the war, so I'm afraid to end up cooking in an army mess somewhere, which would be terrible – for me and them."

The little group chuckled.

Katie waved in her sister's direction.

"I'm nowhere as brave as our Tillie here. What she's encountered driving ambulance has been nothing short of astonishing. It would give me horrors. As far as the Women's Auxiliary Air Force, I suppose it's more of the same. I should think I would be of use with my clerking skills, but somehow it just doesn't appeal to me." She stopped for a moment. "Somehow, I feel I'll be closer to Kenny in the Women's Royal Navy Service. Does that sound foolish?"

Walter spoke in his quiet, methodical, and raised voice.

"Not at all, Katie. I'm proud of your choice. And we all understand. You'll do well in any branch of the service. For the record, you are brave and clever."

Tillie jumped out of her chair to hug her sister.

"You'll look smashing too, darling," Tillie joked.

The fitted navy-blue uniform with its double row of gold buttons was the most attractive and glamorous of all the women's service ones.

"Spot-on Tils. And think of all those naval men. Surely, I'll be able to find a husband, an officer perhaps, with a bit of luck." Katie's eyes twinkled. She always fancied a spot of fun and was hoping for some adventure in the months ahead.

"Just be sure it's an English officer," Walter replied gruffly.

"Oh Pops. Don't you fancy me with an American? Surely, I'll be coming across some handsome, well-fed officers from over the pond," she teased.

"Certainly not," Walter sputtered. "A fine British lad will do brilliantly."

"I'll do my best, Pops," Katie replied with a wink.

"I think you're wonderful, Katie. And ever so brave," a little voice arose from the corner of the sofa. Hannah spoke up, eyes shining, with the ever-present Robbie in her lap.

"Thanks ever so much, Hannah. I'll do my bit. It's what we must all do, isn't it?" Katie was touched by the young girl's kind words.

"Who's for a cup of tea? After such an extraordinary night, I expect we all need it." Alice rose to her feet, laying down her knitting.

"I'll help you, Mum," Tillie offered with her usual liveliness.

Alice's heart beat so fast she thought it would burst from her chest. Her hands trembled as she turned the kettle on. Another child in uniform. How would she cope? She leaned over the sink, trying to collect herself.

Tillie squeezed her Mum's shoulder.

"It'll be alright, Mum. The Americans coming over will be a turning point. 1942 will be different, you'll see."

"Aren't you the sly one, then?" Tillie slipped upstairs to Katie's room after they'd done the blackout and everyone had gone to bed. "No one knew what you were even thinking, love."

Katie lay on her bed, reading. She put down the book and smiled at her older sister.

"Come on, Tils. You've all been wondering when I would settle down and decide. Nothing like the last minute, then?"

Tillie was ready for bed, having put on her blue dressing gown and her hair in the usual pin curls. She dropped down on the bed, smiling. Hot water bottles had been placed in both their beds to fend off the December chill.

"I suppose it has to be right, doesn't it? But you don't have any daft ideas about finding Kenny or rescuing him, I suppose?"

Katie shrugged.

"Not really. I have no idea of where I'll be posted. You never know if I might come across an unidentified sailor in a naval hospital. A handsome lad who has lost his memory?" Katie twitched a loose thread on her coverlet.

"Oh darling. The chances of that are so slim. Please don't think that could really happen. You're bound to be gutted."

Katie shrugged again. As the two youngest, Katie and Kenny were close. She'd missed him terribly since he'd been reported missing in action and had cried herself to sleep many nights. During the day, she'd kept up a brave face. It didn't help anyone to be glum. The whole family ached for him.

"I suppose you're right, Tillie. But I have to join up somewhere…and soon. It might as well be the Women's Navy." She shivered and pulled the coverlet over her shoulders. It was a frosty night.

"In a way, I rather envy you. You'll likely be posted somewhere quite glamorous. And you are a wretched letter-writer. You must do better, please love?" Tillie begged her sister. "We at home count on letters more than you can imagine."

"Now, don't go getting tearful, Tils," Katie gave her a push, seeing her sister become emotional. "With the Americans in with us, it can't be long now till victory is in our reach. And life will return to normal. Won't that be bliss? And in the meantime, just think of the WRNs uniform?"

"You will look stunning, darling. Now, shall we creep downstairs for a cup of cocoa? The nights are really getting chilly."

Katie threw back the coverlet and pushed her feet into her slippers. "You're on!"

* * *

Christmas 1941 was a quiet affair. Neither Trevor nor Maggie were given leave, so it was a small group that gathered around the Kingston's dining room table. Everyone tried not to notice the empty chairs, and the less than bountiful tabletop.

The family had been elated to discover that Hannah had a knack for cooking. With the Kingston's housekeeper Faye long gone as a war nurse, the family had suffered from Alice's dubious attempts to feed them. Hannah was thorough, precise, and inventive. And she loved baking!

"This plum pudding is a marvel, Hannah dear," Alice gushed, sinking her teeth into the sweet confection. "I don't see how you sorted it with this wretched rationing."

Hannah gave her a broad smile.

"Well done, you," Isla praised. "You've got the makings of a terrific cook." This was high praise, as Trevor's mum was an excellent baker herself.

"Thank you, Aunt Alice, Mrs. Drummond. It puts me in mind of Mama, and all she taught me. Paying keen attention to the recipe, and making use of replacement ingredients when needs must, can make all the difference."

"So, how is our Maggie getting on as an ack-ack girl?" Shirley asked to fill in the sudden silence. No one wanted Hannah to feel gloomy thinking about her parents on Christmas.

"She looks proper sharp in her ATS uniform. And she is ever so dedicated. She takes her job seriously – just like everything in life," Tillie reported proudly. "She's getting a fair load of practice, and daily drills, but not much live action. At the height of the Blitz, her station had four bunkers and eight teams manning the guns around the clock. They've reduced it to just one."

"I suppose she will be deployed elsewhere before long, then." Walter added thoughtfully. "With bombing in the London area seeming to pause at the moment, she's not seeing much action overhead, is she?"

Alice's voice shook.

"Do you really think so, Walter? We just got her back from basic training. I don't want to lose two of my girls at the same time."

"She's in the army, dear. She'll have no choice as to where they send her. And you wouldn't want her to shirk her duty, would you? She's performing a vital role in the war effort," he said.

"Yes, of course you're right, dear." She straightened her shoulders. "I'm not being asked to withstand anything that thousands of other mothers aren't also facing."

This was all getting too somber for Tillie's liking.

"Mum, have you forgotten about this daughter? I need help in planning my wedding. It's only a few short months away." She smiled at the women around the table. "At this rate, I'll be wearing my ambulance uniform on my wedding day. Who has a brilliant notion of a gown for me?"

"Darling, certainly we'll help. I still have my wedding gown. It's rather old-fashioned, but with a bit of alteration, it might do," Alice rushed to propose, happy to be of help.

"Ta, Mum," Tillie replied warmly. "But I'm at least three inches taller than you. It would need major fixing up."

"I fear my dress is the same," Shirley added glumly. "We older sisters are much shorter than you and Maggie." She paused and gave a little shriek. "Our WVS group is holding a Make Do and Mend gathering next week. I'm sure one of the ladies will have something that would suit you." She beamed.

Tillie was dubious. A Make Do and Mend wedding frock didn't sound romantic or alluring in the slightest. The government initiative to help the weary public find fresh ways to adjust old clothes was a great idea. But for a wedding dress?

"What about my gown?" offered Isla slowly. "We're of a similar height, and albeit a bit old-fashioned, I should think you could make something of it. It's lacy and fitted. And white, of course. And I still have my veil."

"Mrs. Drummond, I'm gobsmacked. What a kind offer. Are you sure you would want to loan it to me? That's far too generous." Tillie's eyes opened wide.

Isla stood up, and sat next to Tillie in Maggie's empty spot, taking the younger woman's hands into her own.

"I don't have a daughter of my own. I hope one day to consider you more than a daughter-in-law." She threw a questioning look towards Alice, who nodded encouragingly. "In point of fact, I already do. I couldn't be more delighted that Trevor has chosen you for his bride. It would just be my small contribution to the day."

Tillie hugged her future mother-in-law.

"In that case, I'd be chuffed to try it on, and see what we can make of it. Thank you, Mrs. Drummond." She turned to her Mum and Aunt Shirley.

"And perhaps the Make Do and Mend group can sort dresses for Maggie and Katie? Or we can try to find something off the peg? Assuming they can get leave, I want them both to look beautiful. It's so grim trying to make a wartime wedding with all the shortages and people away. But Trevor and I want more than just a registry office ceremony in uniform."

"And you should have it, darling. We'll all do our best to make it a wonderful day – a wedding you will never forget," Alice was getting into the spirit of things. And what a welcome distraction from tearful farewells and longing for letters.

"With that, Thomas and I will take our pipes and port to the library. A special Christmas fire has been lit for the occasion and we don't want to waste it. There's more to talk about President Roosevelt and the Americans. Enjoy your organizing, ladies."

"Shall we take our tea to the drawing room and sort some plans?" Alice offered eagerly. Now this was a topic she was delighted to discuss amongst all the dreary war talk. "I'll make a tick list."

An hour later, the family reconvened to listen to the King's Christmas Message.

"I am glad to think that millions of my people in all parts of the world are listening to me now. From my own home, with the Queen and my children beside me, I send to all a Christmas greeting.

Christmas is the festival at home, and it is right that we should remember those who this year must spend it away from home. I am thinking, as I speak, of the men who have come from afar, standing ready to defend the old homeland, of the men who in every part of the world are serving the Empire and its cause with such valor and devotion by sea, land and in the air.

I am thinking of all those, women and girls as well as men, who at the call of duty have left their homes to join the services, or to work in a factory, hospital or field. To each one of you, wherever your duty may be, I send you my remembrance and my sincere good wishes for you and for yours.

…My heart is also with those who are suffering – the wounded, the bereaved, the anxious, the prisoners of war. I think you know how deeply the Queen and I feel for them. May God give them comfort, courage and hope.

All these separations are part of the hard sacrifice which this war demands. It may well be that it will call for even greater sacrifices. If this is to be, let us face them cheerfully together. I think of you, my peoples, as one great family, for it is how we are learning to live. We all belong to each other. We all need each other. It is in serving each other and in sacrificing for our common good that we are finding our true life.

In that spirit, we shall win the war, and in that same spirit we shall win for the world after the war a true and lasting peace. The greatness of any nation is in the spirit of its people. So it has always been since history began; so it shall be with us.

The range of the tremendous conflict is ever widening. It now extends to the Pacific. Truly, it is a stern and solemn time. But as the war widens, so surely our conviction depends at the greatness of our cause.

God bless you, everyone."

As the broadcast ended, the BBC played *God Save the King*. They all got up and stood in silence, each thinking of a loved one far away on this cold Christmas Day.

CHAPTER ELEVEN

February 1942

Tillie stamped her feet and rubbed her arms to fend off the cold. The train station was freezing, and Trevor's train was late. Of course.

The latest graduate of the RAF's School of Firefighting was due leave before being assigned to a unit somewhere in the United Kingdom. At least that's what Tillie hoped. Even though the bombing over Britain had eased off, there were still air attacks in the south of the country. And aircraft returning from missions over the continent that ran into trouble created lots of fires to be extinguished by qualified firefighters.

Please, please let him be stationed somewhere in England. She blew on her fingers. I can't bear the thought of him being shipped overseas.

The war had taken a nasty turn, which had brought everyone down. Singapore, a British military base and economic port in South-East Asia, had been seized by the Japanese in a surprise attack. The British had been forced to surrender, and tens of thousands of troops became prisoners of war. Tillie feverishly hoped they'd be treated well, but as the Japanese had killed thousands of civilians just three days after the surrender, there were great fears for these prisoners of war. Prime Minister Churchill had called it the worst disaster in British military history, and that was all anyone was talking about these chilly February days.

Lost in her thoughts, she almost missed the train whistle. Jumping up, she got as close to the platform as possible, straining her eyes to see Trevor's tall frame, shock of black hair, and bright smile.

Soldiers and pilots of all shapes and sizes burst out of the railway car doors, all eager to reunite with their loved ones.

Finally, she saw him! Dressed in a blue uniform with his cap set at a jaunty angle, he spotted her at almost the same moment.

"Trevor!" She called, waving frantically at him.

Within seconds, she was in his arms, as he enveloped her in a warm embrace. He kissed her hard on the lips, then stood back.

"Tillie, you are as lovely as ever," he dipped his head to kiss her again. "But your lips are like ice."

"It's freezing here in the station. Trev, I've missed you so, darling. You look fit and well."

He grinned at her, slung his kitbag over his shoulder, and squeezed her into his shoulder.

"Just early morning drills, lugging heavy equipment and mates around in exercises, and plenty of plain fare. But I've missed my girl."

Tillie raised an eyebrow and punched him in the arm as they walked out of the station.

"Fiancée, you mean? And soon-to-be wife."

"Not soon enough, darling. I've waited so long to make you Mrs. Trevor Drummond." His blue eyes flashed, his dimple twinkled, and a broad smile swept across his face.

Tillie's body hummed and throbbed with her familiar longing for him. She was constantly astounded by her feelings – deep, intense love coupled with an easiness to be around him. It was an intoxicating combination.

"As much as I want to marry you, love, I also want our day to be special – as much at it can be with this dreadful war going on and on. Plans can wait till later."

He kissed her again as they joined the line for the underground.

"And it will be extraordinary, I promise. But for now, we have forty-eight hours together before I'm posted." He held up his hand. "And don't ask me where, sweetheart. You realize I can't tell anyone until it's official."

Tillie opened her mouth and then closed it.

"That's my girl. All right, then. I can say that I should be staying in Britain – at least for the present."

"Trev, what a relief. I won't ask anymore, I promise." She beamed at him and snuggled against him for warmth. "Your mother is waiting rather impatiently at the flat with tea. It won't do to keep her waiting." Tillie looked deep into Trevor's cobalt blue eyes, willing herself to enjoy every moment of the next forty-eight hours with him. The ambulance, her family, even Singapore and the war would fade into the background for two whole days. It would all come crashing back to reality before long.

"Sounds grand, Tils. But we are going out for supper tonight – I want you to myself after all this time apart," he growled.

A delicious thrill chased up and down Tillie's spine.

"You're sure you don't mind the Corner House? I want to sort the wedding cake with my actual bridegroom present." Tillie and Maggie had both been Lyon's Nippies before the war. One benefit of the job was the promise of a free wedding cake for any current or former employees, of which Tillie planned to take full advantage. She and Maggie shared fond memories of their time at Lyons and the friends they'd met.

"Brilliant. After one of Mum's teas with homemade baked goods, we shan't be that hungry, I expect."

"Splendid, darling."

They both laughed, excited with an enticing forty-eight hours together stretching ahead luxuriously, all the while being fully aware the time would fly.

Isla was delighted to greet her only son. They caught up over tea and condensed milk cake.

"Mum, this is delicious. You must have been saving your butter and sugar rations for weeks," Trevor enthused.

"It's worth it to see you tuck in with gusto, Trevor."

Isla couldn't wipe the smile from her face.

"You are a tremendous baker, Mrs. Drummond," put in Tillie. "I adore your sweets."

"Please have another piece," Isla urged.

"No, ta, Mum. We're off to supper after a walk, right Tils?" Trevor cocked an eyebrow.

"Right. But tea was lovely. And I'll see you tomorrow at ours for lunch?" Tillie stood with Trevor.

He kissed his mum, as she forced herself not to hug him tight.

"I'll see you later tonight, Mum. Thanks for letting me kip here." He winked at her.

"Where else, I shouldn't wonder. This is your home!" Isla pretended indignance.

They all laughed, and within moments, the bright couple was gone, leaving Isla to clear away with a smile.

Being such a frosty day, the couple couldn't enjoy their walk. The wind had picked up as the afternoon slipped into early evening, whipping around them as they traipsed around the park near Trevor's flat. Large snowflakes floated and drifted around them. Still, they were happy just to be together, and chattered while huddling closely.

"Dare we sit for a moment or two or will we freeze to the bench? I want a proper kiss and cuddle." Trevor looked down at Tillie, who nodded.

The park was deserted at this late hour. Not very romantic with the sandbags piled everywhere, and no green in sight. Even if it were spring, no buds would be blooming. Every spare inch of growing space across London – England in fact – was being appropriated for growing vegetables and fruits to feed the hungry Britons. But the chilly and gray surroundings couldn't dampen their desire for each other. Amorous embraces heated them both up, Trevor kissing her until she could scarcely breathe.

"It's a good job it's so cold out here. Otherwise, I'd be trying to get inside your sturdy coat to discover what's underneath," Trevor said in a shaky voice, coming up for air.

"And I'd likely let you, darling," Tillie gazed at him with longing and tenderness.

"Alright, we'd best get a move on, then. Your nose is looking blue." Trevor kissed the end of it.

"And Alfie is expecting us," she sighed as she stood, huddled in her woolen coat.

The couple breezed into Tillie's old Corner House restaurant at Coventry and Rupert Streets. Resisting the urge to rush up the staff back steps, Tillie led Trevor into the main dining room.

"Two cups of tea to start, please," Trevor ordered as they scanned the menus. "We need something to warm us up before even thinking about food."

Tillie's rosy cheeks just enhanced her lovely look. Tonight, she'd worn her golden hair in a Victory Roll. Her dark green velvet dress hugged her curves, despite it being a pre-war frock.

"You look rather fetching tonight, Tils. Especially once we stop you from shivering."

"I'll be okay, Trev. I'm starting to thaw."

After a filling supper of spam fritters, parsnips, and peas, the pair enjoyed tea and a treacle pudding.

"So, the dresses are sorted, but that's all you need to know about that. You'll be in uniform, so that's simple enough. We're meeting the vicar at St. Luke's tomorrow. He will talk us through the service, and how it will all go on the day. We are slotted in for 11:00 a.m. ceremony time. There are two other weddings after ours, so we'll have to nip out smartly once we are man and wife." Tillie took a deep breath. She, a married woman! Imagine.

"Mum, Aunt Shirley and your mum are organizing all the food for the guests who can make it back to our house for a bare-bones wedding breakfast." Tillie methodically ticked off items on her fingers. "Everyone will save up their coupons, but I fear it may be a dismal affair of spam dressed up as mock duck or some such. And masses of garden veg to make the table look like it's crammed with food. Mum has promised some form of sausage rolls – that I will somehow be able to recognize."

"Don't look so glum, sweetheart. I won't even notice the food or drink. I'll be that happy to be married at last. And the rest of the guests will just be chuffed for a knees-up." He grinned back, showing his dazzling dimple. "And no one can identify what meat is in a sausage roll anymore, so don't bother about it."

Tillie threw him a grateful smile.

"I almost forgot. The boys at the London fire station offered to get in some pints – watery as they are – from the local pub. And somehow – a bottle or two of champagne. I'm not to ask questions on that score."

"Black market?" Tillie raised an eyebrow, then shook her head. "Never mind. On my wedding day, I don't want to know. I just want it to be special."

"And it will be, Tillie. I have my eye on the wedding night, myself."

"Me too, love. But I haven't yet told you about the flowers and the music…"

"I expect I've heard enough for now. I suppose this really is a woman's domain." Trevor sipped his tea. "I wouldn't have thought of half of that lot."

"With a war on, we must keep it simple. Even so, I want it to be memorable."

"Tillie Kingston," boomed a voice at their table.

"Alfie," Tillie jumped up and embraced her former supervisor.

"Sit with us, please," Tillie smiled at the gruff older man. He had been so kind to her when her first fiancé had been killed early in the war.

"Well, just for a moment. I was that pleased when you said you were coming in. Trevor, good to see you." The men shook hands. "How are you two getting on? You're looking fit as fleas."

"Brilliant now that we're together," Tillie answered for them both. She squeezed Trevor's hand.

"Smashing. How was your supper?"

Tillie made a face.

"It wasn't too rubbish, I suppose. We almost went to one of those new British Restaurants, but decided to give Lyons a chance," she said, eyes open wide with innocence.

"Yes, for just 9d, I hear you get a proper three-course meal," Trevor joined in. "Filling and nutritious."

"British Restaurant. I should say not," Alfie objected, his face contorting in indignation. "That's all well and good for those bombed out of their homes, or run out of ration coupons. But it's not a proper restaurant of the standard of Lyons Corner House."

Tillie's tinkled laughter merged with Trevor's guffaw.

"We're just having you on, Alfie," Tillie sputtered between laughs. "British Restaurants provide a needed service. But naught compares to Lyons."

"That's more like it," Alfie replied, slightly mollified.

British Restaurants had sprung up in 1941 to address the need for simple, inexpensive meals for those in need. The Ministry of Food, sponsored by Prime Minister Churchill, opened up dozens of restaurants, many of them in London. Some served out of central depots, or even churches or deserted school dining rooms. They performed a valuable service, and almost 200 were scattered around London. It was an excellent way to get a hot meal off the ration.

Alfie sat back, running his hand through his gray hair.

"On to more important matters. I've spoken to Chef, and we're going to make you a fine wedding cake. May 2nd, is it?"

"Yes, that's what we are planning on." Tillie looked anxiously at Trevor. Please let nothing stand in our way.

"Excellent. I can't vouch for the number of layers, but it will be a delicious fruitcake, with as close to a buttercream frosting as Chef can muster. We'll deliver it on the day."

"Thank you so much, Alfie. This means the world to us. Could you manage sending it the day before? Just to be sure, everything is all right? There will be loads of bits and pieces to pull together on the day."

"Righto, Tillie. You can count on me. And Lyons. Now, have you heard the one about the customer who confused chutney with a pickle?" Alfie was famous for his puns, most of which made his audience groan.

"Do tell us, Alfie," Tillie played along.

"It made him chuckle," Alfie roared at his own joke, turning his face a bright shade of red.

"Very funny. You haven't lost your touch, Alfie." Tillie gave him a kind-hearted smile.

Alfie beamed and turned to Trevor.

"How is the RAF treating you, young fellow? It's heartening that an experienced firefighter like yourself is keeping our planes in the sky."

"Thank you, Sir. I've just finished with my training and I'm being shipped to my new base this week. Loads of marching, drills, early mornings, PT. I expected I was in rather good shape fighting fires in London, but the RAF puts you through your paces."

"Have you been drilling firefighting itself, yet, son?"

"Oh yes," Trevor continued. "They take destroyed planes, and set them on fire again, so we can put them out. It's a tad trickier than burning buildings, but most of the methods are familiar. Except that we'll be rescuing RAF pilots, not civilians and passers-by. And lectures too, of course, but I find them dead boring. I fancy using my hands and wits to learn on the job, not from books." He obviously loved his work. Tillie, on the other hand sat quietly tense, trying not to imagine her beloved climbing into a burning aircraft to save another pilot.

"Just so," replied Alfie, as he motioned their waitress for more tea. "I should think you will do just splendidly, young man. Take good care of yourself. This young lady here has quite the soft spot for you, I reckon."

Tillie mustered a smile as she gazed around the war-worn but still elegant restaurant. It still bothered her to see gray-haired Nippies, but they were just as jolly and efficient as the younger girls had been.

"I'd best get back upstairs. I must keep an eye on the girls. You'd be surprised what they get up to if I'm not there." His deadpan expression belied the twinkle in his eye.

Trevor and Tillie said their goodbyes, and hurried home in the chilly, February night.

Mounting the steps to the front door, it burst open before Trevor could give his sweetheart a goodnight kiss.

"Tillie, you won't believe it. Kenny is alive. Kenny is alive!"

CHAPTER TWELVE

"Kenny's alive?" Tillie screamed as she pushed through the door and clutched Katie, whose face was aglow with joy. "But how?" She sputtered.

"Come through, come through. Uncle Thomas is here and can explain it much better than I can. Oh Tillie, our brother is coming home!" Katie was rosy with excitement, her eyes flashing.

Rushing upstairs to the drawing room, Tillie and Trevor found the whole family gathered, looking confused but radiant.

"Hello everyone. What's happened, Uncle Thomas?" Tillie and Trevor made cursory greetings and sat down on the nearest couch.

"Good evening, you two. Well, it's nothing short of a miracle. Your brother has been found alive in northern Africa." Even Thomas' normally calm demeanor was replaced with an unexpected elation.

Tillie clapped her hands and conjured up the youngest Kingston. Tall with the same golden hair and liquid brown eyes as the twins, Kenny had been underage when he signed up for the Navy, against his parents' wishes. Ultimately, they'd supported him in joining the fight against the Nazis. He'd been serving on the *HMS Dainty*, patrolling North African waters, when the ship had been attacked from the air, which started fires that ultimately sunk it. Kenny had been reported MIA, and the family had hoped and prayed that he'd somehow made it to safety. That was February 1941. It has been over a year since they'd heard from him.

Tillie hugged Trevor in disbelief.

"Details are sketchy at the moment, but this is what I've been told. The ship left Torbruk in the late afternoon of February 24, 1941, for a patrol alongside the *HMS Hasty*. Three planes out of Sicily, Italy approached in the early evening, strafing other targets in nearby waters. A low-flying Heinkel attacked, dropping a 250-kg bomb on the destroyer. It detonated in the captain's cabin, starting a serious fire straightaway. It spread rapidly, causing the ammunition of the stern gun to explode, perhaps a magazine blast. Commander Thomas ordered the crew to abandon ship immediately."

Shirley and Alice clutched hands. Hannah fixed her gaze on Thomas. Tillie and Trevor were spellbound.

"While abandonment was in progress, torpedo warheads began detonating and scattering fragments all around, sinking the motorboat which *HMS Hasty* had lowered to collect men in the water. *Hasty* herself, with skillful handling, came alongside *Dainty* and rescued the majority of the survivors before *Dainty* sank. The death toll amounted to sixteen, with eighteen injured and two reported missing – Kenny and one of his mates."

Alice put a hand to her mouth, thinking of her poor son, suffering through the explosion. How frightened he must have been.

"After a thorough search of the waters and surrounding area, both midshipmen were officially reported Missing in Action. Torbruk, Libya has been a major battleground. We've wrestled it from the Italians, but it's far from secure.

I've just had word from one of my naval contacts there that Kenny has been found – alive. Evidently, he and his mate Harvey Ward swam to shore, holding on to debris from the ship.

Here's where it gets a bit foggy. They were discovered on a beach by a local fisherman. Both men were delirious, with some injuries, the extent of which are unclear."

"Oh, my word," Shirley exclaimed, as she hugged her sister. Alice's eyes never left her brother-in-law's face as she sat motionless.

"Steady on, dear," Thomas soothed his trembling wife. He smiled at Alice encouragingly.

"Sadly, Kenny's mate didn't make it, succumbing to his injuries. However, Kenny survived, albeit he sustained a head injury that caused him to lose his memory. He also broke an arm. The family recognized he was a sailor, but without knowing who he was, they've nursed and cared for him until he recovered.

Just a little over a fortnight ago, his memory started returning. It's spotty, but he was able to recite his name, rank, and ship, and insisted on reporting to the local British authorities. The long and short of it is that he's returning within a month, and will continue to convalesce here at home, until declared fit for duty again." Thomas sat back.

"Surely he won't be required to go back?" Alice was aghast at the thought. She started shaking and couldn't stop, despite hugging herself tightly.

"Only if and when he is fully recovered will they redeploy him, dear. Perhaps the war will be over by then," Walter encouraged gently.

Alice nodded, gulping.

"I for one, think it's brilliant. Let's not borrow trouble, Mum. This is marvelous news, Uncle Thomas. How did you find all this out?" Tillie was almost jumping up and down with delight.

Thomas smiled and laid a finger next to his nose.

"I can't give away my sources, my dear. Rest assured I have been making inquiries for a year now, with no leads. I hadn't quite given up hope, but I'm more than relieved to bring the family such brilliant news."

"I've been hoping and praying for this moment," Katie said, her voice unnaturally hushed. "I've missed my brother so much," she wiped a tear from the corner of her eye.

"Darling, this is good news. The best. Don't be sad. We need to celebrate. Pops, what do we have in the cellar to bust open?" Tillie was grinning from ear to ear, hugging everyone in the room.

"I should think we might just have a bottle of something. I've been holding back a few bottles for the end of the war and other significant markers. I'll have a look." The weary look that Tillie hadn't realized her father had worn for the past year, seemed instantly lighter. "And yes, our son is coming home. We have so much to be thankful for." A slow smile spread across his face. He went to his wife and kissed her on the cheek. "All will be well, my dear."

Alice shook with excitement, picturing all four of her children in this room together in a matter of weeks. Would her sleepless nights finally be over? She busied herself with glasses and the drinks tray as the little family reveled in the news that they could hardly believe.

"Mum, it's almost Kenny's birthday – the 13th. It's fate. The best news ever."

A wide smile spread across Alice's face.

"The best ever."

"We must send Maggie a telegram straightaway," Tillie cried out. "She'll be over the moon."

* * *

Still, Trevor and Tillie's parting was gloomy, even though both were happy at the thought of seeing Kenny soon and having him at their upcoming wedding.

* * *

"Kingston, the GPO wants to see you," one of the girls brought Maggie the message. Maggie put down her sketchpad, abandoning her drawing of her fellow soldiers polishing their boots. She liked to send Micah drawings of her daily life in the hut.

The blood drained from her face. There were no circumstances under which this could be good news. Snatching up her cap, she jammed it on her head, shoving her loose hair up underneath it. Thanking the soldier, she was out of the hut in a few strides, and in the GPO's tent within minutes.

Waiting to be seen, Maggie ran through the list of possibilities in her mind. She dismissed her own performance. They'd had no attacks lately, and her record was clean in terms of lecture attendance, inspections, and drill.

It had to be something from home. Had something happened to Tillie on an ambulance call? Oh no. Was it Pop's health or Mum's? Had a stray bomb hit Uncle Thomas and Aunt Shirley's new home? Or Katie, had she taken ill? Maggie was frantic thinking of everything awful that might have happened back home.

She ticked through the family members in her mind. Oh dear, please let it not be Kenny. I couldn't bear to hear he's been found dead. Not Kenny, please. She started to feel sick.

"Kingston, thank you for waiting. I have a telegram for you," Sgt. Griffiths called her into the office.

Maggie took off her cap, and entered, standing.

"You may sit, Kingston, and don't look so stricken. It's good news."

Maggie let out her pent breath and sank into the hard-backed chair in front of his desk.

"Thank you, Sergeant."

He handed her the buff-colored envelope. He nodded, and she opened it as quickly as she could rip it open.

"THE BEST NEWS EVER STOP KENNY FOUND ALIVE STOP COMING HOME IN FORTNIGHT STOP ARRANGE LEAVE STOP TILLIE STOP"

Maggie read it twice and burst into tears.

"That's alright, then, Kingston. Congratulations on the splendid news. You are dismissed." The sergeant looked uncomfortable.

Maggie was mortified, and mopped her tears with her army-issue handkerchief.

"I'm so sorry, Sarg. I don't know what came over me."

He waved her away.

"Not at all, Kingston."

Maggie got the distinct feeling she couldn't get away quickly enough for the Sergeant. So, she did.

"Pip, you won't believe it. My brother is still alive. I don't know how or where, but he's alive," Maggie burst through the door of the hut.

"That's smashing, love. But how? I thought he was missing in the Mediterranean Sea?" Pip sputtered. She snatched the telegram from her bewildered friend and scanned it.

"Nothing more than that? But it must be true, love. Or they wouldn't have sent the telegram. How wonderful." Pip hugged Maggie, still looking slightly dazed.

"That's all I know. But I must ask for compassionate leave. I haven't seen my brother for a year. And now he's coming home. Oh, I hope he's not too injured. I wonder where he's been. What he's been doing. So many questions and this short telegram doesn't say much."

"But it says the most important thing, Mags. Take heart in that. Just think, you will see him in two short weeks." Pip couldn't be happier for her.

* * *

A fortnight turned into a month, but it didn't matter to the Kingston family. The day finally arrived when Kenny would come home – for good if his mum had anything to say about it.

Maggie had somehow procured compassionate leave and had a six-hour pass. Katie had been shattered when she'd received her papers for basic training and would miss her dear brother's homecoming. She had been gone a week and made everyone promise to give Kenny her love.

They decided that only the parents would meet Kenny's train so as not to overwhelm him. They turned up at the station early and waited anxiously. But it didn't matter. Once Walter and Alice saw their son, they sagged in relief. It was a poignant reunion, as the three clung together.

Tillie and Maggie had made a Welcome Home sign and waited impatiently at home for Kenny to arrive. Shirley and Thomas planned to come over later for tea. Hannah was in her room, playing with Robbie.

"Darling, it's marvelous to see you. You've given us all quite a fright," Tillie mumbled, trying to hide her shock at seeing her brother. Kenny was gaunt, his hair had grown long, and he looked older than his nineteen years. He'd grown in the last year and looked taller. He licked his lips, and his eyes darted nervously around the room. But he was still dear Kenny.

"Let him come through, Tillie. Don't muddle him with your fussing," Alice scolded.

"Sorry Mum, Kenny. We're just that thrilled to see you."

"Hullo, Tillie. It's good to be back. Maggie, your uniform suits you." A ghost of a smile flashed across his face, but didn't reach his eyes.

Maggie blushed and gave him a kiss on the cheek.

"Welcome home, Kenny," she said quietly. Where was the exuberant boy that was always up for mischief? Where was the happy-go-lucky young man that teased his sisters unmercifully?

"Where's Katie, then? She's not here to greet the returning hero?" His tone had an edge, as he scanned the room.

"Remember, darling. I told you she's gone for basic training. You'll see her when she's home for embarkation leave." Alice put a hand on his arm.

"Right," he responded tersely. He perched uncertainly on the armchair in the living room while the winter sun peeked through the windows.

Tillie and Hannah ran down to the kitchen for a pot of tea and Kenny's favorite biscuits.

It was a subdued group, not sure what to ask the returning son.

"Can you tell us what you recall, Kenny?" Tillie finally asked gently.

"I remember who I am, but nothing about the explosion or what happened just before or after. Bits and pieces come to me – sometimes in nightmares, but it's all so frustrating when I can't recall simple things." Kenny raked a hand through his hair.

"There, there, darling," Alice soothed. "Give it time. You've been through so much. I'm sure it will all come back to you. Don't rush yourself," she said.

"How was your transport home?" Maggie changed the subject.

"It was alright, I suppose. The navy arranged my passage on another ship, and then an airplane, then a train. I should have thought being on board another ship would help to remember what happened that night, but naught. All of that is still wiped out," he shrugged.

"And of your time in Africa? Uncle Thomas said a fisherman rescued you in the water. That was so kind of him to take you in," Tillie inquired gingerly.

"I don't remember the rescue, as I've explained. But the fisherman and his wife were more than charitable. They got in a doctor who set my arm. Apparently, I was in and out of consciousness for some time, so they fed me delicious fish soup, and the woman nursed me back to health."

He wiggled his left arm.

"See? Good as new!" He attempted to lighten the mood.

Maggie noticed Kenny didn't mention the names of the people who had cared for him. Had he forgotten? Or didn't he want to dwell on painful memories? It was impossible to tell, but it was clear Kenny would need tender attention to fully recover.

"Were they sorry to see you go?" Tillie asked. She was always the one to go where no one dared to tread.

"I suppose so. They had no children of their own and lived simply off the sea and land. Sparing with words, but generous in deed. I don't even know if I can write to them, but they gave me their address – such as it is – and I hope to correspond with them once my memory returns." He gave a lopsided smile that reminded them of the old Kenny. "If it ever does."

A chorus of encouragement boosted him a little.

"Thanks everyone. I wish I had more strength to talk and explain what happened. But I just get so tired. And it hurts my head to force myself to remember."

"Would you like to rest? We've tidied up your old room, and it's just as it was. You've had a long journey."

"Perhaps I might, Mum. It has all been a bit much."

He stood up, a trifle unsteady.

"But I am glad to see you all. And to be home. Truly." He walked slowly towards the stairs.

They all understood that they'd need to give Kenny time to heal. As always, the Kingston family would rally round him to make it as smooth as possible.

"Come on, Mags. Let's have a chinwag with Hannah before a proper twin talk."

"And Robbie. I've missed my sweet kitty."

Maggie and Tillie went up the stairs together. They found Robbie where they expected, in Hannah's lap. The young girl had a cardigan over her brown jumper to ward off the cold seeping through the house.

"Is he okay? How is Kenny?" Hannah looked up from brushing Robbie.

"He will be okay," Tillie answered carefully. "Right now, he's rather in a state of shock, a mild shock perhaps. He remembers some things, but not everything."

"Will he remember me?" Hannah asked, worried. The last thing she wanted was to be a nuisance to the family.

Maggie scooped up Robbie and petted him. She stole a glance at Tillie.

"I'm not quite sure, but I believe he will. His memory is patchy, but coming along splendidly. So, if he doesn't recognize you straightaway, he soon will. And remember – you have changed heaps since he last saw you early in the war. You are quite the young lady now."

Hannah brightened.

"Can I ask you something?" she looked steadily at Maggie.

"Of course, darling. What is it?"

"Do you reckon now that Kenny is safely home that Micah, Mama, and Papa will come soon?"

Maggie gasped, then caught herself.

"I wish I knew, sweetheart. I don't want to give you false hope. I wish for that with all my heart, too. But the situation in France is much different. All we can do is wait and hope. And be brave. That's all any of us can do."

"I understand, Maggie. I'll try to be brave." Hannah nodded. It broke Tillie and Maggie's hearts.

"And as for this big old puss, what have you been feeding him? He weighs a ton. I can see you've spoiled this sweet boy. Do you even remember me, Robbie?"

He purred in response, and they all laughed.

CHAPTER THIRTEEN

The reunion supper was subdued, yet everyone was in a good mood. Tillie was all wedding talk, and Kenny ate ravenously of the Woolton pie, potatoes, turnips, and Bakewell tart. He had little to say, and no one pressed him.

While the others lingered over tea in the drawing room, Uncle Thomas took Maggie aside.

"Maggie, I've been hearing disturbing rumors in France – in Paris – and even the unoccupied zone in the south. The Vichy regime has been planning roundups of innocent Jewish people intending to deport them to work camps. For no apparent reason aside from their faith. I believe a significant roundup is coming in a few weeks' time. Most probably men, of all stations in life. I'm sorry, Maggie. France is not safe for Micah and his parents."

"But Micah is British born," objected Maggie, turning pale. "Surely they can't round him up or send him away?"

"My dear, they are seizing men of esteem – doctors, lawyers, business owners, politicians, some of whom aren't even practicing the faith. But if they appear on the census record as Jews, that's how they are counted."

What Thomas didn't tell his agitated niece was that the situation was considerably worse. There had already been several roundups, Nazis pounding on doors in the middle of the night, screaming in German for men to pack a case and depart at once. They'd been taken to central locations, by force if necessary. Any excuse to scream at or beat the prisoners was an excuse to bully the men into submission. No talking was allowed, so none of them could work out what was coming next, or what they could do.

Left in large, cold, empty rooms with no food, water, or proper facilities, these men could not understand why they were there, or what was going to be their ultimate fate. Sitting stoically for hours or days, eventually they hungrily consumed what little watery soup was provided, sometimes accompanied by moldy bread.

Later on, the men were roughly pushed and prodded into crowded train cars and deported to unknown destinations. Some were allowed to take their cases, others were stripped of everything but the clothes on their backs. After endless train trips, sometimes with hours-long unexplained stops, the starved and thirsty prisoners disembarked at an unknown location, and left there under terrible conditions for further unspecified times.

The treatment of these innocent men was brutal, sadistic, and inhumane. It was the model the Nazis had perfected by taking over prisoners in other European-occupied countries. All with the same aim – to break the prisoners' individuality, instill relentless fear, and make them feel less than human.

What happened next to these poor men was murky. Reports were unclear, but extremely disturbing. It seemed the prisoners were eventually piled into overloaded rail cars and sent to labor camps in Eastern Europe – Poland and Germany. Labor shortages in the German war economy had become critical, and Jewish captives were increasingly used as forced workers. They arrived at labor camps to snapping dogs and fully armed Nazi guards who rapidly sorted the newcomers into two lines, one for prisoners fit to work, the others for men too old, sick, or unable to work. What happened to them Thomas didn't know, but given the treatment he'd heard of all the prisoners, he realized it was very bad.

Would Micah survive such severe conditions? Could he withstand stark and unrelenting heavy physical work? And what of his parents? They were bound to be separated, with women being sent – where? How would this devoted couple cope with what could possibly be their final parting? Would Samuel be sent with Micah? Considered fit for work or to a more terrifying outcome?

Thomas heard it from an excellent source that in addition to Jews being persecuted on the streets, their businesses were being closed down. And that within a matter of months, Jews would, in all likelihood, be forced to wear a badge that set them apart and branded them as Jews. The situation was ominous. Although Maggie was a level-headed and mature twenty-six-year-old woman, her uncle didn't think he should tell her all that, at least not yet. Perhaps the situation wasn't as appalling as the reports suggested. Maybe it was part of a larger propaganda campaign to confuse the Allied countries. Hitler couldn't be this cruel and malicious, could he?

"Maggie, you must write Micah and implore him to leave while he still can. I can pull some strings now – because he is English. In a few months' time, or maybe sooner, I won't be able to help him. It will be too late." He took her by her slim shoulders, resisting the urge to shake sense into her. "You understand, don't you, Maggie? You must."

She felt helpless. Her head started to pound and her temples throbbed.

"Our letters aren't getting through most of the time, even now, Uncle Thomas. And even if I could convince him to come home, he's been quite clear that he won't leave his Mama and Papa. Ever. Can't you do something to rescue Mr. and Mrs. Goldbach as well? Hannah needs them."

Thomas' shoulders sagged as he let go of his niece.

"I should think the time for that is past, my dear. They are French-born and Jewish. Unless they somehow escape illegally, I can't see how to liberate them. Just do your best, Maggie. You truly care for your young poet. He's a clever young man. Perhaps he'll find a way."

Maggie nodded, a ball of dread forming in her stomach.

Her short six-hour leave flew by. She needed to be back at base by 1900. She helped clear up, saw to the blackout, and made her goodbyes.

"I'll see you soon, Kenny," she whispered to her brother as she placed her cap on her head. "Take it slow."

* * *

Back at base, Maggie threw herself into her job in order to avoid thinking about Micah too much. The new squad was starting to work as a team, improving their speed. What originally had taken approximately five minutes from spotter identification of a German aircraft to a gun being fired into the sky was now reduced to the required thirty seconds or less. In actual combat, they would need to be even quicker.

It was a complicated dance between interconnected partners. At the first signal, the spotter grabbed her binoculars and identified the Luftwaffe aircraft overhead. Pip was excellent at this, and recognized all the enemy planes at first sight, as did most of them. Her voice was perpetually hoarse from shouting out names of German planes. Then, Addy operated the height and range finder by pinpointing the aircraft through a viewfinder. She was a little slow but improving daily.

Finally, Maggie and Louise turned the dials to calculate the precise distance the guns would have to fire. Then it was over to the men, to set the fuse at the optimal moment for maximum damage, then the searchlight operator shouted the read, the predictor would automatically relay the information to the guns, and the gunner shot. The predictor was the first fully automated machine that could aim a gun at an aircraft based on observed speed and angle to the target. Maggie was extremely proud of her important role in the squad.

The women stayed in their assigned positions, but the men rotated to relieve boredom. So far, they hadn't actually shot down any planes, but they trained daily under the exacting Sgt. Griffiths. Maggie worried about shooting down a plane with an actual pilot inside. It was a real person in that plane. A man with a family, perhaps a wife and child. She forced herself not to think about it. She had a job to do, and was determined to do it well. The team was starting to build a genuine camaraderie, and spent most of their off time together.

"Oi, it was cold out there today, wasn't it Mags?" Pip moaned as they huddled near the barely warm stove in the middle of the hut.

"I can hardly feel my toes," Maggie grumbled, grateful for her teddy bear coat. They'd taken to sleeping in their uniforms with coats piled on top of the skimpy blankets they'd been assigned. Yet they still froze with a stove that constantly smoked and never had enough coal. But they'd all learned how to fall asleep wherever and whenever they could. They were that exhausted by the end of their shift that sleep came instantly.

"I don't know if I'm more whacked or hungry. Cold is winning out," Louise mumbled from under her covers.

Addy pulled the blankets off the shivering Louise.

"We've got ter eat, girl. We needs our strength fer drill early termorrow." Addy was an East End girl, no nonsense and sturdy. She had curly light brown hair which she stubbornly tried to straighten, and freckles dotted generously across her nose and cheeks.

Louise groaned and struggled up. At eighteen, tiny, with goldish red hair and green eyes, she was the youngest. Her eyelashes were so pale that they were almost invisible and a long fringe hung down over her eyes. Addy was determined to bring her out of her shell.

"Come on, then. Let's brave the elements. The mess is not that far. We'll sleep better in this frigid hut with at least something down us," Maggie urged. She was always hungry.

"I wish we could order a shandy or pint with our supper," Pip sighed. "After a long day of duty, it would go down a treat."

"Pip, you know that's against regulations," Maggie said. "We can't operate our equipment safely with any drinks in us."

"I know," Pip shrugged. "I'm just wishing, is all."

"I'm too young to drink," Louise whimpered, making them all laugh.

"Here we are, then."

The foursome rushed into the mess, which was thankfully slightly warmer than outside.

Over a dish of mixed sliced meat, pickled beetroot, carrot roll, apple pudding and weak tea, the gunner girls talked about life before the war.

"Working at Whiteley's department shop, I had more propositions from men than sales," said Pip through a mouthful of apple. Particularly when I worked in the women's departments – jewelry, perfume or dresses. The men would pretend they were purchasing something for their wives' birthdays and ask me out in the next breath. It was exhausting and made me fed up to find an honest bloke."

"Well, yer do 'ave loads ter offer," Addy said with a wink.

Somehow, even in drab khaki, Pip filled out the uniform in a way that caught second looks and whistles. And she was forever getting in trouble for wearing too much lipstick.

"Addy, that's rubbish. Chaps are interested in more than just a woman with a bosom," Maggie said.

"It's okay, Mags. I'm used to it. Sometimes it comes in rather handy. Now that the Americans are in it with us, maybe I'll snag a fancy one for myself. Perhaps a lad from somewhere down south where it's always warm. I hate this blooming cold."

"I didn't have a proper job before the war," little Lou, as they had nick-named her, ventured. "I just helped out on the farm – with everything from milking, to feeding the chickens, bringing in the hay, putting up preserves, and more. It was work every day from sunup to sundown."

"Bollocks," Addy protested, her mouth a giant O. "Yer never milked a cow or baled 'ay. Yer as tiny as a mouse."

Louise jutted out her chin.

"I may be small, but I'm strong. And there was no one else to do it. Just Ma and Pa. And a few farmhands. But none of them ever stayed long. Couldn't stand the work, that's what Pa says. I didn't mind, though. I suppose the farm will be mine one day. I'll need to find a solid husband to help me run it, that's what Pa says."

Maggie was starting to believe that little Lou was strongly influenced by her father.

"Pa was that cross with me for joining up. He grumbled and whined about having to apply for a land girl to take my place. But I'm meant to do my duty, aren't I? Just like everyone else."

"Too right, Lou. Yer pa sounds like a mean bugger ter me."

"No, he isn't, Addy. He's just looking after the farm is all. Ma wrote in her last letter that it takes two land girls to do the work I once did. Maybe Pa will be proud of me now."

Some 200,000 girls and women had signed up to work farms as Land Girls across England, freeing up men for crucial war jobs. They were essential to the food production, which had been a massive issue since the start of the war. Since most of England's food was import-ed, there had been shortage of many food items since the German U-boats regularly torpedoed incoming supply ships. The girls, in their bright green and beige uniforms, could be seen all over the countryside, doing the heavy farm work left behind by departing soldiers, sailors, and airmen.

"I'm sure he is, love. You're doing a smashing job of the ack-ack guns,"

Maggie remarked. "And we'll all be on the lookout for a stout farmer, for you, right girls?"

"One with an enormous nose to keep off the rain," Pip added with a giggle.

"And a glass eye ter stare down ter rats," Addy laughed.

Lou shuddered.

"I don't miss rat-catching and that's a fact. I had one run up the leg of my dungarees once."

"Eek," the other girls shrieked.

"Enough of that," Maggie said with a grimace. "Addy, you worked in your father's shop before the war, right?"

"Too right. It weren't nothin' as excitin' as yer girls. We had a small corner shop in Woolwich. I 'ad to work all ter hours God sends, and mostly it were dead borin'. Especially once coupons set in. House-wives bickerin over a rasher of bacon. Back when we 'ad bacon," she said matter-of-factly.

"I'd raise my skirts for real eggs and a plateful of bacon," Pip sighed.

"Go on, yer never would," Addy contradicted. "Leastways, I never would."

Pip loved to shock, so Maggie just ignored her.

"And how did you meet your fiancé?" She asked.

"'orace worked at ter butcher shop. He ain't no Cary Grant, but we suit. I'll 'elp 'im in ter shop once ter war is over, and we get married."

"What does he look like?" Pip asked. The girls wanted to stay back in the relatively warm mess as long as possible.

"Well, 'e's about my height. With brownish hair. His teeth be a tad crooked, but 'e's a good lad, and 'e loves me." Addy seemed almost defiant, daring Pip to make fun.

"He sounds dreamy," Lou piped. "I wouldn't say no to Cary Grant myself, though," she propped her chin in her hand, gazing dreamily into the distance.

"When will you get married, Addy?" Maggie asked.

"After ter war, I expect. No use now. With 'orace fightin in Italy, and me 'ere, we wouldn't be tergether anyroad. We'll 'ave our time when ter war ends."

Maggie wished she could be as optimistic and confident about her own future with Micah. She constantly stopped herself from thinking of planning a wedding or setting up a home with him. At this moment, getting him and his parents safely home was her all-consuming concern.

"What about you? Are you sweet on anyone?" Pip seemed to read Maggie's mind.

"I do have a childhood mate who is in France. We write to each other, but I'm not sure when I'll see him again." Maggie was beyond uncomfortable talking about Micah.

"So, it ain't serious, then?" Addy asked.

"I don't think we can tell properly till the war is over. Can any of us?" Maggie evaded.

"What did you do before the war?" Lou asked curiously. "You never said."

Maggie sat up a little straighter.

"I worked as a Nippy at Lyons Corner House. Both me and my sister. Pops was none too happy about it at first. He has an accounting firm and wanted us both to work in the office. But once Tillie and I had the idea in our heads, we wouldn't be dissuaded."

"That seems like so much fun, Mags. I've never eaten in a Corner House. I hear they are beautiful, with music playing and ever so posh curtains and fittings."

"I hardly noticed that," Maggie chuckled. "We were run off our feet, mostly. But I loved it. We were meant to be bright and breezy with every customer, and I tried my best." She paused for a moment, remembering the carefree days balancing heavy trays and serving endless meals. She tucked a stray blonde hair up her cap.

"One time, a Scottish gentleman and his wife came in. They'd never been before, and you could just see on their faces they were that bothered the prices would be too dear. The problem was when I came to take their order, I couldn't understand a word they said. Their accent was that thick. I asked them politely to repeat the order, but still couldn't make heads or tails of it. The man got red in the face. I quickly asked my day supervisor to help out. I was beyond embarrassed. Especially when all they wanted was two cups of tea and scones with jam."

The girls erupted into laughter.

"Girls, did I ever tell you about the time that Tillie and I served at a Royal Garden Party before the war? Tillie even met the Queen. And her future husband." Maggie started.

"Do tell," Pip said as the girls leaned forward.

So, Maggie told of the day the Nippies served tea in the tents at a garden party in 1938. A woman had cut her hand, and Tillie jumped in to help. They went to the medical tent, where the Queen had kindly come to ask after the poor injured woman. She suggested to Tillie that she should join the ambulance force. Trevor had been on duty as a firefighter in case of an outbreak, and the two had met.

"How romantic," Lou breathed.

"And he's a terrific bloke. They're getting married in May," Maggie finished. She then went on to speak briefly of her WVS work early in the war.

They lingered over another cup of tea discussing what they would all do when the war ended, a topic of endless fascination for them, and all Britons.

CHAPTER FOURTEEN

May 1942

"My goodness. I'm glad to have that lot sorted," Maggie sank onto her bed, still wearing her ATS uniform. She tossed her cap on the nightstand, and fluffed her golden hair, pushing a strand behind her ear.

"Thanks, Mags for pitching in the moment you turned up today. I never dreamed it would be so much bloody work putting on a wedding," Tillie sat on her own bed, kicked off her shoes, and massaged her foot.

They'd been busy since Maggie arrived, decorating the house with paper streamers, bunting, and dried flower arrangements dropped off by the WVS women. The dining room table had been set with the best linen, dishware, crystal, and silver that Alice had saved from before the war. Kenny had been convinced to hoover, Hannah had polished all the wood surfaces, and everything gleamed and shone.

"Well, it has to be right, doesn't it? Even with a small number of guests coming back for the wedding breakfast, we must make it special for you and Trevor," Maggie smiled, as she got ready for bed.

"Why do they call it a wedding breakfast when it's a full meal?" Tillie shrugged. "It will be odd just having the family and a few chums. But that's what war weddings seem to be. In the event, I have my chief bridesmaid. And I have my bridal gown," she spun to face her sister. "You don't think it's ill-chosen to wear a white dress, do you, ducks? So many war brides are wearing uniform or saving up coupons for a useful suit."

Tillie was right. It was unusual for brides to wear wedding gowns in wartime. For one thing, you couldn't find one even if you had the vast number of coupons required to buy it. And some felt it was inappropriate to splash out on a big wedding gown in grim times.

"But darling, you've had Mrs. Drummond's dress made over for you, which has cost almost nothing – a few pounds, if that. The WVS have clubbed together altering it to make it more modern. You'll be smashing, and Trevor won't be able to keep his eyes off you." Maggie rushed to reassure Tillie, who chewed on her lower lip.

"It does look a bit of alright, doesn't it, darling? I so want Trev to see me as a beautiful bride."

"He will, love," Maggie replied softly.

Tillie beamed.

"And it's remarkable to see how Mum, Aunt Shirley, Mrs. Drummond, and all the WVS ladies have saved up their rations so we can have a decent meal. It means the world to Trev and me."

"Indeed, it is. And Alfie has come through with the Lyons cake. It's brilliant." Lyons had come up trumps with a complimentary wedding cake – even during wartime.

It was a lovely confection. Three tiers of real cake and no cardboard bottom layer to give the illusion of height. Figures of a happy groom and bride perched on top, and the Lyons motto was delicately etched on the side: *Happy to Help You*. Tillie had been so touched, in fact, she'd been on the verge of tears all day. Everyone had been so kind to her and her future husband. It was all a bit overwhelming.

"It looks delicious, Tils. The white icing with little roses and silver balls are so pretty," Maggie had changed into her nightie, and was applying ponds cream to her face. She turned to her sister. "No doubts, sis? This is our last twin talk before you are a married woman."

"Not a one, Mags. I love Trevor with all my heart and can't wait to be his wife."

"Are you nervy about the wedding night?"

"A little, but largely, I'm just excited. The last few months it's been hard keeping ourselves pure. We've had to hold back on many occasions. But, it's important to me we save it for our wedding night. It's hard to imagine how wonderful it will be to finally give myself totally to Trev."

Maggie couldn't help thinking of Micah. Would she ever have this moment of anticipation about her own wedding night? She shook her head. It was Tillie's time, not hers.

"Right, we'd best get your hair into pin curls, so you have a proper do for tomorrow. Then you can have your weekly bath. It won't do to be smelling of smoke and cordite on your wedding night. Then I'll do your nails. I have pearly white nail varnish for you," she held the tiny bottle up.

A gentle knock interrupted their laughter.

Alice appeared with a tray, two cups of cocoa, and a plate of short-bread biscuits.

"May I come in, girls? I brought provisions."

"Ta, Mum. That's kind. Come in," Tillie motioned for her to sit on her narrow bed.

"How are you feeling, love? Excited for tomorrow?" Alice handed the cups round.

"Very happy, Mum. I'm marrying my dream man," Tillie answered, blowing on her hot cocoa.

"He's a terrific bloke, Tillie. I hope you two will be very happy." She took a deep breath. "But we have something important to chat about."

Tillie raised an eyebrow. She hoped Mum would not delve into anything delicate.

"Have you sorted your something old, something new, something borrowed, and something blue?" Alice asked.

A hand flew to Tillie's mouth.

"Oh, Mum. I never even thought of it. What are we going to do?"

"Don't fuss, dear. You already have something old – Mrs. Drummond's lovely dress and veil."

"And something new – didn't you buy new white court shoes with your clothing coupons?" Maggie asked.

"Yes, that's right. Now for something borrowed, I suppose I can also count the wedding dress?" Tillie offered dubiously.

"Nonsense. I have something for you to borrow, love." Alice produced a beautiful set of pearls. "I wore these for my wedding to Pops, and I'd be honored if you'd wear them tomorrow." Tears glistened in Alice's eyes.

"Oh Mum," Tillie gushed. "Are you sure? These are just lovely."

Tillie gingerly rolled them between her fingers.

"Absolutely, Tillie." She fastened them around Tillie's slender neck.

"I expect they will look a tad better with your wedding dress, darling, but they are lovely," Maggie laughed. Even with her flowered nightgown, the pearls looked stunning on Tillie.

"Thank you, Mum. I'll take proper care of them."

"I hope they bring you good luck and happiness," Alice said simply.

"All we need now is something blue," mused Maggie.

Silence fell as they thought about it.

Maggie snapped her fingers.

"I've got it. We'll tie a blue ribbon around your flower bouquet."

No fresh flowers were available during wartime. Most had been dug up long ago to plant Victory Gardens of needed fruit and vegetables. Alice's WVS had aced it, creating decorations and a modest bouquet from dried flowers, ribbons, and other bits and bobs they could get their hands on. A piece of blue ribbon should be easy to find.

"Well, that's sorted then. I'd best get off to bed. Tomorrow is a big day," Alice yawned. "You two — don't stay up late chatting. Tillie needs her beauty sleep." She smiled at her girls, as she picked up the tray.

"I love you, Mum. And thanks — for everything," Tillie kissed her mother on the cheek, feeling slightly weepy. The emotions of the day threatened to overpower her.

"I love you, too. Both of you." She quietly closed the door.

The next morning was a bustle of activity getting ready for the 11:00 a.m. wedding. Trevor had a five-day pass and had arrived and been met by his mother last night. Tillie hadn't seen him today. Wasn't it bad luck for a groom to see his bride on their wedding day? Maggie only had a twenty-four-hour leave, so would have to return to base after the wedding. Katie was at the old Royal Naval College in Greenwich. She was deep into her basic training with the WRNs and could not get any leave.

Alice and Maggie helped Tillie get dressed. The old-fashioned drop waist of Isla's satin gown had been altered to fit around her bodice and waist. The lacy long sleeves had also been taken in to suit the more tailored look. The full-length antique lace veil had been shortened, allowing the extra lace to be used for hankies for the women, and to smarten up Maggie's pre-war dinner dress at the collar and cuffs. The veil framed Tillie's lovely face to bring out her natural beauty.

Tillie wore her wavy blonde hair loose down to her shoulders. In addition to the pearls, Alice had loaned her matching earrings. The overall look was breathtaking.

"You look lovely, darling. Enchanting," Alice whispered, fighting back tears. "The length is spot on, and you look so happy."

"I am, Mum," Tillie said calmly, her eyes shining. "I'm ready."

The family crowded into two taxis for the short ride to St. Luke's. As chief bridesmaid, Maggie stayed with her sister as the rest went into the church. Alice kissed Tillie on the cheek and walked in on Kenny's arm, her heart bursting with tenderness for her daughter. Hannah stood nervously, waiting to walk in front of Tillie and Alice gave her a nod of encouragement.

"Are you ready, love? You are a beautiful bride, inside and out." Pops offered his arm, blustering a little to hide his emotions.

The organ began playing. Everything was happening so fast.

"That's my cue." Maggie was lovely in pink with lace trimmings. She kissed her twin and turned to walk down the aisle behind Hannah. "Trevor will be gobsmacked."

Tillie placed her hand on her father's arm, and the pair strode confidently into the church. They paused just inside the door. Pops surveyed the small crowd of family and friends, and Katie! She'd somehow made it. She winked at them both.

But Tillie only had eyes for her bridegroom. Trevor looked impossibly handsome in his RAF dress uniform. Their eyes locked, and Tillie's final nerves suddenly faded away. She floated down the aisle to make her vows to her one true love.

The May sunshine flooded the stained-glass windows of the seventy-year-old stone church. The vicar was resplendent in his colorful robes. The joyful couple exchanged vows, and Trevor placed a gold band on Tillie's left hand. No trembling! After the blessing, they kissed tenderly. No one in the church was left wondering if they were in love. Their light filled the church, and for a short while, war was forgotten. Hand in hand, they walked up the aisle as the organ music played. No church bells rang out – and hadn't since the start of the war – but they were used to it by now.

"Katie, darling, however did you get leave?" Tillie hugged her younger sister, charming in her new naval uniform.

"I've only got an afternoon pass. And even that I had to wheedle out of my CO. I mustn't be late for the 16:33 train – I mean the 4:33. I couldn't miss my sister's wedding, could I?" Katie's words bubbled over in delight.

Uncle Thomas has somehow managed to secure a photographer to capture a few pictures of the occasion. He snapped one of the happy couple, Maggie and Tillie alone, and the entire Kingston clan. But the photograph that Alice would treasure for years to come was the Kingston family and four children. Walter, Alice, Maggie and Kenny were in their wedding finery. Katie was in uniform, and Tillie glowed in her wedding gown. At last, Alice had all four children with her. She insisted Hannah join in – after all, she was family now too.

Back at the house, Alice was in her element, hosting her entire family, friends of Tillie and Trevor's from school and Lyons, and everyone's mates from the ambulance and WVS that could make it.

"Ernie, I'm so glad you could make it. You and I have been through loads in our ambulance adventures. I wouldn't have missed it for the world. Remember our first call when I ran pell-mell into a burning building to make a rescue?" Tillie clinked glasses with her driving partner.

"How could I forget? Jasper tore a strip off you a mile long. I don't think I've ever seen your face so red. But you learned. And Jasper was impressed with your courage, despite your foolhardiness." Ernie's driving experience had made him an invaluable partner. With so many streets damaged by bombs, his cabbie knowledge helped them navigate the broken London streets.

Tillie smiled and looked around the drawing room.

"Where is Jasper, by the way? Mum sent him an invitation."

"He's on duty, Tillie, and sends his regards."

Tillie nodded. In wartime, even the best of intentions were interrupted or abandoned by happenings out of an individual's control.

A superb wedding breakfast of carrot soup, sardine rolls, beef ragout, and assorted vegetables was enjoyed by all. The women had outdone themselves with the food, and the twins grinned at each other over the sausage rolls. Tillie and Trevor cut the wedding cake and served each other a bite without smashing it. Pops and Trevor both made short and poignant speeches thanking everyone for coming and drinking to those who couldn't be there. Watery beer flowed, and a couple of bottles of champagne mysteriously appeared, and were distributed so that everyone got a tiny taste for the toasting. As the afternoon wore on, couples danced to popular songs played by Maggie on the piano. Uniforms in all hues blended with wedding outfits after being mended, clothes swapping, and a kind eye by the guests.

Maggie was kept busy refilling glasses, removing dirty plates, and generally making herself useful. She kindly put one of Trevor's intoxicated firefighter mates in his place when he made an awkward pass at her, leering drunkenly that she was almost as pretty as the bride.

Noticing Hannah was missing, she went in search of the girl, concerned she was thinking of her own family on this joyous day. She found her in the re-opened library, gazing out the window.

"Darling, are you okay? It can't be easy on you, seeing everyone so jolly, and your family isn't here."

Hannah turned, tears in her eyes.

"It's just so hard, Maggie. Not knowing where they are, if they are safe, and most of all – will I ever see them again?"

Maggie longed to pull the young girl close, but hesitated. She didn't want to overstep her bounds.

"I think about the same things every day, love. I miss Micah so much it hurts. But we must be brave and hold on. We can't lose hope."

"Micah loves you very much, Maggie. He told me so."

Maggie's heart surged, despite the glum exchange.

"He did?" She squeaked.

"More than once, Maggie. He spoke of getting married one day, back here in London. He is resolved to it, Maggie."

Maggie gave her a gentle hug.

"Thank you for that, darling. It means the world. Now, let's dry our tears. This is meant to be a joyful event. We mustn't let Tillie and Trevor see wet eyes."

"Thank you, Maggie. I promise I'll show a cheerful face. I just had a weepy moment."

They rejoined the party, no one the wiser. Maggie decided to keep in closer touch with the lonely girl.

As the afternoon wore on, Tillie and Trevor exchanged a look across the room. Trevor nodded at his bride. She excused herself from her sisters and moved to her husband's side.

"Are you ready to set off, wife?" He whispered in her ear. A shiver ran through her. She nodded.

The two slipped away unnoticed by all but Maggie, who smiled at her twin from across the room.

Isla had offered up her apartment for their wedding night. She would stay with the Kingstons. The next morning, the newly married couple would leave for a short three-day honeymoon in Scotland.

They treasured every moment.

CHAPTER FIFTEEN

"...and after we caught the train to Glasgow, our honeymoon truly began. Oh Mags, it was as if time stood still. And yet, it raced by. We walked for hours every day and even took a train trip to Loch Lomond. The views were spectacular.

We tried several local restaurants, but hardly noticed what we ate. The nights...oh my goodness. I wish I could say how marvelous married life is, but I suppose you'll just have to wait and discover the bliss for yourself. I'm blushing even as I write this..."

The sound of an air raid signal blasted through Tillie's honeymoon letter.

Pip and Maggie locked eyes, as everyone in the hut sprang into action. She and Addy had been playing cards. Pip was losing, so happily dropped her cards on the cot, and grabbed her kit. Lou had just finished polishing her boots. She quickly put them on and was out the door in seconds. Maggie shoved Tillie's letter into the top drawer of her bedside table, grabbed her helmet and coat and ran with the rest of the girls to the Ack-Ack Command bunker.

"Do you reckon this is the real thing?" Louise shrieked. They automatically looked up to the sky. No enemy aircraft in sight, but the searchlights were already probing the night, trying to locate the German bombers.

"Full moon," Morris groaned, as the men staffed their stations. "Just like Jerry likes it."

"Maybe it's another false alarm," Simon shouted.

Maggie and the rest of the squad moved quickly into position. Her heart thumping against her chest, Maggie waited for Pip to locate the incoming aircraft through her binoculars. Maggie didn't even look up to see how many Luftwaffe were heading over the river.

"Engage," Sgt. Griffiths roared.

"Dornier," Pip called. "No, there's two of them," she screamed.

Louise and Addy rotated the height-and-range finder until the aircraft was visible through the tiny eyepieces. Staying fully focused, they quickly adjusted their instruments until the images were perfectly lined up.

"Read," Lou shouted.

"Read," Addy repeated.

It was time for Maggie to swing into action. She took a deep breath.

She took the information and measurements and started adjusting the knobs and dials on the predictor and then called out the fuse length.

"Set," Gordon yelled. The men loaded the shells into the guns.

"Fire," Simon shouted.

Maggie felt as though she were moving in slow motion, even though the entire operation lasted only seconds. Even though it was a chilly May night, Maggie felt sweat dripping down her back and forehead.

The guns blasted, deafening in their noise. The air was filled with smoke and the smell of cordite. The ear-splitting shots were followed by the clank and jangle of metal shell casings hitting the ground. Maggie couldn't help but duck down, pushing her helmet down her head.

Everyone scanned the sky, looking for a German plane on fire. All they could see were the London searchlights, and barrage balloons in the distance. Damn, they'd missed their shot.

"Dornier," Pip shouted again, her binoculars plastered to her face.

The squad immediately jumped into action again, their weeks of training plunging into gear, as drills met instinct. Within seconds, more booming shots were fired. Again, they missed.

"Bloody hell," Morris swore. "Come on, we've got to strike at least one of those damn planes."

Maggie found herself reassuring the older man.

"We'll get them next time, Morris. Steady on."

But there was no time to waste. The planes were coming fast and furious.

"Stand down," Sgt. Griffiths shouted.

The soldiers immediately stopped, more than a little confused. Looking up at the sky, Maggie was perplexed. Even from this distance, she could still see bombers in the air. Explosions sounded all around them, so what was happening?

"It's one of ours," Simon spat out. "We can't shoot until our plane is in the clear."

Maggie and the team stood by, grabbing whatever binoculars were available to see what was going on.

Pip provided a play-by-play.

"It's a Spitfire – looks to be attacking a formation of enemy bombers. There are seven, eight, no, ten of them. The Spit has a bomber in its sights. He's fired. Wait, no; the German plane fired, but missed."

A low cheer came from the bunker.

"It's a dogfight," Pip barked. "A Heinkel and Spitfire are circling each other. The Heinkel is swerving, the Spit is following close."

All eyes were on the sky, tensely watching the deadly dance in the air.

"Come on, come on," Maggie moaned.

"I see an explosion," Pip yelled. "Smoke everywhere. I can't see who is hit."

Seconds later, they all saw a plane spiraling down, smoke pouring from its tail.

"It's the Heinkel. Bloody hell, he got him."

The enemy plane left a trail of black smoke as it swirled and twisted downward. A blob of white appeared, the pilot bailing out in his parachute.

"Look," pointed Lou. "It's heading into a steep dive."

Suddenly, the plane broke into a thousand pieces in mid-air.

"We did it, we did it," Maggie jumped up and down, hugging Addy, Gordon, and whomever else she could reach.

"One for blighty," Addy cheered.

"The Spit is going higher. He's falling back. He's safe." Pip reported, her eyes glued to the binoculars.

"Stations, everyone," Sgt. Griffiths ordered. "It's far from over."

Relieved to be of use again, the team waited for the callout, which came in seconds.

Pip constantly shouted out throughout the night. The planes just kept coming. The deafening sounds of the ack-ack guns, and the explosions in the sky boomed and crashed all around them. Cordite and dank smoke filled the nostrils of the squad, causing choking and spitting. The light in the sky came from searchlights and explosions.

With hardly a moment to breathe, there was no chance for a bathroom break, a drink, or even a glance away from the equipment.

Maggie's hands were slippery from spinning the dials over and over, doing her best to pinpoint targets for the guns. Her back ached from hunching over the predictor. She didn't think. She just performed her duty to the best of her ability.

By the time the all-clear sounded at four a.m., the squad were exhausted, hoarse, and covered in a mix of grime, sweat, and pride.

"Blimey, we shot down two of 'em," Alfred beamed as they dragged themselves towards the mess for a well-deserved cup of tea.

"And did you see the one with the engine fire crash into another one?" The men were bursting with pride.

The women lagged behind.

"I don't know how I feel, girls," Lou said in a small voice. "I'm ever so pleased we carried out our duties as we've been trained, but…" her voice broke.

Maggie hugged her.

"What happens to the ones who bail out?" Lou asked.

"If they're not dead, I expect they'll be picked up by local Home Guard, who will turn them over to the police. Then they'll be arrested and escorted to a nearby POW camp – Lancashire, I expect," Gordo said shortly. "If they broke a leg or whatnot, they'll be treated medically – and quite well – until they recover."

"Then what?" Lou almost whispered, her throat so sore she could hardly speak.

"I heard they'll likely be shipped to Canada," Gordo said wearily, as he removed his tin helmet.

"That'll teach 'em," Addy snorted, tossing her grubby hair. "No chance 'o escape from over there, bloody Huns."

"I suppose that's not too bad. Better than burning to death in a plane set on fire." Lou had a heart of gold and struggled with this part of the job.

"It's hard to cope with shooting down a real person. Who has a family, a mother, maybe a sweetheart." Maggie herself felt a bit sick – being a party to taking a life. "And some of them are barely out of short trousers themselves – so young, and probably scared to death." Her legs felt like rubber.

"But that's our job, girls. And that's fewer enemy bombs killing British pilots and civilians, destroying our beautiful country," Pip sniffed. For her it was all straightforward.

Charged up with adrenalin and the evening's success, the crew hashed over the operations' accomplishments over tea and sandwiches.

"We can do even better next time," Alfred said in his halting voice.

"I suppose we did rather well," Pip defended huskily. "But I agree. We can improve our time and accuracy now that we've seen real action."

"I'm frightfully sleepy," Maggie said with a yawn. "And the sun is almost up. I'm for bed." She drained her teacup and dragged herself to her feet. She and Pip walked in silence, the sky turning from a dull gray to a pale pink.

Back at the hut, Maggie gave her face a cursory swipe with her flannel, changed into her pajamas, and collapsed on her cot, pulling the blankets up to her chin.

"Goodnight, Pip," she whispered. "Well done, you."

"Well done, you too, Maggie," Pip rolled over.

As exhausted as she was, Maggie couldn't fall asleep. Her mind darted from image to image. Tillie and Trevor at the front of the church in their wedding finery, declaring their love for all to see. Kenny's face as he struggled to remember people at the wedding. Uncle Thomas taking her aside for a quiet word, urgently warning her again of the looming roundups in France. The German bomber falling out of the sky, trailing fire as it spiraled to the ground. Pip's voice getting raspier and croakier as she shouted out her spotter's calls. Robbie's purr as he snuggled into her shoulder at night. Hannah's shadowed eyes that were slowly learning to trust again.

The image she had the most difficulty conjuring up was Micah's face.

It had been so long since she'd seen him, and he was getting harder to picture. Slender, serious eyes, spectacles, sandy brown hair, and a kindly smile that she had dreamt about for over two years. But it was fading. How brown were his eyes? What was his nose like? Maggie worried she would forget him over time if she didn't see him soon. She longed for a picture of him to hold close to her heart. Many RAF flyers kept a picture of their loved one in the cockpits of their planes for good luck. Micah had no picture of her, either. Would that have given him more luck?

Sighing, she willed her body to relax. Finally, she drifted off to sleep, only to be awoken a few short hours later.

With succinct thanks for a job well done, the squad was informed they were being redeployed to Exeter in two days' time.

"What?" Pip squealed. "But we've hardly been here."

"That's enough, Murley," Sgt. Griffiths snapped. "It's not for you to question orders. Or any one of us. All I can tell you is that your ack-ack battery is more needed nearer the coast. The army is shoring up resources. Come back tomorrow at 0800 sharp for your rail passes. In the meantime, pack your kit, and be ready to depart at 0900 Thursday morning. Lorries will take you to the train station. Good luck to you."

Murmurs started within the group.

Morris raised his hand.

Sgt. Griffiths nodded.

"Quimby?"

"Will this station be closed?"

"Not your affair, Quimby. But I believe it will be abandoned for the moment. None of us knows where this war is going," he gave a brief smile. "The army thanks you for your service so far. And good show."

The little group felt bewildered. They wandered to the canteen for a cup of tea. Maggie struggled to make sense of her thoughts and feelings. Being in London meant she was close to home, should she be needed. And her half-day leaves allowed her to look in on Kenny and Hannah, and Tillie of course. And Robbie, she gulped. But she must go where she was needed. And she would be closer to Micah. There was that. She was lost in thought when she heard the sounds of a huge gasp, followed by weeping.

She turned to see Louise doubled over, sobbing uncontrollably.

"Darling, what is it?" Maggie pulled her up and into her arms.

"I don't know. I don't know. I'm scared. The Germans," she wailed.

Maggie looked at Pip and Addy, who both looked puzzled.

"Let's sit, Lou." Maggie pulled her to the shelter doorstep. "Whatever is causing you so much distress?"

Lou tried to stop her tears, brushing them from her cheeks, desperately trying to regain control.

"It's just that somehow in London, I feel safer. I see it's daft, but if we're in some remote place, the Nazis will strike us easier."

"But you realise, darling, that London isn't safe. Think of all the bombs that have dropped, people killed, and buildings destroyed. We'll be no less safe anywhere else, by my reckoning. And we're together. We'll look out for each other."

Lou nodded, hiccupping.

"You're right. I don't know what came over me. I'm ever so sorry." She turned pleading eyes to all three girls. "I'll be fine, really."

She stood up, straightened her shoulders, and walked towards the hut.

"I'm going to start packing up my kit, girls. You go ahead without me."

Maggie nodded. The young girl needed some time alone. Because of her fearful outburst, she was frightfully embarrassed.

"I'll bring you a cuppa back, Lou. Take your time."

The three young women set off for the canteen.

"Well, I never," Addy said with a low whistle. "Where in bloomin 'ell did that come from?"

"We are all under an enormous strain. This war is such a hodgepodge of monotony, loneliness, shortages, and fear. Sometimes it gets the better of us and it just boils over. I feel jumpy at times, and every little noise bothers me," Maggie confessed.

"Sometimes I can't fall asleep for an age. My mind just whirls in circles and won't settle. It's awful when we have such early mornings and demanding days. I need to sleep, but it just won't come," Pip added.

"Now and 'gain, I'm that worn out that me temper is short. I take it out on people round me," Addy said shortly.

"We never noticed, did we, Mags?" Pip guffawed.

"Worry takes different forms," Maggie responded slowly, thinking of Kenny and his nightmares. "It's bound to get to all of us, never knowing when we'll be attacked again. We must just get on and do our best."

Pip and Addy nodded. What else was there to say?

CHAPTER SIXTEEN

Maggie and the team said goodbye to their London base and hopped on the train for Exeter. She was grateful to be traveling with their squad, albeit Sgt. Griffiths was posted somewhere further north.

"Seeing the tents being dismantled that have housed us these last weeks was a bit sad," Lou observed a trifle forlornly as they bustled onto the train.

Pip snorted.

"One base is the same as the next. I'm just that glad to see the back of that hut with another moody, smoking stove."

"Oi, 'ere's 'oping our next digs are warmer," Addy agreed.

"Well, no bother about that for the moment. Who knows? Maybe we'll be moved again before winter," Maggie added philosophically as they crammed into the jam-packed train. "Where is everyone off to? We'll never get a seat."

And she was right. The train was packed with uniformed passengers.

Pip added a dash of lipstick.

"Not if I can help it." She cast her eye around the crowded car and spotted American uniforms. "Hey, if it ain't the Americans joining us. Hello boys," she gave them her broadest smile.

"Hello, young lady. Where are you headed?" A tall, dark-haired American with bushy eyebrows removed his cap.

"We're not to say, are we? But it's at least a four-hour journey for my friends and me. Without the inevitable stoppages. Don't they teach any manners where you're from?" She smiled again to take the sting out of her words.

He immediately jumped up.

"Private Hughes, at your service, Ma'am." He jostled his neighbors. "Come on you yokels. Stand up for these fine ladies of the English military."

Within moments, Hughes and his friends shuffled good-naturedly out to the corridor.

"Thanks ever so much," Maggie smiled at the soldiers.

"Ain't it true that yer Yanks 'ave nylons an chocolate, an all?" Addy asked fearlessly.

Lou and Maggie elbowed her in embarrassment.

"Give over, Addy," Lou shushed her, ten shades of red.

"No nylons, I'm afraid, but how about a Hershey bar?" A fresh-faced soldier scrambled into his pocket to produce half a bar.

"Ta, thanks Yank," Addy snatched it out of his hands.

The Americans guffawed as the bar was painstakingly split into tiny pieces and shared all around.

"That's heaven," Pip declared rapturously.

Maggie had never tasted anything so delicious. At least not for years. She hadn't had any type of candy since rationing came in.

The Americans also passed out Lucky Strikes. The girls all passed except Addy, who was game for any handout.

Two hours later, the G.I.s disembarked, not before flirting outrageously with Pip and Addy while a red-haired lad tried unsuccessfully to pull Lou onto his lap.

"Addy, you are shameless," Maggie chided good-naturedly once the car was clear.

"The cheek of you," little Lou laughed. "But I'm not moaning. The chocolate was brilliant."

Addy shrugged.

"All's fair in love and war."

Maggie shook her head and gazed out the window.

Within a few hours, they arrived at Exeter, and from there were driven across dusty roads to a base that seemed to be in the middle of nowhere.

Thirsty, tired, and travel-weary, they were met by an order-barking sergeant, and assigned to their barracks, all of which were starting to become drearily familiar. They chose their iron cots and dropped down their kit, surveying their surroundings.

"I were 'alf 'oping we'd bag a billet in a cast-off manor or swish 'otel," Addy moaned, removing her dusty shoes, and rubbing her feet.

Lodgings across the country took all shapes and forms, so Addy was not far off the mark. From rooms in private homes to abandoned schools, to requisitioned country houses. As did their hosts – some hospitable, others grudging, and some downright rude. Schoolchildren had experienced this during the initial evacuations of 1939, and now all branches of the military were finding themselves in the same circumstances – in cramped quarters with long daily walks to base, or the lucky few in posh estates – some with indoor plumbing.

"Not this time," Pip laughed. "But we know what to expect at least." She unpacked her kit. "Spam for supper, girls?"

They made do with a light wash-up before a hurried meal at the canteen.

"This place is crawling with soldiers. Did you see all the Americans, too?" Lou asked as they toured the base before bed.

Maggie nodded.

"If the number of troops count for anything, we're meant to be proper occupied here," Maggie observed. "We'd best toe the line. The army is depending on us."

They settled in for the night, which was a warm one. No stove needed!

Saying their goodnights, most of the girls fell asleep straightaway.

Maggie stole a few moments to pen Micah a letter before turning in.

"Dearest Micah,

I hardly know where to start with this letter. Life has been a whirlwind of late.

Tillie and Trevor's wedding was all that you can imagine and more. Even though it was a small war affair, Mum and Aunt Shirley made it ever so lovely. Tillie was beautiful, and she and Trev were lucky enough to have a brief honeymoon in Scotland. Needless to say, it was short-lived, as Trevor was due back on base. He's just about finished with his basic fire training. Tillie is hoping he'll be based somewhere close to home, but needs must, and he'll go willingly where he's sent.

You'll want news of your sister. Hannah is becoming quite the young lady. She takes her studies proper serious, just as you said. She was a bit skittish when she first arrived, but has quietened down. I'm not sure if it's the busy Kingston household, or the plentiful but plain food, but she seems to be sleeping better. You can see she longs for news of you and your parents, but she waits in silence, as do we all.

An unlikely friendship has formed between her and Kenny. Perhaps because they are close in age – she's almost fifteen, and Kenny turned twenty in February. They spend loads of time together, walking and talking about who knows what. Between them, they have taken over Robbie's care. I admit I miss the little mite, but am more than relieved that he's been loved and spoilt! My brother and your sister need him more than I do at the moment.

As for me, I have news as well. Our battery unit has been transferred to a new location (I hope the censors won't black this out). Being in the south of England makes me feel closer to you, dear Micah. I can't help fancying you and your parents somehow escaping France and appearing on a boat nearby. Foolish, isn't it?

I suppose I should get back to the here and now. We were stationed here to protect our location from fresh attacks by the Luftwaffe. They've been bombing historic targets as part of what's being called the Baedeker Raids – something to do with famous sites in the travel guide. I suppose they reckon hitting our cathedrals and monuments will grind us down. They don't realize what we're made of. They bombed here in April, as well as a few other cities that I won't reveal. Protecting the British coastline is vital to the war effort.

Our team feels rather experienced at this point. We spend all our time together – eating, sleeping, and working – so it's expected that we should become close. Pip and I have become good mates. She is so different from me. She speaks her mind and is so funny. I marvel at her bravery.

Lou is small but mighty. She's young but has learned so quickly. Addy is into everyone's business, but is generous and kind. It truly makes our awful nights easier to bear with such good chums. I miss my dear Tillie, but am proud to be part of the Royal Artillery, and would do anything to safeguard my mates. The men are protective of us, and proud, too. I expect they were originally skeptical that we could handle the job — especially under pressure. But now, they even brag about what fine work we do to anyone that listens. It feels good, I must say.

I'm tired all the time, Micah. I fight homesickness, and the drudge of living on top of each other, scant washing up facilities, and food that tastes more the same with each passing day. The weather is fair, so we are all thankful.

There are more ATS and mixed-battery units here. There's talk of a dance in a few weeks. Pip is insisting we all go. I'm uncertain.

Micah, I hope my daft ramblings of ATS life reaches you. I think of you as I work my predictor machine, doing my bit to help the Allies win the war. Now that the Americans are truly in, it must soon be over, mustn't it?

I've enclosed a sketch of a few of my crew on the lorry here to Exeter. I hope I've captured a bit of their courage and fatigue.

I miss you desperately and long to see you. Uncle Thomas says I must implore you to find whatever path imaginable to come back to England whilst you can. I understand you won't leave your parents, but please consider how you might make your way back to me.

Mum always says what's meant for you won't pass you by, and I cling to that. I don't see a future without you. It's as simple as that. Please stay safe.

All my love,
Maggie xx"

She put down her pen and looked around the hut, seeing nothing through a blur of tears. She wiped them away impatiently, read over the letter once more, and placed it in an airmail envelope for the morning post.

When would she see Micah again? Was that only a dream? Would he still care for her? Was she worthy of that love?

* * *

"Kingston, snap out of it. Are you ready yet?" Pip's voice penetrated her jumbled thoughts. "Are we going for a walk or not?"

"Keep your hair on, Pip. I'm coming."

Addy stayed back to wash some of her gear, so Maggie, Pip, and Lou set out on a cloudy June afternoon. A lone sparrow whistled in the wind.

"Shall we try to cadge a lift into town on our next day off to see the damage for ourselves?" Maggie asked. "Life on base can be dead boring at times."

Exeter had been bombed twice in the past month, resulting in an appalling 164 deaths and heavy damage to the city.

"I heard the Cathedral sustained a direct hit," said Lou. "Heartless buggers."

Maggie and Pip stopped to stare at young Lou. This was quite a fiery outburst from the shy girl.

"Quite so," Pip agreed. "At least it's still standing, or so I'm told."

"And they've attacked Bath and Norwich. All in supposed retaliation for our boys bombing German targets. But if they think we'll capitulate because they're blasting our treasured cities, they have another thing coming, don't they, Mags? We're going to trounce them soundly."

"No question. It just inflames us all to work together to end this war as soon as humanly possible. So, we can get back to our lives." Maggie said hopefully.

"What do you miss about normal life, girls?" Pip asked. "I want to sleep and sleep, go dancing and to the films every Saturday, and throw out my ration book," she declared. "Never wear khaki again and wear as much lippy as I can buy. And not just *Burnt Sugar* to go with khaki. Oh, and find a nice chap with a bit of money that will marry me. If I don't find an American here on the base first."

The girls laughed.

"I want our housekeeper Faye to come back and cook us a Sunday roast with all the trimmings. Piles of roast beef, mashed potatoes loaded with butter, anything but cabbage or Brussel sprouts for veg. Oh, and a pile of warm biscuits that crumble to the touch. Tea with two heaping

136

spoonfuls of sugar to go alongside chocolate sponge with custard. Two large helpings." Maggie paused, unaware that her friends had stopped in their tracks.

"I don't believe I've ever heard you speak so much in all the time I've known you, Mags," Pip giggled.

Maggie shrugged.

"It's what I dream of at night. Won't it be heavenly after the war to eat whatever we want, when we want?"

"What I fancy more than anything is to see my parents. To be at home in my own bed in Hereford, being woken by the cows," Lou's voice shook with emotion. "And to not be scared all the time. To never be afraid again." She pushed her fringe out of her eyes.

"It's the simple things we crave, isn't it girls?" Pip strove to keep it light. "Deciding what we want to do each day. We can look to our own futures – finally."

"We all just want life to be normal again, I expect," Maggie sighed.

"Whatever normal is," Pip retorted wistfully.

"What I don't fancy is things going back to the way they were. Men coming back to their jobs, us settling for the local boy that we've known since grammar school. We've grown older, we've lived, girls. And look what we've accomplished. We've worked shoulder-to-shoulder with the men, and kept up our own. We deserve better, don't we?" Pip burst out with passion.

"I should think we do," Lou replied quietly. "We've earned it."

"It's going to be strange, just keeping house, and raising babies, if we're lucky," Maggie mused. "That will be something of an adjustment."

The trio continued walking in silence.

"Who's for a cuppa, then?" Pip asked.

CHAPTER SEVENTEEN

August 1942

"Well, what do you make of that, then?" Pip remarked, as she wiped her face in the scorching sun.

"Ain't we fancy? Royalty comin ter see us," Addy joined in.

"It's grand that the Princess Royal is touring the ATS bases across England," Maggie said, staring up at the blazing sun. "I hope it cools down some, or we'll fry to bits while on inspection."

"Did you hear Sgt. Plath? We're to scrub down every surface till it gleams, polish up our buttons and boots, and go on parade each day for an extra hour. I hope Her Royal Highness is worth it," Pip whined.

"Of course, it's worth it," Lou stopped on the dirt path to the canteen. "Princess Mary is the King's sister, isn't she? And the Controller Commandant of the ATS? It's dead brilliant that she's paying us a visit," her voice trailed off.

"Look at you, taking us to task. You're finding your voice, love," Pip joked.

Lou blushed and kicked a stone in the dirt.

"Leave off, Pip. I'm just proud of our work is all."

"Don't let this daft cow knock yer down," Addy jumped in. "I'm 'appy ter give a little show to ter Princess. We all be doin our bit, ain't we?" She put a hand on Lou's shoulder.

Lou threw her a grateful smile.

Maggie thought back to her last brush with royalty. When she and Tillie had been selected in a group of Lyons Nippies to serve at a royal garden party, they had been so excited.

Tillie had been the lucky one, being chosen to serve in the Royal tent, near the King, Queen, and the little Princesses. Tils had remarked on the beauty and graciousness of Queen Elizabeth, and the exquisite manners of Princesses Elizabeth and Margaret Rose. The King had looked splendid in his uniform.

After an accident with a broken glass, Tillie had come to the Queen's attention when she quickly tended to the bleeding patient. In the medical tent, Her Majesty had done a double take when she spotted Maggie, who had appeared in the doorway, looking for her sister.

Maggie smiled to herself, as the girls settled at a table. How prophetic the Queen had been when she suggested Tillie take a post as a nurse or ambulance driver. This had been just before the war, but Queen Elizabeth had realized it was coming. And what a splendid job Tillie had done driving ambulance – particularly during the Blitz – when the bombs rained down for almost three months straight. She had put herself in danger over and over again, as she and her partner Ernie had been called out to live sites where fires and bombs threatened everyone in their paths.

She, herself glossed over her own heroic efforts during the Blitz. As a volunteer for the Women's Volunteer Service, she had employed her Nippy skills serving in a mobile canteen. Night after night, she and her crew were parked in dangerous locations around London bringing tea, sandwiches, biscuits, and comfort to ARP wardens, firefighters, policemen, ambulance workers, and all those who risked their lives to rescue Londoners in danger. Her own life had been in danger countless times, only partially protected by the truck's metal roof. But for Maggie, it was the least she could have done – helping others as she hoped others were helping Micah and his family in France.

Thinking of Micah, she smiled. She missed their quiet times together, playing music, reading, and walking together.

"And what are you so pleased about, love?" Pip teased, as they sipped their lukewarm tea. "Fancy loads of marching about then?"

"Sod off," Maggie shook her head. "Just woolgathering, I suppose."

"Maggie wiv 'er 'ead in ter clouds agin," Addy commented.

"I suppose so, Addy," Maggie just smiled again. "Sgt. Plath said one of the mixed batteries would be giving Her Royal Highness a demonstration of the equipment and guns."

"Wouldn't it be brilliant if they chose us?" Pip exclaimed.

"Smashing," Lou echoed.

"Cor, it be bloody 'ot," Addy swore. "Wot can we do to cool down?" She fanned herself with her cap.

"I'm going to nip to the showers. It's not my day for a hair wash, but I'm that desperate that I don't care if I get caught," Pip breathed out and wiped her neck.

"Whilst you're at it, give your kit a good clear out," Maggie suggested mildly. "You'll never pass inspection with that jumble in your locker and under your bed. How you find anything, I don't know."

Pip shrugged.

"It doesn't seem to matter how often I sort it, it's in a muddle in no time."

"I'll get a start on polishing. And I've a loose button I need to mend," Lou said, rising. "I don't have energy for much else."

"Fancy a walk, Mags?" Addy turned to her.

Maggie shook her head.

"No, thanks just the same. I've letters to write. Maybe a breeze will magically appear." Maggie got up.

"Chance is a fine thing," Pip guffawed. "By the time we're on duty, maybe. I expect it will be a hot night on the guns."

They all nodded, not looking forward to the close quarters, heat, and smells of the ack-ack station in August.

"Dear Hannah,

It's a warm afternoon here on base, and everyone is searching for a way to cool down. How I wish we could be back at Brighton Beach, splashing in the cold water, and walking on the windy pier in search of ice cream.

Do you remember that afternoon, just before the war? None of us wanted to believe it was coming, even though the signs were all around

140

us. We just wanted to put aside all thoughts of it, and enjoy the day – and the amazing picnic food. It was smashing, wasn't it?

I suppose I shouldn't dwell on the past – we must always look forward.

How are you getting on? The Kingston household can be hectic, with so many comings and goings. Tillie can fill up a room with her presence, and Mum is always fussing around.

I trust they are taking good care of you. I expect you are well-fed, even with ration food. Isn't Aunt Isla's baking just wonderful? I don't know how she manages with all the butter and sugar shortages, but she creates delicious confections. My mouth is watering as I write this. Now that chocolate and sweets have been added to the ration at just two ounces per person a week, how will we cope? It doesn't bear thinking about, does it dear?

Are you settling in at school? It must be strange to be back at a desk learning, but Micah and your parents want you to get an excellent education, and you won't let them down. You might even be Dr. Goldbach someday? Wouldn't that be splendid?

How is my dear Robbie? I miss him dearly, but I sleep well knowing you're taking marvelous care of him. Does he still fancy a cuddle into your shoulder at night? Give him a kiss for me.

Some thrilling news. Her Royal Highness, the Princess Royal will be touring our station in a fortnight. We shall all have to shine up and march smartly around the camp to make our best impressions. I'll write later with all the details.

Darling, I must go. I have a few other letters to write, and I don't want to miss the evening post.

I'm so relieved, little sister, that you are safe at home. This will all end someday, and we'll plan for the future. University for you, I hope. No more khaki uniform for me, I'm counting on that.

Please write soon, and tell me how you're getting on. I love you, sweet dear.

Love, Maggie xx"

Maggie chewed the end of her pencil, hoping she'd struck the right note. She didn't want to linger on the past, and what poor Hannah had been through. She hoped she would make Hannah smile.

Concentrating on sealing the wafer-thin paper into an envelope, she went on to write to Micah and Mum. She wasn't any cooler, but felt better about connecting with loved ones at home.

A fortnight later, the camp was abuzz waiting for the royal arrival. All hands had been employed in painting, tidying away, and cleaning every nook and cranny that might come under scrutiny.

The Princess Royal was expected at 11:00 a.m.

Astonishingly, Mixed Battery 677 was selected for special notice by Princess Mary, Countess of Harewood. The team had trained for hours for the short demonstration that would present the Squadron in action.

"I'm that glad that it's not so bloody hot today," Pip exclaimed as they all washed up, brushed their dress uniforms, and examined the buttons and boots to ensure they gleamed.

"You and me both," Addy agreed, as she smoothed her hair under her cap.

"Do I look alright," Lou asked nervously. The one mirror in the hut had so many soldiers swarming around it, that no one could get close.

"You look fine," Maggie encouraged. She was already warm in her woolen khaki jacket. At least it wasn't raining.

"I can't eat a bite," Addy groaned. "Me tummy is that clenched."

"Let's all give it a try," Maggie said. "We'll need our strength to stand and parade, and then the demonstration." She looked at Pip. "And go easy on the lippy, love."

"I can't help myself," Pip laughed, as she brushed some across her lips. "There. Is that better?" She turned to her friend.

"Much. Alright, let's get a move on. The canteen will be crammed with soldiers and airmen."

A few hours later, the company stood at attention in the makeshift quadrangle as a convoy of army vehicles approached the camp. A trumpeter played as the procession stopped. An ATS soldier opened the back door of the car bearing the Princess Royal, and she bounded out, in full ATS dress uniform.

"She is tall, isn't she?" Pip breathed.

"Shhh," several voices shushed her.

The next hour flew by as the princess inspected the soldiers, visited the airfield, and had lunch with the senior officers on the base.

Battery 677 had been told to be at the gun park by 1200 sharp, in position and ready for the demonstration.

At 13:30, the visiting party strode purposefully towards the gun bunker. Alfred had been selected as spokesperson, and for that Maggie was relieved. She didn't think she could even speak, let alone lead a demonstration.

He introduced the squadron, and all the girls remembered to curtsey to Her Royal Highness. Princess Mary looked at each soldier in turn, and made small talk about the equipment, life at base, and even the weather.

"Lance Bombardier Kingston, is it?" Oh no, the princess had stopped to speak to her.

Maggie bobbed into a curtsey.

"Yes. Good afternoon, Your Royal Highness."

"And what is your position with the anti-aircraft crew?" The princess asked, looking directly at Maggie.

"I operate the predictor machine, Ma'am," she answered shortly, not sure how much detail the princess really wanted to hear.

"I understand that takes a great deal of skill and concentration," Princess Mary said.

"Yes, Ma'am," Maggie didn't know what else to say. "We've undergone a great deal of training."

"Yes, just so," the princess replied. "And how do you find working on a squadron mixed with men and women? Have you been treated properly?"

Seeing as how this was all she'd ever experienced, Maggie hesitated over her response.

"It's brilliant, Ma'am. When we first started, the men showed us the ropes, and have looked after us ever since. We've been treated just like any other soldiers."

"Excellent. Carry on. You are doing a superb job for the war effort on behalf of the King and Queen. You should be proud."

Maggie curtseyed again, feeling rather uplifted.

The princess turned to Lou.

"And where are you from, Private?" She asked Lou politely.

"Hereford, Your Majesty...I mean Your Royal Highness," Lou fumbled a curtsey, turning crimson red.

"Farming country, then? First-rate. England needs to grow as many crops as possible to feed our people. Why did you decide to join the ATS?"

The princess had stopped directly in front of little Lou, who somehow shrunk even further.

"I heard you on the radio Ma'am, saying every girl wearing an ATS uniform replaces a soldier, which increases fighting strength." She almost whispered.

The Princess Royal took a step back. Her chest puffed proudly. Up close, she wasn't actually that tall, but had a formidable posture and carriage – just like her mother, Queen Mary.

"That's remarkable, Private. And you can manage this heavy equipment, a little bit of a thing like you?" She asked gruffly.

"Yes, Ma'am, I get by," Lou managed to squeak.

Princess Mary turned to one of the officers leading her party.

"It's quite extraordinary what these women are accomplishing in the field. Vital work. Tremendous."

With that, the squadron simulated an attack, with Pip spotting, Addy and Lou on the height and range finder, and Maggie pretending to operate the predictor. Having called out an imaginary enemy aircraft, the crew sprang into action, though no actual shells were fired. Alfred explained the process as it happened. The entire demonstration took less than a minute, so the princess insisted upon a repeat performance.

Just then, an officer ran up to the Princess' aide, who turned to speak to her. The trio looked serious, indeed.

"That's all we have time for today. Thank you all. I'm quite struck with all I've seen. Excellent job." She nodded and hurried away, her aides rushing to follow behind.

The team almost collapsed after she left.

"She thinks we're extraordinary," Pip jumped up and down, hugging Addy.

"That was quite something," Maggie tried to catch her breath. "Well done, all of us. Without sounding smarmy, I'm ever so proud to be a part of the Royal Artillery."

"I called her Your Majesty," Lou said gloomily. "I'm such a gormless ninny."

"Oh, give over, Lou. I'm sure it happens to her all the time," Pip's enthusiasm could not be squashed.

"And we're all to go the NAAFI for free beer tonight," Alfred exclaimed.

Maggie felt proud that her team had done well for such high royal company. Something to tell my children someday, she thought to herself.

"Wot are we waitin' fer?" Addy linked arms with Maggie, as they were dismissed from duty, and went off to celebrate.

Maggie and the girls later heard that the reason for the Princess Royal's abrupt departure was tragic news. Her brother-in-law, George, Duke of Kent, had been killed in an RAF plane crash en route from Scotland to Iceland. All the passengers and crew were lost, apart from one rear gunner. The duke was only thirty-nine and left behind a wife and three children. His son, Edward, took over as the new Duke of Kent, at the young age of six.

Despite wartime, a family service was held for the King's brother at St. George's Chapel, Windsor. He was the first royal family member in 500 years to perish in active service. The Windsors were devastated, but had to carry on. Just like everyone else.

CHAPTER EIGHTEEN

October 1942

"How does Lord Woolton dare think we can eat this rubbish bread?" Tillie grumbled. "I bet his family isn't trying to make toast out of this mess."

Hannah looked up in surprise. Tillie was usually so cheerful.

"Tillie, it's hardly that bad, is it?" Alice looked at her.

The National Loaf had been introduced earlier that year, in part to save precious space in shipping food to Britain. Its whole grains and reduced sugar allowed it to stay off the ration. But it also rendered it gray, mushy, and tasteless, which added to the general weariness and disillusionment of the British people.

Germany and its partners were fighting against the Soviet Union, with both success and failure. Advances had been made, but the Germans had grappled with the harsh winters, sustaining heavy losses. Rallying, they had fought their way into Stalingrad last month and secured the Crimean Peninsula. Having also penetrated Egypt, Germany seemed poised for triumph. It was crushing to the Allies.

Tillie put down the knife she'd been using to cut the thick and heavy loaf.

"Sorry, Mum. I'm just out of sorts. I miss Trevor and Maggie. And Katie too, I suppose." Tillie had put her hair up in a red turban, which matched her Victory red nail varnish.

Alice turned off the stove and poured the boiling water over the tea leaves. She paused to study her daughter.

"You do look a bit peaky, love. Rough night in the ambulance?"

"Not so bad. Only called out twice – one was a house fire started in a kitchen in Putnam. No casualties, thank goodness. An older woman on her own who left the hob on. She was unconscious, with smoke inhalation. We passed her on to first aid. I'm sure she'll recover nicely. The other was two sisters and their father in Fulham. A fire started in the old man's bedroom when he knocked over a lamp. The neighbors called for us, and the fire brigade, whilst the sisters tried to rouse their father. When we arrived and examined him, I suspected a heart attack, so Ernie and I loaded him in the ambulance straightaway and got him to hospital. I hope they can save the poor dear." Her tone was matter-of-fact, but every case meant something to her. It was difficult at times, transferring patients to hospital, never knowing the outcome of their injuries. Sometimes she returned a day or two later to look in on those that touched her heart.

"Are you getting worn down driving ambulance, Tillie?" Hannah asked curiously as she brought three bowls of porridge to the table. Her fair hair hung in long braids and she had grown a couple of inches since joining the Kingston household. She hardly looked like a young girl any more. Only the braids and school uniform gave her away.

"A little. Not that I wish the Blitz back for a second, but I really felt I was making a difference then. We saved so many people, and really pulled together with the WVS, ARP, and local fire stations," Tillie spread a little margarine on her toast, then pushed it away. "I don't miss steering the shuddering ambulance with air raid sirens, anti-aircraft fire and bombers whomp-whomp-whomping all round. Nor do I long to feel shrapnel dropping like tin cans on the roof as we swerved to miss potholes, broken glass, and rubble. The crump, crump of the bombs overhead. Cordite burning our nostrils and throats as our eyes streamed from smoke. The conditions were horrific, Mum. I still hear those sounds and smell those odors sometimes when I can't sleep."

Alice clucked.

"My poor dear. The sights you have seen are too much for a young woman your age. All of you. You younger generation has been robbed of youthful fun and carefree days. I really hate that for you." Alice shook her head, her brown-gray curls bouncing on her collar.

"It's alright, Mum. We're all doing our best. And before you can say it, yes, I do miss running into Trevor as he fought fires in the East End. Or even the thought of seeing him. It could perk up even the most wretched shift."

"Aren't you going to eat, love? The bread is not that dreadful," Alice knitted her brows together.

"Just tea, Mum. My tummy is a bit wobbly today."

Alice looked at her sharply but said nothing. She glanced at the clock and then over at Hannah.

"Hadn't you better get off to school, dear?"

Hannah gobbled the rest of her porridge, snatched Tillie's toast from her plate with a wink, and picked up her satchel.

"Thanks, Aunt Alice. See you for tea. I'll help with supper. Ta." In a flash she was gone.

"Another cup, dear?" Alice lifted the knitted tea cozy off the brown pot. "Or maybe some Horlicks to perk you up?"

"Another cuppa is lovely, Mum. I have some letters to write, but they can wait."

"You're quite missing your new husband, aren't you, darling?" Alice asked quietly.

Tillie raised bleak eyes.

"Mum, I'm trying not to, but I really am. I know it's daft when he's safe, and so many men are…not, but I'm miserable without him. I trudge through each day, but it's the sameness that gets to me. And the loneliness." The telltale flush crept up her neck.

"Love, I'm so sorry. It can't be easy for you. You're young and in love. This should be the happiest time of your life. You and Trevor should be making a home together and planning a future with excitement. I hate this bloody war." She tossed her napkin on the table, infuriated.

"Mum, language," Tillie tried to tease her mother.

"Sorry, darling. I just feel so helpless at times. You and Trevor, poor Maggie desperate for word of Micah, Kenny and his lingering fears, and now Katie in the fray. All I can do is offer cups of tea," she finished bitterly.

"Oh Mum, you do so much more than that. You are the rock of the family. You keep the chaos under control, and you provide the calm and security we all need."

"And here's you comforting me, when you are bereft of your dashing young husband. But thank you, Tillie. That means so much."

"And I'll be just fine, Mum. I find I'm a bit weepy these days. Don't pay me any mind. We're all under strain, aren't we?" Tillie patted Mum's hand, seeking comfort.

The weak October sun streamed through the window, as the two women sat in silence.

Alice rose to clear away the breakfast things and put on the kettle for more tea.

"Hannah seems to be settling in. It's a pity that she's missed so much school being in France. It can't be easy having younger classmates." Mum changed the subject.

"Surely, she'll soon catch up and overtake them. Do you think there's a chance she'll do well enough to go on after she passes her 'A' levels? Or more's the question – will there be a likelihood of her being able to attend university?"

Alice sighed heavily.

"It's ridiculous to imagine that this war will still be waging then. But if it is, she will be conscripted."

"She may even enlist at age eighteen, Mum. I haven't spoken to her about it, but every able-bodied man and woman is needed. I'm just hoping against hope that this madness will all end soon, and we can get back to normal."

Tillie inadvertently echoed her twin's sentiments.

"You and me both, love," agreed Mum.

"You and me both what?" Kenny asked as he sauntered into the kitchen. "And what's on offer for breakfast?"

Today looked like it was going to be a good day for her son. Mum smiled.

"Good morning, Kenny. How did you sleep?" She jumped up to fetch him a cup for his tea.

"Passable, Mum. No nightmares."

Kenny's night terrors were slowly declining. Some nights he still woke up sweating and screaming, reliving the explosion on *HMS Dainty*, struggling to get to shore, and the painful days since. Sometimes, he

149

welcomed a cold pack and a comforting arm. At others, he shied away, wanting to grapple with his demons himself.

"Porridge, and toast is all," Alice offered. "A bit of powdered egg, perhaps? Sorry I can't give you the full English, darling."

"Oh, how I dreamt of that in northern Africa, Mum. Eggs, bacon, sausage, baked beans, bubble and squeak, fried tomato, fried mushrooms, black pudding, and fried bread." Kenny licked his lips.

"Oh Kenny, please," Tillie groaned. "You are making my stomach turn. That sounds disgusting. I'm off to write Trevor. Mum, I'll join you to queue for the shopping. It always goes faster with company."

"Ta, love. Now, young man, let's get something sorted for you. But put the full English out of your mind. A spot of blackberry jam from our allotment do you on your toast?"

"Smashing, Mum. Just eating British food is good enough for me," Kenny smiled.

He was looking healthier, too. He had filled out a bit, losing the gray pallor and gauntness from his face. Now the tallest in the house, he had the same golden hair and chocolate-brown eyes as his twin sisters. Even his cocky personality was starting to re-emerge. The girls will be crazy about him, Alice thought as she put the toast on and brewed a fresh pot for her son.

"Mum, I'm starting to remember more about my time with the fisherman and his wife," Kenny said softly.

Alice's teacup clattered.

"Really, darling? Would you like to talk about it?"

"Just to say, Mum, that Jafi and his wife Raefa treated me very well. I believe I was in a high fever for some time, and I remember Raefa bringing me strange but lovely tea, and cooling me with cloths on sultry nights. Jafi was busy with the fishing boat most days – leaving before the sun rose each morning, and returning at sundown, sometimes with few or no fish. There was little talk because we couldn't understand each other. But we somehow communicated through hand motions. We ate fish most days, soup, and bread. Plain fare, but it helped to build my strength.

I had no idea who or where I was, and this began to vex me as time wore on. Who were these people? Who was I? I could tell from the differences in our skin colors that we weren't related, had the language barrier not already provided that substantial clue." He raked a hand through his messy hair.

"It was a peaceful time, if that doesn't sound too odd. Once my arm healed, I helped Jafi with the fishing. At first, I bumbled around, but after a time I watched and learned." He grinned. "I'd like to think I gave some aid to him."

"What finally released your memory of your identity, dear son," Alice asked gently.

"It came to me at night. In dreams. I began to see fragments of images of home, of British faces, and the *Dainty*. I took up long walks to jar my memory, and I suppose it worked. Looking out at the sea one day, the name Kenneth burst into my mind. It was such a thunderbolt, Mum, that I fell in the sand."

"Oh, my dear. It must have been so harsh for you," Mum sympathized.

"By then I was relieved to finally realize who I was. It all came rushing back over the next few weeks. I managed to make Raefa understand I needed to see the doctor, who spoke some English. Once he arrived, and I reclaimed my name and military rank, matters moved quickly after that. And here I am."

"Darling, I'm so comforted that you were well looked after. I owe so much to that wonderful couple." Alice could not even imagine the picture her son painted.

"And the explosion. Do you recall anything of that night?" She asked delicately.

Kenny shook his head.

"Just the vague nightmares. Nothing more. And in some ways, I hope I never do."

Tillie re-entered the kitchen, having overheard a little of the conversation.

"Sometimes the mind protects a person," Tillie ventured. "I've seen it time and again in traumatic accidents. It's as if the brain somehow grasps how much a body can take, and shuts down to help the healing. It's naught to bother about. It will recede over time."

A smile flashed across Kenny's face.

"I'm home and healthy. And the nightmares are waning. I want to put my best foot forward now. And Mum, that means I need to get to sea, and do my bit."

Alice tried not to gasp, knowing this day was coming.

"I understand, love. And when the time is right, that's what you need to do."

Kenny was grateful she didn't make a scene. He'd had enough emotion for one morning.

Uncle Thomas appeared unexpectedly that evening after supper. Kenny and Hannah had gone for a walk. Walter read his newspaper while Tillie struggled with her knitting, trying to make a pair of mittens for Trevor. Mum patiently unpicked her last mistakes, showing her where she went wrong.

"Ta, Mum. But I don't think I'll ever cope with this bloody knitting."

A loud knock startled the quiet atmosphere.

Walter let in his brother-in-law and showed him to the drawing room.

"Thomas, what a lovely surprise. Can I get you some tea?" Alice half-rose out of habit.

He shook his head tersely, removing his felt hat.

"No thank you, Alice. I'm here to impart some news. Some disturbing news."

Alice sunk back into the wing chair, while Tillie gave up any attempt at knitting.

"Please sit, Thomas," Walter said quietly, as he joined Tillie on the sofa.

"It's about Micah and his family," Thomas started slowly. "We've been hearing rumors for the last several months about roundups happening in France – in both the occupied and unoccupied zones. Most of it has been kept out of the papers to keep up morale here." He paused and looked at the anxious faces around him.

"I can confirm that the rumors of the Vél d'Hiv roundup is true. There was a mass arrest of something around 13,000 men, women, and children."

Tillie gasped and clutched her father's hand.

"The Vichy government in the southern unoccupied zone has been actively collaborating with the Nazis and did nothing to impede the roundup. British Jews were meant to be exempt, but I've learned that Micah and his parents were part of that arrest. The most I can find out is that they were shipped by train to Drancy in northern France."

"What is Drancy?" Tillie asked, holding her breath. The drawing room suddenly felt stuffy and airless.

Walter looked steadily at his niece.

"There's no easy way to say this. It's a transit camp, my dear. From there, Jewish people are being deported to Auschwitz, a work camp in Poland".

Tillie felt as if she were going to faint.

CHAPTER NINETEEN

"Tillie, you're white as a sheet. I'll fetch you some water," Alice jumped up.

"I'm okay, Mum. It was just such a shock. Please sit down. Uncle Thomas, do go on. I'm sorry."

Alice sank back down, keeping a worried eye on her daughter. She hadn't been herself lately.

"What else, Thomas?" Walter interjected. "What are the facts?"

"I will tell you what I know, but I must warn you it's rather grim. Drancy is near Paris. It is an unfinished housing project that has been converted to a transit camp." He paused, looking at the serious faces around the room. "It's a harsh place, poor living conditions, and limited food. From what I understand, it's rather a holding base.

There's no gentle way to say this. Jewish people are collected by Nazis in roundups across France. Against their wills, with no notice, scant time to gather things, and no information about where they are going or for how long."

Tillie stifled a gasp. How would Micah and his parents cope with such rough treatment?

"They must be so frightened," she couldn't help saying.

"Indeed, you are right, Tillie. The entire experience is terrifying, so I'm given to understand."

"What happens to them, then?" She asked, her voice almost a whisper.

"They are treated as prisoners, with callous disregard for their status or positions. In fact, hardly regarded decently as human beings. They are sent to Drancy via train and are temporarily held there for days or perhaps weeks. Then, these poor souls are loaded onto trains and sent to work in German camps."

"What kind of work?" Alice asked. Her hands were trembling so she picked up her knitting to calm herself.

"It's unclear, but some kind of physical labor. Building sites or perhaps some type of war production. It seems that the Germans want to use the dispossessed Jews in some sort of workforce capacity."

"But how?" Tillie sputtered. "How can they just take a group of people out of their own country and put them to work against their will? It makes little sense." Now Tillie was getting furious.

Thomas raised his hands uncertainly.

"The Germans have control over France – at the moment. It's becoming apparent that they have a plan for the Jews. We just don't comprehend what it is. Hitler has made no secret that he has an enormous prejudice against the Jewish people – why is hard to tell. It is all rather distressing."

"So, are the Goldbachs still in Drancy or have they been shipped to Poland? It all sounds so callous, cruel even," Tillie was aghast.

"That I don't know, but I continue to make inquiries," Walter replied.

"What are we going to tell Hannah?" Alice asked weakly. "That poor girl. She's already been through so much."

"I should think we tell her nothing until we learn more. Surely, we'll get news soon. I don't want to burden her any more than necessary."

Tillie nodded.

"And what of Maggie? She's an adult and should be told."

"I agree. I suggest we send her a telegram. There's no need for her to come home – there's naught for her to do. But she needs to be told, poor dear."

"I'll do that straightaway," Walter said. "This is grim news, but we must keep hope."

Yet, they all felt a dreadful sense of foreboding.

* * *

Maggie read, and then re-read the bold type on the thin, yellow paper with Post Office Telegram letterhead.

"GOLDBACH FAMILY HELD AT FRENCH TRANSIT LOCATION STOP MAY TRANSPORT TO GERMAN WORK CAMP STOP NO FURTHER NEWS STOP TAKE HEART STOP POPS AND MUM STOP"

Maggie sat on her narrow metal cot, oblivious to the sound of women buzzing around her. All she could hear was the fierce pounding in her head. The telegram dropped to her lap.

"Bad news from 'ome, love?" Addy asked with sympathy.

Maggie couldn't speak. She needed to think. She pulled on her coat and left to walk and sort her thoughts. The Goldbachs in a holding location? Maybe being sent to work at a camp for Jews? Why? What had they done wrong?

Maggie walked for an hour; her thoughts tangled in her head. What would happen to Micah? His Papa and Mama? They were in their late forties. Could they cope with a work camp? Would Micah be able to protect them? How long would they be there? How would they be able to return home? When would she see her beloved Micah again?

A cold autumn drizzle permeated Maggie's foggy mind. Looking at her watch, she swore under her breath. She'd missed dinner and was now late for a lecture on German aircraft recognition.

She slipped into the lecture, hoping no one would notice her tardiness. For the next two hours, she tried to focus on Henkels and Junkers. She took detailed notes, as usual trying to block out the thought of Hitler and the Nazis rounding up innocent families like Micah's. It stoked a fire in her to do her absolute best to help shoot down every enemy plane that dared to enter the sky on her watch.

"Are you alright, Mags?" Pip whispered Pip with concern. "Addy told me you received a telegram."

Maggie nodded.

"Eyes ahead, Kingston, Murley," Sgt. Plath snapped.

"Sorry, Sarg," Maggie mumbled.

Maggie refused to discuss the telegram or its contents with her friends. All she said was that someone she cared about might be in trouble in France. Pip, Addy and Lou were deeply anxious for her, but couldn't cheer her up.

"What do you think of these Americans, then?" Pip asked at the NAAFI a week later.

"I like 'em," Addy declared with a wink. "They be ever so friendly, and their flyers are proper cheeky."

"Who can say no to chocolate?" Pip added. "What a delight!"

"I'm that grateful they are here to join the Allied effort," put in Maggie. "But they are a trifle loud."

American troops in all service branches had been arriving steadily since the beginning of the year. Landing first in Ireland, they had been flowing to air force bases, naval command centers, and dozens of departure points for North Africa, France, Italy, and Germany. Most Britons welcomed the soldiers, sailors and pilots. They brought a breath of fresh air and renewed hope to a weary, rundown, yet undefeated nation.

"Second Lieutenant Ray Phillips is rather dashing in his leather jacket," Pip grinned.

"Oi, do tell," Addy cooed over a cup of tea and a bun.

"Not much to tell – yet," Pip shrugged. "He's taken me for a few coffees is all. He's from a place called Chicago in America."

"Is he the tall one with the slicked back brown hair and devilish blue eyes?" Maggie asked.

"Ain't they all devilish?" Addy giggled. "They're that forward."

"That's him," Pip smiled. "I might fancy him – just a bit."

"If you do, then hold him tight," Maggie said vehemently. "Grasp your happiness whilst you can. Who knows what tomorrow will bring." She squeezed Pip's hand.

"Ta, Mags. That's my girl."

Maggie's heart was raw, but she just had to get on with it. Until she had further news, she could only keep working, doing her best, and trying not to imagine the conditions under which Micah and his family were forced to live. She cried herself to sleep many nights, but stuffed a hankie in her mouth to muffle the noise. The pain was too great to be shared. She must bear it alone.

She kept writing to Micah, but without knowing where he was, it seemed senseless to post the letters. It gave her comfort to pour out her feelings, and share the day-to-day details of ATS life. She wished she had a poetic soul to so she could express herself in verse to Micah. The next best thing was to draw. In her rare private time with hoarded paper remnants, she sketched the ack-ack gunnery, her mates at rest, and whatever outdoor beauty she could find.

She kept writing to everyone at home and paid special attention to Hannah. During frosty nights in bed, she couldn't fight off the panic about the future. If something were to happen to the Goldbach family, something truly awful – she would have to take responsibility for the young girl. This didn't scare her in terms of having to look after her - she loved her dearly. But the thought of being totally in charge was rather daunting. Of course, her parents would help at every turn, but she herself would feel obligated to take over. It would be the least she could do to honor the memory of Micah and Hannah's father and mother. These dark thoughts crept into her mind, though she tried hard to push them away and remain hopeful. After these sleepless nights, she dragged herself out of bed in the freezing cold hut and went wearily about her duties.

Just before Christmas, Maggie received another telegram from home – this one from Tillie.

"HEART IS BREAKING FOR YOU STOP BIG NEWS STOP BABY COMING MARCH 1943 STOP CHUFFED TO BITS STOP TILLIE STOP"

Maggie shrieked. She couldn't help herself. Tillie having a baby! She herself would be an auntie.

"Bloody 'ell. Wots 'appened, ducks?" Addy inadvertently called Maggie by the nickname that Tillie used with her. Maggie burst into tears.

"There, there, love. Is it more dreadful news from home?" Pip, Addy and Lou circled protectively around her.

Maggie was laughing and crying at the same time.

"No, girls. It's brilliant news. The best. My sister Tillie is expecting a baby. In the spring. I couldn't be more delighted."

Maggie sprang to her feet and started dancing.

"I'm going to be an auntie. I'm going to be an auntie."

The girls were thrilled – not just for Maggie's twin, but to finally see a genuine smile on their friend's face. She seemed lighter than she had in weeks.

"1943 will be a better year, girls. I just know it!"

* * *

"I had my suspicions, darling. You've been off your food, especially breakfast. And you haven't been yourself – a little more impatient than normal." Alice was grinning from ear to ear.

"Mum, I had to tell Trev before you. And the doctor just confirmed it. But I was fit to bursting holding in the news." Tillie smiled too. "But what do you mean, impatient?" Tillie pouted.

"It's nothing, dear. It's all part of having a baby. How are you feeling now?"

Alice and Tillie sat in the kitchen, having a mid-day cup of tea and biscuit. Tillie had shared her and Trevor's welcome news the night before, and it had been a cause for celebration.

"My tummy is still a bit dicky, but feeling better each day. I had a few queasy mornings that were hard to bear. I'm just that tired all the time, Mum. Especially when I'm on nights, I'm finding it taxing to keep up my end at times."

Alice tsked.

"Are you sure you should be still working, love? Your job is so physical – and dangerous." Alice's smile faded.

"Oh, it's fine, Mum," Tillie waved her hand, regretting confessing this to Alice, who tended to worry. "And what would I do, in the event, if I didn't work? I expect to do my bit until nearer the end. Every pair of hands is needed."

"I suppose," Alice said doubtfully, recognizing she had little sway with her grown-up, married daughter.

"But Mum, now that the news is out, we can start planning for the baby. I wired Maggie too – I couldn't keep it to myself any longer."

Alice held her knitting needles up, soft white wool already taking the shape of a tiny baby bootie.

"In between my war knitting, I'm working on some things for your layette. So is Aunt Shirley. For now, we are sticking to white and yellow. After the baby is born, we'll complete the layette with the appropriate pink or blue. I'm keen as mustard, Tillie. With all the grim news around us, the idea of a new baby in the house is the best early Christmas gift we could ever want." She clicked away.

"Speaking of a new baby in the house, Mum, that's something I wanted to talk to you about. Are you all right with me staying here with the baby? Houses are impossible to find these days with all the rebuilding going on. Trevor's mum has kindly offered her flat to give Trev and me more privacy. But I feel cozier here at #40 – at least whilst Trev is serving away from home."

"Darling, I wouldn't have it any other way. You can stay as long as you like. I couldn't cope if you took the baby away – and he or she isn't even here yet." Alice couldn't wipe the delighted smile off her face.

Tillie laughed.

"Well, once the war is over, we'll need to find our own home. But for now, this is where I want to be. And Trevor agrees."

"That's sorted then," Alice patted her daughter's hand. "Another bikkie?"

CHAPTER TWENTY

December 1942

Christmas 1942 was even more subdued than 1941. Neither Trevor nor Katie were granted leave, but the family was thrilled that Maggie had a twenty-four-hour pass. She spent a fair part of it traveling, but was still home to celebrate Christmas with the family, and gratefully sleep in her own bed.

Rationing being even tighter meant the feast was modest. Mainly comprising winter vegetables such as, cabbage, sprouts and parsnips, Alice and Shirley had done wonders to dress up the meal. Aunt Shirley had somehow procured a small turkey that was declared delicious by all. Tillie suspected it she got it in the black market, as for weeks, the butcher had no fresh allocations, despite the long lines. The women had saved and combined their sweets ration. Isla Drummond had produced a Christmas pudding that was more carrots than dried fruits and sultanas, but was nonetheless appreciated by all.

With coal rationed since 1941, the family mainly gathered in the drawing room. Alice had reluctantly closed off the morning room and library to save on heating. Another belt-tightening measure that no one fancied. But with coal on the ration, they all suffered the chilly house – for the war effort.

"This time next year, there will be a little one at the table," smiled Isla. She was just as eager as Alice to welcome her new grandchild.

"Perhaps crawling, but just waving a rattle, more like," Tillie responded, tucking into the pudding with gusto.

"I can't wait," said Alice and Isla together. The room erupted into laughter.

After the clearing away of the table, which Tillie avoided saying she had to put her feet up – Maggie and Tillie escaped to their room for a long-overdue twin talk.

"For once, I'm the thinner twin," joked Maggie as the two settled in for a long chat. Robbie had found her, and was purring contentedly in her lap.

Tillie groaned.

"Give over, Mags. We're identical – if not at the moment. Why can't you see yourself the way I do, you daft girl?"

Maggie shrugged.

"What are you feeding this puss? He's gigantic."

"Nice try. You didn't answer me, ducks. Why don't you have more faith in yourself? You are such a kind, wonderful, and brave woman. I marvel at what you do every day as a gunner girl." Tillie looked intently into her sister's eyes.

"Now you give over, Tils. You're embarrassing me. I'm just doing my job. You are the shining star in the family. You drove ambulance in the Blitz. Now you're a married woman about to have a baby. It's no secret who is the more accomplished twin." She avoided her sister's gaze.

"Bollocks, Maggie. It's not a competition, for God's sake. Now you are making me proper cross."

"Sorry, Tils. I just wish I were as confident as you, sometimes. Never afraid to speak up. I'm getting on decently with the ack-ack guns, I suppose. I admire you, that's all. Don't be cross with me." Maggie tried to pacify. She mustn't upset Tillie in her condition.

"I admire you too, Mags. You may not always be the most talkative person in the room, but when you do speak, people listen because what you say has meaning. You don't blab on and on like I do. And if facing Nazi air attacks every night by returning fire in a bunker in an open field isn't brave, I don't know what is."

"That means so much, Tils. It really does. If I'm honest, I'm just that terrified for Micah and his parents that it makes me edgy. Please forgive me."

"Naught to forgive between us, ducks. Now, something top of mind. Will you be home when my time comes?"

Maggie shook her head slowly.

"I'm afraid not. It will be too difficult to manage without knowing exactly when baby Drummond will arrive. The best I can do is put in for emergency leave at the time. Will they give it to me?" She held up her hands. "It will all depend on the enemy action at the station. If I'm needed there, they won't release me unless it's bereavement leave – and sometimes not even then."

Tillie looked crestfallen.

"But I'll do my best. I really will. And if not then, I'll cajole, beg, and plead for emergency leave once he's born."

"He? How do you know it's a boy?" Tillie asked, cheerful again.

"I just know," Maggie replied simply. "We're twins."

"I don't have a feeling either way. Trev and I will be chuffed no matter if it's a baby girl or boy. As long as he or she is healthy."

"Me too, Tils. I just can't wait to see his face. What a wonderful pick-me-up during this drudge of a war."

Tillie and Maggie, like all Britons, were thoroughly sick of living in wartime. As the years ground on, the tolls of loved ones lost forever or not seen in far too long and increasingly strict rationing were harder and harder to bear. And, it showed. Strains and tensions made people snappish and short-tempered. Frayed nerves caused loss of appetite, sleepless nights, stomach pains, headaches, jitters, and other physical manifestations of the grinding worry.

To lift the spirits of the American Allied Forces in Britain, Westminster Abbey opened for a special service of Thanksgiving in honor of the American soldiers away from home. It was the first secular service held in the majestic Abbey, home to the Church of England since the 1500s. Some 3,500 soldiers filled the cathedral, where *The Star-Spangled Banner* and *America the Beautiful* were played in their honor. A feast was later held, and people across Britain celebrated. It brought a little light to the dreary days.

A new baby, hope and a delightful distraction were just what the Kingston family needed to carry on.

"I long to see his or her face too. And to hold his tiny body in my arms. But I'm that nervous about the actual birth. Even though I've seen it several times, and Trev and I even helped deliver a baby – it's quite another thing altogether to go through it myself. And most likely on my own. It would be a miracle for Trev to have leave at just the right moment." Her voice caught.

"I'm so sorry, sis. But men aren't much use when a baby is born, are they? They wait outside pacing and waiting for news. You'll have Mum and she'll be a brick. You know that." Maggie tried to bolster her sister.

"I suppose you're right. But it's not right that Trevor won't be the first to meet his son or daughter. This damned war!" Tears splashed down her cheeks.

Maggie hugged her twin, patting her hair, as Tillie cried months of pent-up frustration, loneliness, and fear.

After a reviving cup of cocoa, Maggie fetched them both hot water bottles. They talked into the night, with Maggie finally confiding her fears and panic about Micah.

They got little sleep, but when Maggie put on her uniform the next morning and left for her train, the sisters felt a sense of relief for having shared intimacies.

"A trouble shared is a trouble halved," Tillie whispered as they hugged one last time.

"Write soon," Maggie nodded.

And then she was gone.

* * *

"Pops, may I have a word?" Kenny interrupted Walter's newspaper and pipe.

"Sounds serious, son." Walter put down his *Daily Express*, and gestured for Kenny to sit down.

"It is, rather. Pops, His Majesty's Naval Service has written me about resuming my duties. I don't have a valid reason for medical leave any longer. And I want to do my bit. Bollocks, if the Yanks are fighting against the Nazis, I must take up service again."

Walter paused for a moment, realizing this decision would crush his wife.

"Son, I understand. But are you truly recovered enough for active service?"

"My memory is going from strength to strength, Pops. Physically, I'm fit as I ever was. I had a medical last week and passed A1. Not only do I think I am in excellent health, the Navy does as well."

"Kenny, you are a grown man. I respect your decision. And I'm proud of you for stepping back into the skirmish. It won't be easy, son. I fear you will have some setbacks. But there's a war on." They both smiled. "We are having some victories in Egypt and North Africa at the moment. But this war is far from over. The Navy needs you. But so does this family. So be safe."

"What about Mum? She wants to keep me wrapped in cotton wool." His tone was a trifle impatient.

"Leave Mum to me. When do you report?"

"A fortnight's time. I'll enjoy my soft bed and home-cooked meals a tad while longer."

* * *

"Kingston, you're needed in the common room," Jasper barked.

It was Tillie's last day driving ambulance. The baby was due in about six weeks, and she was having difficulty performing her duties. She couldn't lift patients onto stretchers without loads of huffing and puffing. And running into burning buildings and kneeling over fire victims was taking a toll. Her ankles were swollen and the night shifts were just too much for her.

But she wasn't expecting to feel so weepy today. She kept thinking of all the memories of the last two years – all the Blitz nights speeding around London picking up injured civilians trapped under buildings and burnt by incendiary bombs. She had met Trevor while working as an ambulance driver – in fact, they had met up during one of his firefighting shifts and run into one another from time to time on fiery London streets.

Mentally shaking herself, she walked into the room where she had spent so many hours in panicky anticipation of call-outs and utter exhaustion after twelve, fourteen, and even sixteen-hour nights.

Opening the door, she stopped short. The room was hung with newspaper streamers, and homemade signs wishing her and Trevor well.

"Jasper, I…" Tillie's hand went to her throat, and she felt the familiar and uncomfortable rush of red spreading up her neck and across her face.

"For she's a jolly good fellow,
For she's a jolly good fellow,
For she's a jolly good fellow,
And so say all of us."

Tears sprang into Tillie's eyes as she looked around the room at her fellow drivers, mechanics and dispatchers. Jasper, her supervisor with his usual scowl and ever-present cigar. Ernie, her retired cabbie partner who navigated the ravaged streets of London with her. Other crew members who had swapped shifts with her, laughed with her, and shared stories over endless cups of tea. And the shadows of those who were missing – killed in the line of duty. Sorely missed and never forgotten.

Her mates came forward, shaking her hand and making jokes to keep things light. A cup of tea appeared at Tillie's elbow, which she gratefully gulped.

"Sit, sit. Shove over, mates. Tillie, I've never seen you at a loss for words," Ernie shooed people away and offered his partner a seat on a hard chair.

"I didn't expect anything like this. I'm knocked for six, if I'm honest. I should have thought today would be quiet, and I'd just slip away."

"Not bloody likely," Jasper boomed. "You were one of our first women ambulance drivers during the Blitz. We weren't going to let you go without a proper knees-up."

Someone started playing show tunes on the piano, and a small crowd sang along. A side table was loaded with baby gifts, and a small cake was brought out.

After talking with everyone, Tillie began to wilt. Once again, her partner Ernie came to her rescue.

"Tils," he pulled her aside. "Your Pops is here to fetch you and the gifts. Whenever you're ready, you can say your goodbyes. We don't want any early babies coming into the ambulance station."

She threw him a wan smile.

"Everyone," she shouted over the din. Someone whistled to get everyone's notice.

"I'm overcome that you would do all this for me – for us. I wish Trevor were here to thank you in person. Your kindness and friendship over the last years means more than I can say," her voice broke but she carried on. "Thank you all, and I'll be sure to bring baby Drummond to visit."

"We'll get the little fellow his own helmet," someone shouted.

"It might be a little lass," Tillie retorted. They all laughed.

Tillie turned in her uniform, helmet, and kit to Jasper, and left with her father a short while later. They took a cab to carry all the baby gifts.

It was time for a new chapter – motherhood.

* * *

For the next few weeks, Tillie prepared for the new baby. She folded and refolded the knitted booties, blankets, jumpers, and caps she'd received from her ambulance team, and from a WVS do that Aunt Shirley had recently hosted. Alice had also knitted complete outfits in pink, blue, and yellow – just in case. Nappies had been folded and stacked in the dresser and Tillie fussed over the bedding for the tiny cot and marvelled at the baby rattles and toys that Alice had saved from her own babyhood.

"Mum, I can't see my feet. I can't fall asleep, and when I do, I wake up every hour to go to the loo. Has anyone ever had a bigger tummy than me?"

Tillie had kicked off her slippers and was rubbing her tummy under a voluminous red and white plaid smock. Her face looked a little more filled out than usual, but she still glowed – despite her complaints.

"Darling, everything is as it should be. You are meant to be fed up at this point. Wanting to get the baby out, and finally meet him or her prevails over the fear of giving birth."

"Well, I wouldn't go that far, Mum. But I can't wait to meet this little darling. I hope he or she looks just like Trev. Do you reckon he'll be able to sort some leave once the baby is here?"

"I'm sure he will, love. And remember, Maggie is due home in two days. If you use your twin powers, maybe you can bring about the birth while she's home. How about a pot of tea? I'm sure we can both do with a spot of comfort."

"Ta, Mum. Any sweets to go along with it? Baby is hungry again."

"By all means, Tillie. This granny won't be denying our precious baby a thing."

"Indeed, Mum. You'll be a smashing granny."

CHAPTER TWENTY-ONE

May 1943

As it turned out, Maggie appeared almost in time. Her train had been delayed, and she arrived home to an empty house save for Kenny.

"Hello, sis," he smiled as he bounced to greet her. "You've almost missed all the madness." He kissed her on the cheek.

"What do you mean, Kenny?" She shrugged off her coat, and hung it on the hall rack. Besides the unexpected tranquility of the house, she was so pleased to see Kenny almost back to his old self – lively and full of energy.

"It's Tillie. She's having the baby. She and Mum have gone round to the Princess Beatrice Hospital. Tillie barely slept all night, and Mum called the doctor early this morning. He's meant to meet them there."

Maggie picked up her coat again and hastily put it on.

"How was she? Was she alright?"

Kenny shook his head no.

"She was in heaps of pain, but I expect that's what having a baby is all about," he replied nonchalantly.

"Easy for you to say, Kenny. Well, I'm off. With any luck, I'll be there to see my niece or nephew being born – or straightaway after."

When she turned up at the hospital, she spotted Mum in the waiting room – knitting furiously to while away the time.

"Mum," Maggie cried, as she kissed her on the cheek.

"What's happening with Tillie? Is she alright?" Maggie was concerned for her twin.

"She's in with Doctor Harding. I have heard nothing in quite some time. Perhaps you can inquire?" Alice asked fearfully. She didn't like to bother anyone, but under her calm exterior she was deeply anxious.

Maggie took her newly earned confidence and strode up to the nursing station.

"Excuse me, I'm Maggie Kingston, sister of Tillie Drummond. How is she getting on?"

The nurse did a double take. This woman looked exactly like the laboring one just down the hall.

"Yes, we are twins," Maggie smiled.

"Right. Well, your sister is in excellent hands with Dr. Harding. She's getting on quite well, so far."

"Can I see her?" Maggie pushed.

"As a rule, no one is permitted during delivery," the pretty red-haired nurse hesitated. "But we've never had a twin situation like this before."

"She needs me," Maggie pleaded with her winning smile. "Her husband is in the RAF, and can't be here."

The nurse chewed her bottom lip and looked around the station. She straightened, having obviously taken a decision.

"Alright, love. I'll take you to her. I'm sure it would bolster her no end to see your friendly face about now."

The two stepped down the hall and the nurse opened a door and motioned for Maggie to enter.

"Thank you so much, Nurse. This means the world to me." She pushed through the door to see Tillie on the bed sweating and looking drained. The doctor and a midwife attended her.

"Maggie," Tillie cried out as she opened her eyes unbelievingly. She held out her arms to her sister.

"Darling, are you okay?" Maggie rushed to her side.

A contraction overtook her sister, and Maggie held her hand as Tillie was urged to push.

"Your sister is a marvel, Miss…" A middle-aged woman dressed in white said to Maggie, as Tillie's pain subsided.

"Kingston. Miss Kingston. Actual Lance Bombardier Kingston to be exact. We are…"

"Twins, I expect," finished the midwife. "That much is evident. I'm Mrs.

Whistledowne. As I was saying, your sister has been doing splendidly. She's been laboring since last night. The baby should be coming any…"

A low moan came from the bed. All eyes turned to Tillie.

"Another pain, dear? Let's try to push again. Miss Kingston, you may stand on the other side of the bed, and hold your sister's hand. That is, if you are not squeamish?"

Tillie's moan was growing to a low roar.

"Maggie, I'm so thankful you are here. Please, don't leave me." Tillie's large brown eyes entreated her sister's.

"I'm not going anywhere, darling. And I'm not squeamish, Nurse. The army rather numbs you after a time." She shrugged off her coat and held Tillie's hand tightly.

"Just please be quiet, and stay out of the way, Miss," the doctor kindly ordered. "And if one of us instructs you to leave, you must do so at once. Your sister and her baby's health are our top concern."

Maggie nodded, her throat suddenly dry. This was serious business.

For the next forty minutes, Maggie encouraged her sister through push after push. At one point, Tillie wailed she couldn't do it anymore. Maggie clutched her hand, looked deep into her eyes, and firmly insisted that she absolutely could. Finally, after a mighty effort, a red, slippery baby boy slid out into the world. Crying instantly, it was apparent he had a healthy set of lungs.

"It's a boy," declared the doctor. "A fine specimen of a lad."

Tillie and Maggie exchanged a look of pure joy.

"A boy, Tillie. You have a son." Maggie could barely breathe.

"You were right all along, Mags," Tillie cried in awe.

As the doctor tended to the new mother, the midwife washed and wrapped up the tiny, screaming bundle, and deposited him in his mother's arms.

"Oh, little love, you are so beautiful. Maggie, look at him. He is so sweet." Tillie kissed his little fingers and unwrapped him to count his ten toes.

Maggie wiped away a tear.

"You were brilliant, Tils. Just marvelous. And so is your young man. He's adorable. I should think he has a bit of the look of Trevor about him."

"Thank you for being here, Mags. I couldn't have done it without you." Tillie was drained, but bright and cheery, and proud of herself. Somehow, after all the lack of sleep, pains, and effort of pushing, she felt exhilarated and full of energy again.

"Don't be daft. Of course, you could have, darling. But I'm ever so glad you waited for me." Maggie had never felt closer to her sister.

The pair cooed over the newborn, until Alice was allowed in, when the emotions started afresh.

"Mum, are you crying already?" Tillie teased as Alice rushed to her daughter's bedside, tears pouring down her cheeks.

"Tillie, are you okay? I've been that worried. Oh, my goodness, the baby. How beautiful."

Mum gazed at the new mother and baby with adoration.

"He's a boy, Mum. And we are both smashing. Would you like to have a look?" Tillie held up the little bundle.

"A boy? Darling, congratulations. And may I?" Alice gingerly took the fragile package from her daughter, and cooed and clucked as only a grandmother can do.

* * *

Maggie only had a forty-eight-hour pass, so had to drag herself from Tillie's side just two short days later.

"I don't want to leave this proper ray of sunshine. I love you so much, little James Geoffrey." Maggie held him for the last time before rushing to catch her train. "This damned war splits up families so heartlessly. I can't bear it. But with Allied victories in North Africa, perhaps the tide is turning – just a little." She reluctantly handed the little blue bundle to her sister.

"I'm sorry, darling. We're going to miss you dreadfully."

"I'm that pleased that Trevor has gotten leave, so he'll be able to rock his son by the end of the week. I'm thrilled for you both, well the three of you, really." Maggie stood.

"It's lovely you've named him after Trevor's father, and our cousin Geoff," Maggie stalled.

Aunt Shirley and Uncle Thomas still mourned their only son, Geoffrey, killed at Dunkirk. They'd been so touched that Tillie and Trevor had honored them in such a kind way. It made Tillie feel closer to her late cousin, who had been a cheerful bloke who gave the best hugs.

"And where is this adorable boy, then?" Katie burst into the room, clutching a worn but well-loved teddy bear. "I've heard that the most beautiful baby in London is right in this very hospital room."

"Katie," the twins both shrieked. "I never knew you were getting leave," Tillie grinned from ear to ear. "Give us a kiss, then. And is that Mr. Teddy?"

Katie kissed her sisters and waggled the bear in front of Tillie.

"I've only got a twenty-four-hour pass – pinched it on compassionate grounds. I had to see my new nephew, didn't I?" Katie breezed. "I was that held up – your little lad has come on a momentous day. The King, Queen and princesses are at Service of Thanksgiving at St. Paul's Cathedral for the victory in North Africa. I heard the bells pealing. I imagined they were ringing for your brilliant accomplishment, sis."

"You are daft, darling. But how smashing to see you," Tillie gave her younger sister a tired grin. "Did you receive the birthday gift I sent last month? Damn this war – we miss so many special days."

Katie waved away her sister's concerns.

"I did, and ta for the soap – it was heavenly." She waggled the brown teddy bear from side to side. "I should have thought he might fancy my old teddy. These days, it's near impossible to find new toys but Mr. Teddy is almost as good as new. Mum patched him up proper."

The three sisters reunited over new baby Drummond – one in a hospital gown, one in khaki, and the third in a smart blue WRN uniform.

"And me, having to dash off, straightaway. This is rubbish," Maggie sulked. "It's not fair."

The three spent a precious hour together, before Maggie had to rush off. The trains would be running late, and it wouldn't do to be punished when she had a perfectly clean record – so far.

Katie spent every moment possible with Tillie and James until her own pass was about to expire.

"How can I leave this young lad? I'm just that mad for him already,"

Katie was loath to surrender the blue-wrapped bundle of sleeping baby. She smothered his face with little kisses.

"You'll see him on your next proper leave, won't you? Before you are assigned to your first post." Tillie itched to reclaim her son. "How are you getting on, then?"

Katie reluctantly handed the newborn to her sister.

"Pretty well so far. I managed to get passed through my basic training. They've put me on clerking and secretarial duties." She made a face. "It's not thrilling work, but with my experience at Pops, it was a logical fit."

"That's lovely, darling. What about…" A loud wail interrupted the conversation. "I expect this young man needs a feed. He certainly lets me know what he wants." Tillie was distracted by James' crying.

"That's my cue to leave. Aren't you the clever old thing creating such a beautiful boy? Cracking to see you both. I'll try to write soon. Ta ra," Katie popped her cap on her head, kissed her sister and nephew, and hurried out of the room.

"Goodbye, love," Tillie called out as she settled the infant for his afternoon feed. "And who's the loveliest baby in the entire world?" she cooed in new mother bliss.

The rest of the family had stayed away – letting the sisters spend time with Tillie and James before returning to their duties.

But now, visiting time every day was crammed with the Kingston family and other well-wishers. With only one visitor per day allowed just for an hour, they took turns to inspect and admire the newest Kingston.

Pops and Mum managed a visit together after Alice had won over Nurse with her charm and polite ways. She brought grapes for the new mother, and a little outfit for James. Pops somehow managed to find a tiny bouquet of flowers.

"My, he's little," Walter peered over Tillie's shoulder. "But a handsome fellow."

"Would you like to hold him, Pops?" Tillie held out the blue bundle.

A look of alarm spread across his face. "No thanks, poppet. I'll leave that to your mother. Babies are her territory."

"Leave off, Walter. You held your own babies."

"That was a long time ago, Alice. Our Tillie is coping beautifully."

In due course, Hannah, Kenny, and the Fowlers came, bringing small gifts and precious sweets.

And of course, Isla was a frequent visitor. Just as proud of her new grandson as the Kingstons, it brought her new life after constantly worrying about her own son so far away.

"He looks just like Trevor at this age," she exclaimed more than once. "Look at that thatch of dark hair. I'm sorry, Tillie, but I don't suppose he will have your blonde looks." Isla cradled her grandson, softly caressing his soft cheeks and tiny hands.

"That suits me to the ground, Mrs. Drummond. Father and son are my handsome boys." Tillie was looking tired but happy.

Isla looked over at her daughter-in-law with a shy smile.

"Now that little James is here, how would you feel about calling me Mum? Mrs. Drummond seems far too formal for us now. I love you dearly, Tillie."

"Oh, that's so kind of you. I love you too…Mum," Tillie smiled back. "Thank you ever so much. We must look after each other, and James – especially while Trev is away serving."

Isla nodded.

"Well, you'll be seeing more of me, dear. It's going to be hard to keep me away from this delightful boy."

Tillie laughed.

"The help is welcome. A new baby is rather a scary proposition. But first, he needs to meet his father. I miss him so. Even more now."

"Me too, dear. Thursday can't arrive fast enough."

Two days later, Tillie had tidied herself up to greet her husband. Her hair had been brushed until it shone, and she wore a pretty yellow satin bed jacket. She held young James in her arms, impatiently waiting for Trevor to arrive.

He appeared mid-afternoon, when Tillie was near bursting. He looked as dashing as ever in his RAF Firefighter's uniform.

"Tillie," he breathed as he gathered his wife and son in his arms.

For the first time since James was born, Tillie burst into tears.

"Darling, what is it?" Trevor was alarmed.

"I'm just that happy to see you, Trev. I've been hanging on. But I'm fine now," she smiled. "And here is your lovely son, who already has your dimple."

Trevor gingerly cradled his baby boy in his arms, memorizing his face and features.

"Well done, you," he whispered to his wife. "He's smashing, isn't he? And he does rather look like a James, doesn't he?"

The couple had agreed on a girl's and boy's name for their unborn child, and were relieved that James Geoffrey Drummond suited the newborn.

"Look what we've done... Daddy," whispered Tillie tenderly. Her heart practically overflowed with love to finally have Trev and her baby in her arms.

"It's down to you, sweetheart. You've done all the hard work. I'm that proud of you...Mummy."

"Trev, I never thought I could ever be so happy," Tillie radiated contentment.

"All we need now is to dig down deep, persevere just a bit longer, and we'll be together forever."

The threesome spent every spare minute together until Trevor had to leave. Tillie would still recuperate in hospital for the remainder of the two weeks.

Their parting was the hardest yet, with Trevor having no notion of when he'd see his beloved wife and new son again. It was a horrific wrench. Tillie was tearful and clung to her husband until the last moment.

Kenny left for Scotland barely a fortnight later, and only one of four Kingston children was left at home. Luckily, Master Jamie took up an overwhelming amount of time and care for such a little person, which was a welcome and delightful distraction for the women of #40 Longridge Road.

CHAPTER TWENTY-TWO

September 1943

Back at Exeter Anti-Aircraft Command base, Maggie and her friends tried to reconcile the hours, even days of monotony with terrifying and often disappointing periods at the guns.

On a gloomy autumn night, the four friends sipped tea, and joined in the weekly spelling game. It was one of various activities to fend away boredom. Others included debates, singalongs, card games, and the occasional dance. Lou was surprisingly good at spelling, and was having a wonderful night.

"Acquiesce. A-C-Q-U-I-E-S-C-E. Acquiesce," Lou rose to her full 5'2" and recited confidently, her fringe hanging down to her eyes.

"Correct," ruled the two judges, giving Lou another point on the scoresheet. She beamed, and sat down beside her remaining rival, Alva Fletcher.

"Well done, you," Maggie whispered. Lou flushed with excitement.

"Fletcher, your word is chrysanthemum." Everyone groaned.

A tall, broad-shoulder searchlight operator stood and cleared her throat.

"Chrysanthemum. C-H-R-Y-S-A-N-T-H-A-M-U-M.

Chrysanthemum," she repeated proudly.

"Incorrect," boomed the judges. "Please sit down, Fletcher."

"What? Bollocks," Fletcher cried, as she reluctantly took her seat.

Lou rose again as her name was called.

"Chrysanthemum. C-H-R-Y-S-A-N-T-H-E-M-U-M.

Chrysanthemum," she repeated proudly, her voice strong with confidence.

"Correct," the judges said with relish. "Stafford, you've taken the title again for your team. The winner of Exeter Base Weekly Spelling Bee is Anti-Aircraft Division Squadron 677 – again. Congratulations."

Adorned with a tattered red 1st prize ribbon, that had been passed from week to week to the best speller, little Lou beamed with pride. It might as well have been a bar of gold, she was thrilled.

"My parents would be dead proud of me, they would. Pops used to drill me on my spelling words at the kitchen table, where it was warm." She looked wistful. "Maybe I'll be allowed to keep the ribbon after the war, if I win it enough times."

Maggie was amazed again at the young and naïve Lou. She was holding up wonderfully.

The following Saturday, a dance was held at Exeter School in Exeter. It was the first military dance held since the Baedeker Blitz, and everyone was looking forward to a night away from the base.

There was no chance of dressing in anything other than uniform, so fussing over dresses wasn't necessary. However, the girls shared precious makeup, nail varnish, and other bits and bobs to feel as pretty and feminine as possible under the circumstances.

The base had offered two trucks to transport all the army and RAF personnel to and from the dance. This was luxury indeed, as Maggie and the girls didn't fancy trying to borrow one of the communal rickety bikes for the ten-mile return journey on the cool evening.

"On ter other 'and, a gang of soused airmen in a crammed lorry at midnight ain't goin ter be a lark, either." Addy tried to smooth down her curls and dabbed a tiny bit of *Chantilly* perfume behind her ears and on her wrists.

"Add in a few lusty Yanks, and we'll be fighting them off all the way home," added Pip. "If we're lucky," she giggled.

"Not for us, right, Lou?" Maggie nudged her. "We're going to stick together. We don't want any sozzled blokes making a play for us."

"Jolly well right," Lou responded, visibly relieved. At times, she seemed frightened of her own shadow. A truck full of drunk army boys was a terrifying prospect.

At half past seven, two trucks pulled up to the NAAFI, and collected

178

a boisterous assortment of ack-ack gunners, searchlight operators, pilots, ground crew, and even kitchen staff. Those left on standby were promised another night out before long.

The men talked of nothing but war news, especially the surrender of Italy in the summer. Sicily was where the Italian army gave little resistance to the Allies. Mussolini's government had collapsed, and the Allies swarmed the Italian mainland, although Rome proved harder to hold. It was a heady victory, and lifted up the soldiers' spirits. Everyone was in a celebratory mood.

The dance was in full swing when the trucks pulled up, and military personnel of all shapes, sizes, and colors spilled out.

The girls secured a small table in the corner of the crowded room.

"Looks a treat, don't it?" Addy scanned the room eagerly. "Getting away from ter bunker, PT, and drab talks is good fer all 'o us."

"I'll get the drinks," Pip offered. "Shandies all around?"

"I'll have orange squash if they have it," Maggie replied swiftly. She had little head for spirits and wanted to keep a clear head tonight.

"Me too," Lou quickly echoed.

"I'll 'ave a shandy or weak pint, if there be one goin'," Addy ordered, feeling excited in the dance's hubbub.

Maggie lost sight of Pip in the crowd. She gazed around, taking in the smoky air, buzz of conversation, and the smell of stale beer. Couples were already dancing to songs played by a makeshift band on the school stage. Strains of *Run Rabbit Run* had the dance floor jiggling and wiggling.

Almost immediately, two soldiers, Archie and Ned, asked Maggie and Lou to dance and the girls shrugged and stepped to the dance floor with them.

Ned wanted a second dance, but Maggie declined, so he escorted her back to the table where Pip had returned with the drinks.

She sat out the next few dances despite being in great demand, the men far outnumbering the women. Sipping her drink, her mind slid inevitably to Micah. Where was he? Was he safe? Cold or hungry? Her heart ached for him.

She absentmindedly said yes to a slower dance with her teammate Morris, who was charming, but had two left feet.

"Feels good to be out of camp, doesn't it Maggie?" He tried to spin her around.

"It's a lovely change of scenery, Morris." She tried not to stare at the large mole on his face. "Do you miss the bakery?"

"I don't miss waking in the middle of the night, but I was dead keen kneading and rolling the soft dough for the bread. I reckon it's peaceful, if that doesn't sound daft. The guns are a tad colder and harder."

"Will you go right back to it when the war's over?" Morris almost slammed her into a nearby dancer. The floor was swarming with warm bodies.

"I expect so. It's all I've ever done. I'll need to rebuild – either my old place or somewhere else in the neighborhood – that's where my heart is."

Maggie nodded sympathetically as she neatly moved her left foot to avoid Morris stomping on it. The music stopped, and Maggie breathed a sigh of relief. This was hard going.

He led her back to the girls' table, obviously worked up from the exercise.

"Thanks for the dance, Maggie. You're a cracking girl, and awfully good at your job."

"Aww, give over, Morris. We're all doing our best. You're tops on firing the guns. I daresay we'll be lucky to keep our eardrums after the war. That noise is ghastly."

"Too right, Maggie. Thanks for the dance."

She sat down, sipping her warm drink.

Pip and Addy hardly sat the entire night. Occasionally they returned to the table for a quick sip, and to wipe their brows. The room grew warmer as the night wore on with so many sweaty, heaving uniforms in one crowded space.

At eleven o'clock, food was laid out, and eagerly consumed by the crowd. Maggie and the girls managed to get some fish paste and spam sandwiches, soggy lettuce soup, and potato floddies. For dessert, they had, broken biscuits from who-knew-where, rock cakes, and a blissful cup of tea which were all eagerly gobbled up.

"Are you having fun, Mags? You didn't really want to come." Lou asked between mouthfuls.

"Actually, I am," Maggie smiled. "I'm glad you lot talked me into turning up."

They grinned at each other.

At some point, Maggie found herself blissfully alone at the table. She needed a moment to collect her thoughts.

"Hiya. Care to dance, Ma'am?"

A tall American, an airplane ground mechanic, stood in front of her. He had dirty blonde hair and bright blue eyes with a smattering of freckles across his nose.

Maggie paused.

"It's just a dance. My name is Steve Clayton. From Oklahoma, Ma'am."

"My name is Maggie Kingston. And why not?" Maggie threw caution to the wind. Although there was absolutely no resemblance, somehow his smile reminded her of Micah.

Steve was pleasant, keeping up an easy banter while they danced to Glenn Miller's *In the Mood*. It seemed natural to stay in his arms for *Kiss Me Goodnight, Sergeant Major*.

Maggie learned Steve had been shipped to England after basic training in the US and had only been in England for three months. He was a private and maintained the aircraft as ground crew. In a matter of minutes, she learned more about airplane repair than she ever cared to know. His father was a rancher, and he had two sisters. – one was married with a baby on the way, and the other had just started training as a nurse. He was chatty, which was a relief to Maggie. All that was required of her was to smile and nod. At least he was a divine dancer.

By the time the bell rang for last orders at the bar, everyone crowded the dance floor for Vera Lynn's *We'll Meet Again*. As the band struck up the first familiar strains, the Britons sang the poignant words:

"We'll meet again. Don't know where, don't know when.
But I know we'll meet again some sunny day…"

More than a few – women and men – wiped a tear, thinking of loved ones back home.

Steve kissed Maggie on the cheek as the last notes echoed through the makeshift hall.

"Thanks for a lovely evening, Maggie. You're a sweet gal and I hope to see you around the base."

"It was lovely to meet you too, Steve."

As for seeing him again, she said nothing.

Lou and Maggie squashed together on the way back. As expected, the men were loud, smoking, and making jokes all the way back to base. Addy perched precariously on a gunner's knee, whilst Pip was nowhere to be seen – hopefully safe in the second truck.

There were several sore heads the next day, but everyone got on, determined not to admit they were aching.

"And where did you get up to, Pip?" Lou asked as the girls dressed for PE.

"I went and found myself a bloke, didn't I?" She winked at Maggie.

"Yer don't say," Addy's tone was droll. "I 'ope yer din't get up ter anything dodgy, did yer? Was it an American? Yer danced all night long."

Pip tossed her head.

"And why not? We all need a bit of fun, don't we? And oddly enough, no – not an American. I danced with loads of th em, but the one that caught my eye is from Liverpool. His name is Albie. Albie Webb."

"Isn't he one of the gunners on Squadron C?" Maggie asked. "He's new, right?"

"Brand spanking," replied Pip, grabbing her jacket and cap. "He replaced Oliver – the red-haired bloke from Newcastle who came down with the measles."

"Ain't yer ter fast mover," Addy teased.

"I call dibs and all," Pip replied, eyes twinkling.

"What about Ray? I thought you two were writing each other?" Maggie asked, puzzled.

Pip shrugged. "He wrote one letter, and nothing after that. I reckon he's gone off me or found someone else." She flashed a wobbly smile. "And Albie's here, isn't he? Who knows what tomorrow will bring or if we'll even be here?" Her live-for-today attitude was shared by thousands

182

of Britons. They'd seen too many good people killed so many chose to seize happiness wherever they found it.

"Did you kiss him?" Lou asked softly.

"Maybe I did, and maybe I didn't," Pip replied, a bit defensively. She certainly didn't want to get a reputation around the base as a tart. The ATS girls already fought off this stamp all the time. Somehow, the men thought that army girls were easy but in fact, the opposite was true. The British government was afraid that women in the forces would cause a dramatic increase in loose behavior, venereal diseases, and unwanted pregnancies. A lot of publicity had been devoted to warning of the dire consequences of loose behavior. Still, women endured regular and uncomfortable testing for diseases and stern lectures on these topics.

In fact, the numbers of women with these unwanted conditions were far greater in the general population than in the military. Whether it was the threat of a dishonorable discharge from an important post, family disgrace, or personal pride was anyone's guess. There naturally was ample opportunity and plenty of willing men around. But Maggie and her friends took great pride in their positions and were determined to resist temptation and took care of themselves.

"Spill ter beans, Pip. Yer gave this Albie a proper snog, dint yer? Yer know yer want to tell us," Addy urged.

"It was just a kiss and a cuddle." Pip would not be drawn. "But he is awfully nice. He's an apprentice boat-builder. I could fancy moving to Liverpool with him."

"You are something else, Pip," Maggie laughed. "You just met the lad, and you're already planning a future with him. Give it a chance."

"Well, he was a good kisser," she replied stubbornly. "That's something, isn't it?"

"It certainly is, Pip. You should see Albie again. This war has to end sometime. You could do worse." Lou said.

They all looked at the uncommon many words quiet Lou uttered.

"Well, I never," Pip joked.

"Come on girls, time to march," Maggie rounded them up to a chorus of groans.

183

CHAPTER TWENTY-THREE

November 1943

"Dearest Maggie,

How are you, darling? I'm sure life is hectic on base. Kenny and Katie are both rubbish at writing, but your letters are always so full of cheerful news, and we're grateful for them.

Young Jamie is six months old now, and a going concern. He's sitting up, albeit he often teeters over. Hannah shouts timber each time, and he laughs like mad. He's been beastly at night, but has two bottom teeth to show for it. Mum and Aunt Shirley are spoiling him dreadfully, but I can't stop kissing and cuddling him myself. He's such a little dear, and I just love him to bits. His hair is growing in quite dark, but his eyes are still blue, so I suppose he's his father's son. Trev has a weekend pass in a fortnight's time, and we are counting the days. We both miss him so. I fear Jamie won't recognize his daddy, and this gives me qualms. Trev will be so distressed if the baby cries when he holds him. But Jamie is at an age of making strange. Mum says it will all sort over time, and I'm counting on that.

You're holding your breath for news of Micah and the Goldbachs, and I'm dreadfully sorry to have nothing to report. Uncle Thomas continues to make inquiries. When I pester him, he shakes his head sadly and says the situation is dire. More and more we are hearing about these work camps, and the picture is appalling. Take heart, dear love. We must remain hopeful. I do, for Hannah's sake. She doesn't say much, but she spends too much time in her room with Robbie, who brings her much comfort. She's taken to playing the piano again, but it is mournful sounds we hear from the drawing room. Poor love.

Mum's 50th birthday last month passed with a small celebration. We took her out for supper at Simpson's in the Strand in Covent Garden. I won't tantalize you by describing the delicious roast dinner. Suffice to say — eating at a restaurant that's off-ration is heavenly. They even dished up walnut cake for her. She was pleased with her little party, albeit we missed you desperately.

You may ask if I miss the ambulance. You know what, Mags? I really don't. I adore being Jamie's mummy. And you'd be surprised how much time a little one takes up in a day. Without the two Mums, I don't know how I'd manage. We've decided that to minimize confusion, Mum will be Granny and Trevor's mum will be Nana. If I'm honest, it's rather less awkward calling her Nana than having two Mums — especially as they are both almost always here. At times, I feel I have to wrestle one or both of them for my own son! In the event, I'm the only one that can feed him, so I do have him to myself a fair bit.

Just like clockwork, Master Drummond is loudly commanding my attention just now. I should think it's a wet nappy.

Write straightaway and more importantly — come home soon when you get leave, Aunt Maggie. We miss you.

Love, Tillie and Jamie xx"

Maggie smiled, picturing her twin as a young mum. Tillie would be great, as she was in anything she put her mind to. Despite the fact they were exactly the same age, Tillie seemed to always be the daring one, not afraid to have a go at new things and lead the way. Maggie stood in her shadow, glad to have her sister in the limelight, and relieved to have Tillie go first in all things. Undoubtedly, Maggie would be grateful to learn from Tillie's mothering ups and downs when her own turn came.

She longed to bounce her young nephew on her knee and snuggle him without a time limit. Huddling under her jacket, she fought to stay warm and fought an overwhelming swell of homesickness.

She firmly pushed the lack of news about Micah to the back of her mind. If there was truly anything to share, a telegram would have arrived, or Pops would have gone down to the post office to ring her on base. Best to just stay calm and wait as patiently as she could.

Maggie sighed and opened the little drawer of her bedside table for paper to write Tillie back. She'd done a little sketch of the Exeter dance that she wanted to slip in to amuse Tillie and Hannah. Her letters were dull compared to Tillie's, so perhaps the artwork would cheer her sister.

The loud air raid alarm pierced the hut, and everyone sprang into action straightaway. With no time to pin back her hair, Maggie shoved it under her tin helmet, and ran for the bunker.

"Come on, girls. Maybe tonight we'll actually shoot down an enemy plane," Pip shouted over the din.

The searchlights were already flashing across the sky as the squad leaped into position.

Pulses pounding, Maggie waited for the first spotting of enemy aircraft.

It was a bitterly cold night. Maggie could see her breath, as she sat poised to operate her equipment. No one spoke.

"Spitfire. One of ours," Pip called crisply. She logged it in her book, returning directly to the binoculars.

"Heinkel. Angle 20," she shouted moments later.

Seconds that felt like minutes ticked by. The crew steeled for the attack.

The plane flew low and began shelling them. Light and blasts filled the air as the crew ducked repeatedly but kept working.

As the girls worked the height and range finder, Maggie fed the data into the predictor, and within seconds, the proper fuse length was relayed to the men who loaded and fired the gun. The noise and light from the anti-aircraft gunfire were enormous, but the squad didn't flinch, as Pip called out more aircraft.

Three other gun stations were operating in tandem, all with the same aim to blow German planes out of the English sky. Women bellowed out spotted aircraft to waiting squads. The GPO circulated amongst the four stations, barking corrections as he went.

A tremendous explosion ripped through the sky. Within seconds, the British spitfire was aflame, and spiraling towards the earth. Maggie thought she saw a puff of white and hoped that was the pilot bailing out, his parachute breaking his fall. The earth shook as the airplane crashed about two or three miles away. Shrapnel rained down from the sky, metal hitting metal as plane fragments thumped on gun barrels and pinged off helmets. Smoke surrounded the bunker. And yet the crew carried on.

"Another Heinkel," Pip screamed, her voice starting to rasp from yelling.

Lou and Addy operated the height and range finder, and Maggie spun the knobs and dials of the predictor. Despite the frigid night, sweat glistened on her forehead, and dampened her neck. She never looked up or swayed from her post.

Gordon and Morris set the fuses, whilst Simon and Alfred fired on command.

With bated breath, the crew prayed for a direct hit. The record for shooting the Luftwaffe in the air was depressingly low. Morale would take a great boost if they could actually shoot one down.

A white, ear-splitting explosion blast confirmed the inconceivable. They'd shot down the Heinkel! No one could see the pilot, so they assumed the on-target detonation had taken his life, along with destroying his plane.

"Bloody well right," Gordon shouted with his fist in the air.

"Take that, Jerry," Alfred added.

"We did it!" Maggie shrieked as she hugged Lou.

More shrapnel fell all around them, on the open field, and in the bunker.

"Take cover," the GPO screamed.

Everyone scrambled to get as low as possible. Maggie flattened herself on the ground face down, her cheek pressing into the frigid cement, as she closed her eyes in fear. She hoped the others were safe but didn't dare look up. There was an air raid shelter on the base, but the only time the squadron had been inside it was when they were off duty. Otherwise, the alarm signaled a call to action inside the bunker. They ran towards danger, not away from it.

The hit achieved its aim, to scare the enemy and chase their planes back over the channel. Within a few minutes, the sky was empty of all but searchlights, and the all-clear sounded. Everyone struggled to their feet, brushing dust, dirt, and stray shell fragments off themselves.

"That was brilliant," Pip cheered. "We got one. Everyone alright?" She peered around the dark and smoky bunker.

"I'm good," Maggie confirmed.

"Me too," Addy chirped. "That were a bit o' a thrill."

Maggie noticed Lou was slumped over the height and range finder.

"Are you alright, love? Did you see? We got him." Maggie shook her friend.

To her horror, Lou fell heavily to the ground. Maggie's world spun out of control.

"Oh no," cried Maggie, as she dropped to her knees, her sweat-slicked hands feeling for a pulse. She found none.

"Double-quick, hand me a torch," she ordered.

One was swiftly produced, and Maggie flashed it in Lou's face. Her eyes were glassy, and a large piece of gray metal protruded from a bloody gash on the side of her neck, just under her ear helmet strap. A lock of fair hair fell forward.

"No!" Maggie screamed at the top of her lungs. "Lou, come on, girl," She put her head to Lou's chest, desperately listening for a heartbeat, and finding none. She ripped off her tie, and wrapped it tightly over the wound around Lou's neck, trying in vain to staunch the blood pouring from it. Lou remained lifeless, but Maggie wouldn't believe it.

After a few minutes, Pip gently pulled her off.

"It's no use, love. She's gone."

Maggie sat back on her heels and raised haunted eyes to her friend's face.

"How?" she whispered. "She was just here five minutes ago."

Pip shrugged. She had no words. Tears poured down her face. Addy stood frozen in place.

Someone had run to the hospital tent to report the accident and get help. The medics came straightaway and gently loaded little Lou on a stretcher and took her away. The crew stumbled their way to the NAAFI, where they were served drinks; pints for the men and shandies for the women.

Maggie was white with shock and left her drink untouched. Addy was shaking, and Pip tried to comfort her, but Maggie didn't even notice. She kept replaying the scene where Lou fell to the ground over and over again, when she saw the shrapnel protruding from her neck, blood everywhere. Maggie's hands and the front of her uniform were splattered with Lou's blood. It'll be an ordeal, trying to get the stains out, she thought dully.

The men spoke in a low voice about the German plane they'd shot down, while throwing troubled looks toward the girls. They'd become rather protective of their ack-ack gunners, and understood that this would shake them up.

"Will you be alright, Maggie?" Simon asked, bringing a cup of tea to the table.

Maggie looked up in a daze, recognized her teammate, and gratefully accepted the hot mug. She clutched it tightly to warm her hands.

"I really don't know, Simon," she whispered. "I don't know what to think, what to do. Lou was just here. She didn't deserve to die. She was so brave, just nineteen last month. A baby. She was a baby," Maggie's voice trailed off.

The men walked the girls back to their hut. All three of them were wide-eyed with shock. The medics had checked everyone over, and none of them had so much as a scratch on them. How ironic, Maggie thought almost hysterically.

Pip rallied and helped put both Maggie and Addy to bed. Removing only their heavy boots and overcoats, she tenderly washed their faces, and some of the worst blood from Maggie's uniform.

"Come along, love. There, there," Pip soothed her dear friend as she led her to her cot, laid her down, and covered her up as best she could. The hut was chilly, so she added the teddy bear coat on top. Maggie was still, staring unseeingly at the ceiling.

Pip repeated the process with Addy, who was slightly more animated. Wringing her hands, she began to cry. As Pip tucked her in, Addy rolled to her side, hugging herself, and sobbing into her sheets.

Pip dragged herself to the washbasin, gave her face a cursory swipe with her flannel, and almost fell into her own cot. She felt numb, blank, empty. She lay awake a long time, hearing muffled sobs throughout the hut. Louise had been loved by everyone, and all would miss the quiet and plucky gunner girl.

They were granted the next day to grieve. Maggie wasn't up to sharing stories or going over the gruesome details of the previous evening with her friends. She needed time alone.

After a solitary and frosty walk that did nothing to clear her mind, she pulled out a pen and paper.

"Dearest Micah,

The most ghastly thing has happened. I can hardly bring myself to put it into words, but Louise is dead. We had just shot down a German plane and forced the remainder of the attackers back to the continent. Shrapnel fell everywhere; it was raining metal, so we took cover.

It was an ear-splitting noise, and seeing the plane on fire and hurtling to the ground was more gratifying than I could ever have imagined.

When the all-clear sounded, we were so happy, jubilant in our success. Jumping up and down, and hugging each other, we were so proud as a battery unit.

Then we discovered that poor Lou had been hit with a stray piece of shrapnel. It must have pierced her jugular vein; the medics told us. It was a sudden death, thank goodness. And she wouldn't have suffered. That's a blessing and an enormous comfort to me, Micah.

She was such a sweet little thing, but often scared as a church mouse. It would have been too awful if she'd suffered or been in any pain.

War is so senseless, my darling. One minute Lou was there, working her machine, and the next she was gone. I keep asking myself why. Why her? But there is no answer. No rhyme or reason. I'm fighting the urge to feel bitter and resentful. War can be so random.

I've offered to write to Lou's parents. They will be so devastated. She was an only child. It will be the hardest letter I've ever had to write.

It makes me ache more for you. We mustn't waste a minute once you are home. And you will be home and soon. I believe it, I tell myself

over and over again. It's the only thing that keeps me going some days.
*   Even if you never get this letter, it helps me no end to write you my*
thoughts and feelings. You help me to keep on.

*   All my love,*
*   Maggie xx"*

Maggie insisted on packing up Lou's personal belongings to send back with her body to her parents in Hereford. She'd been dry-eyed since the night Lou had been killed, but broke down in uncontrollable sobs when she found the carefully folded red ribbon Lou had so proudly won at the spelling bee.

"What a waste. What a bloody waste. She was so young. Her entire life ruined. And yet, the Luftwaffe keep coming. They never stop coming."

Pip held her friend, smoothing her hair, and murmuring quiet words until Maggie's shoulders stopped heaving, and she dissolved into hiccups.

No one could say it would be all right, or that everything would be fine. Because no one knew how the war would end. Or when. It just dragged on day after day.

Maggie included the 1st place ribbon with Lou's kit and personal items for her parents. She asked no one for permission.

CHAPTER TWENTY-FOUR

January 1944

Five days after they'd said their last goodbye to Lou, all four battery units were called together.

"We've had word from above that this site is being abandoned. We are not expecting more air strikes in this location for the foreseeable future. You are needed elsewhere. I'll call you in to give you your specific orders. Mixed-battery squads will be redeployed together. Searchlight operators, ground crew and maintenance will be sent where the need is greatest. Be prepared to move within three days."

"Sarg, may I ask a question," Morris asked.

Sgt. Plath nodded.

"We've been hearing rumors about something big coming. Troops marshaling along the coast for a European offensive. Does our move have anything to do this invasion?"

Sgt. Plath rolled his eyes.

"Decker, you know I can't answer that. We are realigning staff in line with what we understand about German air movements at present. That's all I know." He held up his hand to fend off more questions. "Dismissed."

Shortly after that, Maggie and the rest of Mixed Battery 677 were instructed to pack their kit and move to Bristol. They'd be joining an existing base with at least two other batteries.

"Wot do yer make 'o that, then?" Addy emptied the contents of her tiny night table into her duffel bag.

"I expect this is what the army is all about. I suppose we should be thankful not to be sent overseas," Maggie replied with a shrug as she organized her sponge bag, neatly folded her khaki wardrobe, and carefully placed each item into her rucksack.

"No one's about to inspect your bag, Kingston," Pip joked as she haphazardly folded her pajamas and stuffed her underwear into an already overflowing bag.

"Shove off, Murley. I like to be able to find my things when it's time to unpack them. And you can fit more in if it's nicely folded." She looked over at Pip's bag and wrinkled her nose. "Is that underwear even clean?"

"I'm not quite sure. Does it matter?" Pip retorted, then picked up a pair of khaki panties and sniffed. "I suppose so."

Normally, Maggie would have laughed, but she was still too heartbroken about little Lou, so the joke merely warranted a smile.

"We've barely unpacked 'ere," Addy moaned. "I s'pose all these bases look ter same, anyroad."

"Do you reckon that there's a major continental attack in the offing? Could the end of the war truly be in our sights?" Maggie paused, feeling a sliver of hope.

"I won't get me 'opes up yet, but why else would they be shuttin' us down?" Addy asked, sitting on her cot, her packing finished. "This were a bustlin' place jus a fortnight ago, yet we're all bein' shifted. Gotta be good news." Life was pretty simple for Addy. She never speculated, everything was black or white.

"I'm with Mags. This is the start of something big. Maybe this will be our last redeploy before the end of the war. This time next year we could be off rations and no more queues."

"Pip, what a flight of fancy. I can't imagine we'll be demobbed that soon, but … dreams are free, I suppose." Maggie allowed herself a glimmer of hope. Could the war be over this year? Would she be reunited with Micah by Christmas? Hannah might finally see her mother and father again. It was a heady feeling.

"I am that gutted that Albie and I will be separated," Pip lamented. "I am going to miss him something awful."

"Have yer seen much of 'im since ter dance? I see yer makin eyes at ter Yanks all ter time." poked Addy.

"Albie has been on off shifts to mine. But I do fancy him, you daft cow," Pip tossed a biscuit at her friend. "And no harm in looking. I love to dance and all. You know how it is at these social dances. Everyone steps on the floor with everyone else. Even engaged people dance at these affairs. You realize that." Pip defended herself, while taking a shot at her friend.

"Sod off, Murley. I'm engaged, not dead. 'orace wouldn't mind me havin a whirl round the dance floor wiv a cheeky American."

"We're all far from home, and a friendly dance with an agreeable serviceman is harmless," Maggie said smoothly and changed the subject. "You'll write to Albie, surely?" Maggie asked. "The army can ship us hither and yon across the country, and even further. The same with the RAF. It doesn't mean you two won't wind up together."

"I suppose," Pip replied dubiously. "I didn't think I'd fancy him as much as I do. He doesn't even know where he'll be posted next."

"If he feels the same way, you must hold it fast. You must," Maggie gripped Pip's arm.

"Alright, alright. Keep your hair on."

"Sorry, love. I'm proper jumpy since we lost Lou. Moving to another gun park is rather a relief. Too many memories around every corner." Three pairs of eyes strayed to Lou's empty cot.

"I'm ever so thankful we're being shipped out together. I don't know what I'd do without you lot," Maggie said, biting her bottom lip.

"Us too," Addy replied simply.

"Oi, we'd better get on with it. Our transport is due at half-past." Pip jammed the rest of her things into her bag.

Maggie nodded, and they all hurried to finish their packing. Maggie had just enough time to dash off a brief letter to Tillie, telling her of their new location.

The girls wore their warm teddy bear coats on the train and were glad they did. Frost had formed on the inside of the railcar windows, and they could see their breath, as they stowed their kit above their heads.

"It must be a lively base. No space for us in a Nissen hut," Pip hoped chatter would keep the cold out of her bones. "I hope we have a passable billet."

"At least we'll be together. Any luck, it won't be miles from the base. I'm not keen on frigid walks every day," Maggie agreed, rubbing her hands together.

"I'm 'oping for a 'ot shower and warm meals," Addy said, a distant look in her eyes.

"Maybe even hot water bottles," Pip added dreamily.

"And hot cocoa and homemade bikkies brought to our beds each night." Maggie joined the game.

The train jerked suddenly, nearly throwing Maggie onto the lap of an American soldier sitting next to her.

"Hey darlin. You are a looker. Sit right on down." He tried to pull her into his arms.

"Steady on, mate. That's one of our gunner girls. Treat her with respect, mate." Alfred stood up, jumping to Maggie's defense.

"I'll be damned. Are you one of those ack-ack girls we've heard about?" The friendly faced Yank gave a low whistle. He helped her back to her seat. "Sorry, little lady. Don't want to disturb one of England's finest."

Maggie wanted the floor to swallow her up, yet a feeling of pride also ballooned up inside of her. She *was* doing an important job. She was holding her own. A trusted member of the squad. An equal. She gave the soldier a tremulous smile.

"Bloody right," Addy bragged. "We be England's finest."

"You're just too pretty to be firing guns. How does that Churchill fellow put young ladies like you in such danger?" Another American spoke up.

"We don't fire the guns. Only the men are permitted to do the actual shooting. We spot and calculate the height, distance, and projected path of enemy aircraft to help our mates fire at the right target." Pip was happy to explain to the rapt audience.

"We couldn't do it without our gunner girls," Simon said with a mixture of pride and irritation. "And Churchill is a fine leader. He's done a commendable job under the most taxing of conditions."

"No offense, buddy. We're just trying to understand. It's hard to picture our spoiled US gals working on a gun battery." The car erupted with laughter.

"We're tough, but we're still ladies," Pip puffed out her chest.

"We can see that, sweetheart," leered an auburn-haired soldier, staring at Pip's ample bosom.

"That's quite enough, Private," Alfred half-rose again in defense of one of his ack-ack girls.

"It's Airman. I'm going to fly fighter planes. My apologies. No harm intended." He nodded to Pip.

"Alfie, I can take care of myself," Pip placated. "I don't suppose you have a bar of chocolate on your person, Airman? I could see my way to forgiving you, if you could produce that." Pip jumped in.

"You're incorrigible, Pip," Maggie elbowed her, but she readily accepted a few Hershey bar squares. Who wouldn't?

A few hours later, the train pulled into Bristol train station. It was early evening, and the girls were starving. As usual, the train stopped and started for no apparent reason, delaying them enormously. Maggie hoped they'd be met as it was getting colder by the minute.

The army boys were taken by a rickety truck to Filton Airfield, but the girls were left behind. After a cup of tepid tea and a stale bun at the station, they waited, freezing cold. After an endless hour, an older chap with a shock of white hair hurried into the station, hat in hand.

"I'm ever so sorry, girls. There was a calf too stubborn to be born, and I couldn't come sooner. I'm Felix Lowery. You'll be billeted with me and my wife, Ivy, on our farm, alongside our land girls. It's only a two-mile walk, and Ivy has supper on for you."

The girls glanced at each other, said hello to Mr. Lowery, picked up their kit, and dragged one foot in front of the other in the frigid night air.

Maggie couldn't feel her feet by the time they got to the farmhouse, but was relieved to be greeted by a stout woman with grizzled gray hair and a wide smile.

"Come in, pets. Drop your kit, and come by the fire. Let's get something warm into you, then I'll show you to your room. Your fourth girl is expected tomorrow."

The girls didn't hesitate. They were chilled to the bone, and Addy's nose was running from the cold.

An hour later, filled with warm stew and delicious fresh bread, they shuffled up to the farmhouse attic which had been done up to accommodate them.

Ivy huffed and puffed ahead of them.

"It will be a tight squeeze, but it's warm. The bath is one floor below, and you'll share with our two land girls, Lizzie and Maisie. I'll serve you up a nice breakfast and supper each night. No men, mind. Stay out of trouble and we'll get on just fine. The airfield is just two and a half miles north of here. Righto, then. Goodnight, girls."

Maggie, Addy, and Pip dropped their kit, thanked Ivy and inspected their new quarters. Four iron cots sat in each of the four corners of the room, under the eaves. There was a small table and shelf next to each one. An oval mirror was mounted over a table with an old-fashioned bowl and pitcher for quick wash-ups. Pretty flowered curtains matched the covers on the beds.

"Real mattresses. Heaven," Pip exclaimed as she plopped down on one.

"I'll tek this one by ter window, if yer don't mind?" Addy was already putting her kit on her chosen bed.

"I'm happy anywhere," Maggie agreed, as she chose the bed closest to Pip's. None of them looked at the fourth bed, which by rights should have been Lou's.

"I'm done-in, and it will be an early call tomorrow. I'm for bed," Pip spoke for all of them.

After a hearty breakfast of powdered eggs, toast with homemade blackberry jam, two small strips of bacon each and tea, the girls put on their heavy coats and trudged to the base.

"Real bacon. I can get used to this," Pip was giddy from a good night's sleep, a warm meal, and the luxury of an indoor bathroom.

"Too right. I haven't slept that well in months," Maggie sighed.

Reporting to the GPO, the girls found themselves feeling familiar with battery life in no time.

A week later, Maggie's mail arrived, and she was happy to receive a few letters from home. Recognizing Tillie's handwriting, she tore it open first.

"Dearest Maggie,

I'm so sorry to convey this news to you, but I know you would want to hear straightaway. Uncle Thomas has had word that Mr. and Mrs. Goldbach were sent to Auschwitz camp months ago. They were put to work, hard labor, with little to no rations, and appalling living conditions.

Maggie, dearest, they didn't make it. They didn't survive. The last we heard Micah is still in Drancy. We don't know why he's still there, or how long he'll be held. It's unclear if he has been told about his parents.

Darling, this is dreadful news. I understand you only get leave every three months. We'll be waiting with open arms when you come home in a month's time.

All my love,
Tillie xx"

CHAPTER TWENTY-FIVE

Maggie re-read the letter three times before the news sank in. Micah's parents gone. After who knew how many months of ghastly conditions, suffering, and then to perish in unthinkable circumstances. Sketchy accounts of these camps were trickling in, and they were difficult to comprehend. If even half of them were true, the Germans were treating these Jewish detainees appallingly. It seemed Hitler had a contemptible plan for these innocent people. She felt sick.

Sagging onto her bed, she thought of poor Hannah, who was dealt too many blows in her young life. And Micah! What was he having to bear in Drancy? Would he, too, be deported to Auschwitz? He had youth on his side, but this work camp sounded nothing short of evil. Maggie fought her nausea. More afraid than ever for Micah, she forced herself to think of fighting this war to save him from a fate like his parents. She walked for an hour to calm her strained nerves. She turned in early, able only to gulp back some tea for supper. Her stomach was in knots.

After tossing and turning most of the night, Maggie felt depleted, eyes gritty and heart sore. After a breakfast that tasted like sawdust, the girls piled on their warmest gear for the hike to the camp. They presented themselves for the now-familiar medical and dental checkups, and all three were declared A1 and FFI – free from infection.

"At least we needn't undergo more eye and ear testing," Pip remarked in relief. "I suppose we've demonstrated our abilities to the satisfaction of the Women's Auxiliary Territorial Services."

"Fer now," snorted Addy. "Wiv all the muddle in the army, I'm that gobsmacked they even have our service papers."

"Leave off, Addy," Maggie chided. "Who can expect order amongst these shambles? Soldiers being moved every which way across the country, attacks from sea to sea, sorting the Americans coming in. It's astonishing we are organized at all," Maggie said dully.

"Are you alright, love? We don't like to intrude, but we're worried about you," Pip put a tentative hand on her friend's arm.

Addy nodded. "We all took Lou's death 'ard, din't we?" Addy's brow furrowed in concern.

Maggie stopped on the dirt path from the medical tent to the canteen. "Certainly, I'm still mourning dear Lou. Such a meaningless death is impossible to get beyond. But it's more than that. I've received an unsettling letter from home. A dear friend of mine – Micah Goldbach – lost his parents in a German work camp." Maggie's voice broke saying the words aloud. "I've known them since I was a child. They were good people."

Pip and Addy also paused in the frosty winter sun.

"I'm so sorry, love. We've heard of these work camps. If the reports are to be believed, the conditions are atrocious. And it's Jews, Poles, gypsies, and other groups who are being persecuted. The Goldbachs were Jewish, I suppose?" Pip prodded gently.

"Yes, they were part of a French roundup. So was Micah," she added, trying her utmost not to cry.

"Is 'e a special friend, then?" Addy wanted to hear more.

Maggie gulped.

"Awfully special," she confided at last. "We've been writing each other all through the war. He sends me poems," she said quietly. "In the event, he used to. I've haven't heard from him in months."

"He wasn't sent to the work camp too?" Pip asked in alarm.

"The last word I received was he had been rounded up and held in a transit camp in the north of France called Drancy. That's all I've heard."

"You poor dear," Pip put an arm around her. "Perhaps he'll be freed with this big push that's coming. We must fix on that, Maggie."

"Thanks fer tellin us, Mags. Pip and I wondered if yer had a chap back 'ome. Yer alays ever so chuffed when ter post arrives."

Maggie sniffled.

"It's almost if I don't say his name or talk about him, he'll be safe. Daft, I know. If I'm honest, I feel loads better telling you about him."

"Have a care, Mags. Addy will be peppering you with questions about him now," Pip smiled.

"You girls realize I'm not the talkative type, but it's cheering that I can always count on you," Maggie replied softly. "Tea anyone? Perhaps we'll meet our new gunner girl today."

Pip and Addy saw the door was closed for now.

Maggie felt a little lighter having shared her wretched news with the girls. Without Tillie, she had been feeling the lack of a confidante. Pip and Addy were splendid friends. She might even open up more often. Maybe.

Olive Foley was a Yorkshire girl, with a thick accent that was hard to understand at times. But she was cheerful and a quick learner, and didn't dodge her household jobs back at the Lowery farm. She had a fiancé in the navy, stationed somewhere in Northern Africa, and spent most of her free time writing him letters.

Filton Base was a bustling military operation, with four mixed battery squads, and an active RAF airfield. So, in addition to the booming sound of the ack-ack guns and frequent air attacks, the sound of their own fighters and bombers taking off and landing added to the cacophony of the base. Maggie could never say she got used to it, but for all of them, it became routine.

On a frigid February morning after the daily drill, Maggie and Pip chatted on the way to the mess for late-morning tea.

"Hey good looking, fancy a cuppa?" Maggie heard an American accent behind her. She and Pip groaned. They'd heard this line far too many times.

She turned to politely decline the airman, until she saw it was…Trevor! She flew into his arms and hugged him tight. As always, he was an imposing presence – tall, with dark hair, and flashing blue eyes. Tillie was a lucky woman.

"Trevor, what on earth are you doing here?" She was so glad to see a face from home.

"I'm stationed nearby – at RAF Babdown Farm in Gloucestershire. Tillie told me you'd been transferred here, so soonest I could, I pinched a lift to come and see you. I have to be back tonight. Any chance you have a free afternoon?"

"I'm off duty until 2100," she replied with a smile. "What shall we do?" Her brown eyes lit up. "I suppose we could walk to Bristol, or even scrounge up a couple of bikes. There's always a few around here."

"Brilliant. What are we waiting for?"

And that's just what they did. They found a pair of dodgy-looking bicycles, pedaled the thirty-minute ride into town, and stashed the bikes in a safe spot. Wandering the streets, they inspected the bomb damage.

"I love poking about old churches. So many were bombed here – I understand four ancient churches sustained terrible destruction," Maggie shook her head as they stood in front of the ruins of St. James' Presbyterian Church of England. "So much history gone forever."

"It's the same all over Britain, Mags. Beautiful monuments that even if rebuilt will never be the same."

When they were too cold to walk further, they warmed up in a small corner cafe.

They asked the waitress for coffee and whatever sweet was available.

"I've only got chicory coffee, ducks, sorry. But I've scrounged you up a couple of Cornish Fairings. A bloke from Cornwall brought us a tin the other week. They're a tad on the dry side, but just the thing for dipping," she winked.

"Ta," the pair thanked her.

The gingery biscuits dunked into the earthy, acrid coffee were just the pick-me-up they needed on that frigid day.

"When were you home last? I'm gasping for news of the family, and young Jamie of course," Maggie probed.

"Four weeks ago. He's splendid, almost walking, and getting into loads of trouble. I fear he has my mischievous temperament – at least that's what my Mum says." Trevor's dimple twinkled.

"I miss him so. He's growing so fast, and I'm not there for it," Her eyes clouded. "I miss them all. How is Hannah coping with the news of her parents?"

Trevor shrugged, his cobalt blue eyes instantly serious.

"As best as can be expected, I suppose. She's gone very quiet again – as she did when she first arrived from France, so Tillie says. She'd pretty much stopped biting her nails, but has started again. She's not a child anymore, Mags. More's the pity."

Maggie clucked in sympathy. It was the same all over England. Children having to grow up too soon, facing the horrors of war. Maggie couldn't imagine a life without her own dear parents.

"And what of the renewed London bombing? How bad is it, really Trev?" Maggie's eyebrows furrowed.

"They're calling it the Baby Blitz. Back to nightly, or twice weekly air attacks. But we're better prepared this time. Thanks to our birds in the sky, and ack-ack batteries like yours, not many are getting through, and not so much damage when they do. But it's back to the sickening sound of Moaning Minnie and rushing to the shelters. I don't imagine Jamie fancies it at all."

"Oh dear, that's dreadful. Hasn't London suffered enough? Haven't we all?" Her voice caught.

"We have, and yet it still goes on. I'm doing my bit, helping to patch up any of ours getting shot at." He scanned the near-empty cafe.

"Something big is coming, Mags. Allied troops of all sorts are amassing – Brits, Canadians, Americans, Aussies – all getting ready for the big push."

"When is it happening, Trev? Could it really be over soon?"

"Soon enough," he responded non-committedly. "Within a few months, I should expect. The tide is turning, Mags. Hitler is losing steam. It's just a matter of time now until the flap. But we're not out of it yet." He checked his watch and sighed.

"I'd best get you back. I wouldn't want to be responsible for you being called up on a late charge."

"More likely you'd get called up for that rubbish American accent you put on," she teased, as they gathered their things and collected their bicycles.

They rode back to the base in silence, the cold wind stealing their voices and breath.

Maggie was half-frozen when they wheeled up to the station.

"I can't tell you how much you've cheered me, today, Trev. It was so good of you to come and find me."

"We're family, and we must take care of each other," he replied, then winked so as not to be taken too seriously. "Take care of yourself, Mags."

They parted, and Maggie reported for duty, where the work was so demanding that she didn't have time to sort through all her jumbled thoughts and feelings. It had been lovely to get all the news of the family and talk about Micah and his parents. And the thought of the Allies preparing to attack the Germans on a grand scale, was exciting and heartening. It boosted her to try even harder each day on the gun park.

* * *

"Look, there's Aunt Maggie," squealed Tillie at Victoria Station. She held up a squirmy almost-one-year-old Jamie who was waving madly at everyone going by.

Maggie spotted her twin and dashed to hug her and her adorable nephew.

"Darling, did you have to wait long? I'm sorry but you know the trains," Maggie apologized.

"You're here now, and that's all that matters. We have a smashing week planned for you, a birthday party for Jamie, bags of family visits, and ..."

"And some rest," Maggie finished tiredly.

"Of course, Mags," Tillie smiled, as she tried to hold a squirming Jamie who was pointing at the pigeons pecking at the trash on the cement floor.

Maggie swept her nephew from his mum's arms, and gave him a cuddle. At first, he burrowed in, feeling comfortable, thinking it was his Mummy. Then when Tillie started talking, Jamie looked at her, looked back at Maggie, and started shrieking. The twins laughed. Jamie looked confused again.

"He'll get used to you before long, love. He hasn't seen you enough to realize there's two of us. Give him a chance."

The two chattered nineteen to the dozen all the way home. Maggie felt like she'd been reunited with her other half, catching up with all the news in no time.

"It's marvelous to see you at our table again, dear. Even if only for a short time," Walter beamed at his twin daughters in the dining room.

Alice fussed around, happy to have at least two of her four children at home. She refused to think about how long it would be until they were all reunited.

Uncle Thomas and Aunt Shirley joined them, and it felt like a festive occasion, even though there was only offal, winter vegetables, and prune custard. Hannah was subdued, but glad to see Maggie. Maggie had spent an hour reacquainting with Robbie, who took some time to warm to her. He was obviously cross that she'd left him for so long.

"I have some news, and I expect Hannah is mature enough to hear it. After all, you will be sixteen come September. It's for you and Maggie." Uncle Thomas began.

Maggie shot him a fearful look. He held up his hand.

"It's good news, dear. Micah is coming home."

CHAPTER TWENTY-SIX

Maggie's spoon clattered to the table as Tillie gasped.
"But where? How?" Maggie sputtered.
"Let's have our tea in the drawing room. I'll explain it all directly."

They all settled down and waited expectantly. The air was tense. Hannah held Maggie's hand while Tillie and the baby sat with Mum and Aunt Shirley.

"You all understand that Micah has been detained at Drancy since the roundup. Albeit a transit camp, there are a number of prisoners who have been kept behind, performing jobs crucial to operate the camp. I'm given to understand that Micah has been found most useful. His fluency in English and French, his calm demeanor, and his exceptional organizational skills have landed him a post in some administrative capacity. I'm not quite sure what. It may have something to do with keeping track of prisoners' comings and goings."

"Is he safe? Healthy?" Maggie couldn't help but think of his parents starving and being worked to death.

"I have to be honest with you, Maggie. The conditions at Drancy are poor, extremely poor. Enormous groups of people are kept in huge, unheated rooms with no beds, negligible hygiene facilities, and starvation food portions. Most are only kept for a few days before boarding large trains for points east.

Micah will be in marginally better circumstances. But he's been battling for his survival every day, make no mistake about that. And he's been witness to acts of violence and human mistreatment that will surely leave its mark on him."

Hannah smothered a sob.

"My brother. He's all I have left," she cried out.

"And he's coming home to you, Hannah. It seems that the Germans are seeing more and more indications that the war is not going their way. There are rumors that the camp may close in the next several months. They are trying to round up and deport as many French Jews as possible in this short time."

"Appalling," Alice whispered.

Thomas nodded.

"They are planning ahead to how this will look if all goes wrong. When it all goes wrong. As it will. Because Micah is British-born, it's been agreed to release him," he finished simply.

"How much did you have to do with this, Uncle Thomas?" Tillie asked, juggling the fussy baby on her lap.

"I'll take him," Shirley offered.

Tillie smiled gratefully as her aunt took the baby upstairs to put him down.

"Let's just say we've been working on securing his release for some time now."

"Do you have any idea when he'll be coming home?"

"Not precisely, Maggie, but it's a matter of weeks."

Maggie was overcome with emotion. Everyone looked at her for a response.

"I don't know what to say, Uncle Thomas. It's just...wonderful. And yet, awful at the same time. Poor Micah." She clasped Hannah tightly. "Thank you doesn't seem enough, but I'm just knocked for six."

Hannah had been softly crying.

"My brother is coming home. Finally. Thank you, Uncle Thomas," Hannah gave him a shaky smile.

"Oh, and one more point. They are allowing packages to be received for certain prisoners, including Micah. For the present, at least. So, if you can assemble items that you think he might need – food, clothes, and so on – I'll make arrangements for them to be sent to him."

"That's brilliant, Uncle Thomas. We are ever so grateful," Maggie repeated, regaining her voice.

"Please don't mention it, dear. He's a fine young man, and we consider the Goldbachs family, correct, Hannah?"

Hannah nodded, full of emotion.

"Mags, we can spend the day tomorrow gathering food and small items for the package. Mum, could Mrs. Drummond come and help cook and bake? Maggie and I will nip out to the shops." Tillie was organizing everything excitedly.

"Yes, and I'll start on a letter for him tonight," Maggie agreed. Still numb with shock, she couldn't quite believe the sense of power she felt in being able to do something concrete for Micah – finally!

"Wait. Does he know about his parents yet?" Maggie stole a side glance at Hannah, who bit her lip.

"I believe so Maggie," Uncle Thomas nodded soberly. "That's what I'm given to understand. I'm not aware of when he found out."

"I understand, Uncle Thomas," Maggie replied quietly.

"I should think another cuppa is in order. What wonderful news for us all," exclaimed Alice.

"Dearest Micah,

What marvelous news that soon you will be on British soil, at home, reunited with your sister, and dare I say – in my arms?

I must first pass on my deep condolences for the loss of your beloved parents. It must have been such a wrench to say goodbye to them under the dreadful circumstances. And then to hear of their passing. I am ever so sorry, my love. I appreciate it will take some time to heal. I am dedicated to helping you in any way I can.

Uncle Thomas has only given us a sketchy picture of your life at Drancy in the past year, but it all sounds appalling. We will all be here to support you when you return. Hannah is ecstatic to see you again.

I will do my utmost to obtain leave when you return. But I can promise nothing. There is loads happening these days – I mustn't say more or it will be blacked out. So, our battery unit is needed. I will do everything short of going AWOL to be able to greet you.

We've lovingly assembled this package of bits and bobs for you. I truly hope it reaches you. Surely you are longing for things from home, and perhaps these food items will fill your tummy, and the other knitted things will warm you on these cold nights.

Micah, I'm not letting myself get too stirred up about seeing you. I'll believe this is all real when I see your dear face, and hold you. Fair warning, I'm never letting you go!

Be safe, my darling. I will see you in a few short weeks, and we'll never be parted again.

All my love,
Maggie xx"

Led by the twins, the Kingston family rallied together to prepare Micah's package. Loaded with warm clothes, homemade foods and baked goods, knitted socks and scarf, practical items like a new toothbrush, comb, and shaving gear, and many personal items were also added. Letters from almost everyone, writing materials, and everything the family could imagine were loaded into the enormous package. Even a new pair of shoes was stuffed in. Maggie tucked in a poetry book and kept adding postscripts to her letter about the family, Hannah, Jamie, her work, and her love for him. He would be in no doubt as to her true feelings.

Uncle Thomas came to collect it.

"I expect Micah will be flying home on a government or military plane. So, we will have short notice for preparation. I should think he will need time and space after his ordeal. I'm sure you'll give him the love and support he needs, whilst giving him necessary time alone."

They all nodded as Uncle Thomas trudged out with the large package.

Over tea that afternoon, the women discussed sleeping arrangements for Micah when he came home. Jamie was napping, so time was precious before he was on the go again.

"It seems that our rotating bed circumstances will continue throughout this war," Alice commented drily as they considered who to shift where.

"You, Trev, and Jamie should take on our old room permanently," suggested Maggie. "I'm seldom here, and you need the bigger room. I can kip down with Katie, or use her room when she's not here."

"That's awfully kind of you, Mags," thanked her sister. "Now what about Micah? Should we put him in Kenny's room? Both he and Katie are only home on short leaves at the moment. I'm sure Kenny won't mind bunking down in one of the box rooms. Surely, it's more comfortable than life aboard a ship."

"Nana has also offered her flat. She's been on about the three of us to move in with Jamie, but there's not really enough space for us. A baby needs so much gear. Now that he's getting on to a year, it's not just the pram, cot, nappies, and clothes. Now he has so many books and toys – thanks to his Granny and Nana who make such a fuss over him," Tillie said with a smile.

"I've also offered Isla to stay here, to give you some privacy at the flat – if you choose to take it. And just to have her company. I don't like to think of her alone there. But she keeps refusing, saying she wants to stay in the flat for when Trev gets leave."

"It's generous of you, Mum, to offer a place here for Nana. If this Baby Blitz worsens, we should insist. Even though she has a Morrison shelter and isn't ducking into public cover any longer, it would be far safer for her to stop with us. The more the merrier, right Mum?"

"It's no trouble. We love having Isla here. But for now, that's everyone sorted. Let's move your bed upstairs, Maggie. Tillie, we'll have to get you and Trev a larger bed before his next leave."

Tillie blushed.

"Mum, please," she began. "No need to bother about..."

The air raid signal burst into their awkward discussion.

"Oh no," moaned Alice. "Not again."

In an efficient choreography, the women leaped into action, gathering shelter necessities, tea flasks, biscuits, torches, extra blankets, and baby supplies. Within seconds, Alice, Tillie, Jamie, Maggie, and Hannah flew down the kitchen steps, and out the back door to the Anderson.

As they settled snugly onto the familiar, yet freezing cold benches, the buzz of approaching airplanes droned high above them.

"Those are ours," Maggie identified straightaway. "Spits and Hurricanes." Moments later, the engines grew louder.

"Theirs," Maggie named tersely. "Junkers, and perhaps a Messerschmitt or two."

Alice clucked.

"That's amazing, dear. You can recognize them just from the sounds of their engines."

"Too much practice, Mum. And endless lectures. I should hope by now I can identify them."

They huddled together for several hours, hearing the screaming bombs dropping, smelling the cordite, and imagining the damage being inflicted on the city, and worse, the injuries and casualties to the people of London.

"What's the first thing you'll do when the war is over?" Tillie asked desperately in the darkness. "I'm going to take Trevor and Jamie to Hamley's and buy him a brand-new toy. Not that we don't love all the hand-me-downs and homemade things you've given him," she rushed to say. "But a new truck or stuffie as big as him will be just the thing. And then a fancy supper at a restaurant with no rations – a juicy steak, buttery potatoes, and a sticky toffee pudding for dessert."

"My mouth is watering. Leave off, Tillie," Hannah protested. The tea flask had long been empty, and no more food was available. "I want to go to the synagogue with Micah, and organize a memorial service for my parents. Something simple, but a way to honor them."

"That's a lovely idea, Hannah," Alice spoke quietly as the booms and crashes sounded all around them.

"I do too, Hannah. And I'm certain Micah will help."

"After that, I want a big ice cream cone with two scoops – one chocolate and one vanilla," she said with relish.

"Be reckless. Make it three scoops," Tillie added with glee. "What about you, Mum? What will you do first?"

"The most important thing is to have all the Kingstons together under one roof. I have been dreaming about a Sunday roast dinner with all the trimmings. And no one is wearing a uniform. That will make my heart whole again." Alice sighed. "And then, I want to take my sister Shirley to

Claridges for a proper afternoon tea. With cucumber sandwiches, tiny chicken and roast beef ones, too."

"With homemade warm scones, with loads of clotted cream and fresh strawberry jam," Tillie got into the spirit.

"Don't forget the pastries. Little Battenberg cakes, eclairs, berry tarts…my mouth is watering," Maggie added.

"It seems we are all fixed on food," Tillie laughed. "And you Mags. What's tops on your list?"

"After I get demobbed, I will never wear khaki again. And maybe never green either. I want to lie in a bathtub that is filled to the brim with hot water — no lines. And bubbles. Just to stay in there for the longest time, no matter who is knocking on the door."

An ear-splitting screaming noise split the air. Hannah clung to Alice. Maggie was half-relieved, half-jittery not to be able to see the aircraft lights, searching beams, and AA explosions in the sky. Not knowing was killing her. "Then, a hearty meal such as you've all described, before sleeping and sleeping." Her voice came more rapidly. "No early morning PT or drills. Just to put on my dressing gown, and come to a full English breakfast, including proper tea and sugar, real eggs, a rasher of bacon, maybe even a banana or orange," she sighed, and there was a momentary silence. "Heaven. And then a long walk in the park with Micah, looking at flowers — not veg, or artillery making everything look dull and gray."

"Little Jamie here has never even seen a banana or an orange," Tillie said, kissing his head. "Or any fresh fruit, for that matter."

Just then, he woke up from his fitful sleep, and Tillie fed him. Then they passed him around, trying to amuse him with toys and baby songs. He finally fell into a restless sleep.

"It will all be smashing, won't it, when the war is over?" Tillie spoke what was on everyone's minds.

Listening to the blasts above and crashing all around, Maggie couldn't help but wish she was on her ack-ack predictor machine, protecting London with her team's anti-aircraft fire.

At half-past seven, the all-clear sounded.

"I'll stick on the kettle," Alice said, attempting a bright and breezy tone. The rest of the women followed in silence.

CHAPTER TWENTY-SEVEN

April 1944

Maggie asked for compassionate leave when Micah returned to London. Initially denied, but after passionately pleading her case, she was granted a seventy-two-hour pass. She would be too late to meet him, but Uncle Thomas had arranged his transport from the airstrip. Hannah couldn't wait to see Micah, and was the first to greet him. Brother and sister had time to reunite, cry together, and start the long process of healing.

As it happened, Maggie wasn't able to see Micah until five days after his return. She could hardly eat or sleep she was so nervous and apprehensive. Would he be the same Micah she'd known in 1938? Would his war experiences have changed him or his feelings towards her? Was he injured? Traumatized? Would they be awkward together? Did he still love her?

"You're as nervous as a cat," Pip scolded as Maggie restlessly paced the hut, waiting for the transport to Bristol railway station.

"Too right," she replied shortly. "I'm only about to see the man I love, who I haven't seen in almost five years. After he's been through who knows what hell at a Nazi deportation camp. I suppose I should be calm and composed, then?" Maggie snapped and then abruptly stopped pacing. "Oh dear, I'm so sorry, Pip. I didn't mean to shout at you. I'm just that tense."

Pip waved her hand in the air.

"It's forgotten, love. Of course, you are anxious about seeing Micah. There's so much at issue here. But have faith. No matter what the poor man has been through, he has been steadfast in his love for you. Rely on that."

"Thank you, Pip. It's just that I'm the shy one. Tillie is ever so much better at talking and putting people at ease. I fear I will be tongue-tied when I see him."

Pip shook her by the shoulders.

"I wish you would stop weighing yourself against your sister and finding yourself wanting. You are strong and brave – not just the unflinching work you do every day and night, but for your fierce loyalty to those you care about. You are a staunch friend, and I've no doubt you are a caring love to Micah. Have faith in yourself, too, Maggie Kingston."

Maggie couldn't help but brighten. She did have something to offer Micah after all. She was worthy, just for herself. She felt lighter and almost dizzy. She was good enough, even better. She deserved happiness with Micah.

"I suppose you're right. It's just worrisome, having not seen him for so long. I even forget what he looks like sometimes. Has he seen any of my letters? Does he even realize I'm waiting for him, that my feelings are stronger than ever?"

"I'm sure he does, love. Your kind of love transcends time and space. It's had to. And didn't your uncle telegram you that Micah asked to meet you alone first? That sounds proper serious to me. You should stop mucking about in your head, and just get on with it. You'll see in about five seconds how he feels about you."

"Kingston, your transport is here. You can hop on the back of the lorry. But be quick. It leaves in five minutes," an ATS soldier called from the doorway.

Maggie picked up her small holdall, perched her cap atop her head, and smiled at Pip.

"Thanks for the pep talk, love. I feel ever so much better now."

And off she went.

She had asked not to be met at the train station. The army had taught her to move around on her own quickly and efficiently. She was always rushing to catch a train or be back at base by a certain time. And, she wanted to meet Micah alone.

The family had discreetly made plans to be out so the pair could meet privately at home.

It was a cool spring day, one that promised more than it delivered. A few flowers bravely poked their heads out of the cold ground, but the air was still chilly. A lone bird chirped above.

Maggie hurried down the street from the underground, her heart pounding almost out of her chest. She'd freshened up at the railway station as best she could, but wished she was wearing something more alluring than her khaki uniform, heavy lisle stockings, and sensible shoes. But she would go on charge if seen out of uniform.

Bouncing up the stairs to the house, Maggie slowly opened the door to a strangely quiet house. She didn't call out, but just hung up her coat, and walked upstairs to the drawing room where sun poured through the windows. He was there.

Micah stood, held out his arms, and gave her a smile that told her everything would be all right.

Wordlessly, she ran into his arms.

They held each other without speaking for a long moment. Maggie breathed in his scent, his presence, as she clasped him tightly. Her heart calmed and she relaxed muscles she hadn't realized she'd been clenching for years.

"Maggie, little one," he murmured into her hair. She melted against him.

Finally, he held her at arm's length, and drank her in. She saw faint new lines framing his eyes and mouth. Slightly graying hair at his temples spoke of prolonged stress. He needed a haircut. And despite the kindness behind his round spectacles, ghosts haunted his deep brown eyes. He was dreadfully thin. But he was still her same beloved, cherished Micah.

"Micah, I...I don't know what to say. How I've longed for this moment." She found herself choking up as she spoke.

He smoothed her golden hair back from her brow, and bent to kiss her – a sweet lingering kiss that spoke of a mutual ache for each other. His lips were soft, and grew more insistent on hers. He held her tighter and deepened the kiss. He moaned, and it made Maggie's body flutter.

They broke apart shakily, both overcome by the intensity of their emotions. Micah smiled tenderly at her.

"Should we sit? Can I make you some tea?" Maggie was suddenly self-conscious. Damn her shyness.

"Let's sit, but tea can wait," he seemed so calm.

They sat closely together on the sofa, holding hands. Neither wanted to let go of the other.

"How are you feeling? Are you injured?" She examined him closely.

"Not at present," he replied shortly. "But some wounds are deep," he paused. "I'm grateful to be home," he finished simply.

"Micah, I'm so sorry for everything you've been through. And the loss of your parents. We were all devastated. It must have been heartbreaking for you."

"Thank you, darling." He gazed out the window, then was pulled back to her face. "I begged the Nazis to send me in their place. I would have given anything to save them, even my own life. But there's no negotiating with Nazis." Bitterness crept into his voice. "The last time I saw them, my mother was so fearful. They made them wait for hours for their transport with no food or water. Then they filled up a cattle car with hundreds of Jews. All they had was what they wore. Their belongings and valuables had been stripped from them. Mama had stitched some jewels into their coats, so I'd like to believe that bought them a few days of food at Auschwitz." He shrugged. "But I'll never know. Despite many attempts to find out what happened to them and secure their release, I discovered naught. I only received word months later they had died, most likely of tuberculosis."

Maggie held his frail body in her arms, wordlessly. It was his time to speak.

"They were starved, Maggie. Freezing in the winter, boiling hot in the summer. No change of clothes, shaved heads, and numbers tattooed onto their arms. Treated less than human." Tears fell silently down his cheeks.

"The worst is that they were most likely separated at the train station, and almost certainly never saw each other again. Babies are torn from their mother's arms and summarily killed. The weak or infirm the same. Husbands and wives, parents and children – all callously separated.

Poor Mama would have been desolate without Papa. In lice-infested, overcrowded barracks with the harshest of facilities. Papa and Mama, and thousands of others. The world needs to understand what is going on, Maggie. It's evil at its most malignant and vindictive."

Maggie was speechless. Word about the camps had been troubling, but nothing to the horrors that Micah revealed. The British government either didn't acknowledge the level of the atrocities, or chose to censor the most severe reports to keep up English morale.

"You're right, darling. We just didn't know…don't know what is happening on the continent. That doesn't sound like a work camp to me."

Micah wiped his tears and gave her a watery smile.

"Oh, there is plenty of work. Backbreaking hours and hours of it. The sign at the entrance to Auschwitz says *Arbeit Macht Frei* – work makes you free." His voice was harsh. "If you are lucky, you do physical work for twelve, fourteen hours a day, on meager rations of watery soup and a stale piece of bread. If not, you are killed."

Maggie gasped. She couldn't help herself.

"Are you sure of this? Why? How?" she sputtered in disbelief.

"Word seeped through about these camps – they are called concentration camps, Maggie. Hitler wants to exterminate the Jews – all of us. So, he brings us to these camps where we are either worked to death, or killed in the most inhumane ways."

"How is this allowed to happen?" Maggie asked, shocked.

"Because the world doesn't know, can't believe, or won't accept what's really going on," Micah suddenly looked very drained. "But we have to make the world see – and do something."

Maggie held him, utterly dazed.

The grandfather clock in the hall sounded the hour. Micah looked deeply into Maggie's eyes.

"I realize you have questions for me, little one. About my time at Drancy. I just can't answer them right now, and I hope you understand. It's all I can bear to just talk about my poor Mama and Papa. When I'm ready, you are the one who will hear it all."

"I'm just happy you are alive and home safe. And so is Hannah. Take all the time you need," Maggie reassured him.

"Thank you again for taking in my sister. She has told me of all the kindnesses of your family. She's hurting too, but she is young, and has her whole life ahead of her. Thanks to you." Micah smiled a little wider.

"She is family now. We shall always take care of her."

He bent to kiss her again, and Maggie leaned in and poured her heart into the embrace. However long it took, she would help Micah and Hannah heal.

"We have so much to talk about, Maggie. I want to hear all about your war work. I am so proud of you, for doing something so risky. You are the embodiment of wartime heart, my little one," he stroked her cheek.

"And our future together. We have loads to sort. How I am going to provide for you and Hannah for a start. How I can contribute to the war effort. So many plans to discuss. But for now, the precious few hours you are here with me, can we please just spend it together? I want to see you, take in your scent, feel you, embrace you. As I imagined on all those dark nights in France."

Maggie nodded, her heart full.

"I swore that the next time I saw you – if I ever saw you again – I would tell you that I love you. We always danced around this in our letters, but my love for you has been steadfast, and enduring. I love you Margaret Kingston, and one day soon, you will be my wife."

"I love you, too Micah. I always have done, and I always shall do. Everything else follows that," Her brown eyes twinkled. "But I will get a proper proposal, won't I?"

The front door opened, and the family burst in to the sound of tinkling laughter from upstairs.

It was a hero's welcome, but a subdued one, at the Kingston household that night. With the family in mourning for the Goldbachs, everyone was just grateful to have Micah safe in their midst.

Uncle Thomas, Aunt Shirley, and Isla Drummond had been asked not to come this first night. It was boisterous enough with Tillie, Jamie, Mum and Pops, Hannah, and Maggie.

Hannah's eyes never left her brother's face. If he left the room, she followed. Micah tried not to gobble his food, but it was obvious he was still grossly malnourished. He had second helpings of potato soup, Woolton pie, cauliflower, and carrot scones.

Tillie regaled them all with stories of Jamie's adventures learning how to walk, and the tumble he had taken down the stairs to the kitchen. Luckily, he hadn't been injured even though he had practically screamed the house down.

"He can't talk yet, but points at everything and grunts. I'm trying to teach him to say Daddy for the next time Trevor gets leave. He would be so chuffed. But this stubborn little fellow only says Mama. But that also makes me happy," she chattered as she tried to stuff some cauliflower into Jamie's mouth. He promptly spit it out.

"He tries to say Granny," Alice objected. "I'm sure I've heard him say Gaggy or Ganny."

Tillie rolled her eyes at Maggie.

"Sure, Mum. Keep believing that."

Everyone laughed.

"I'm more than a little nervous about this bread pudding. It doesn't have the right amount of sugar, even with us pooling together rations. And you'll have to look mighty hard to find a sultana, but it's the best we could muster, Micah."

"I'm quite sure I shall love it, Mrs. Kingston. Quite sure." He smiled at Maggie, winked at Hannah, and relaxed ever so slightly in his chair.

CHAPTER TWENTY-EIGHT

"How can I let you go, my love? We've just found each other again."

Micah and Maggie held each other tight, ignoring the sights, sounds, and smells of the teeming railway station. Maggie's leave had flown by. Their long-postponed love strengthened with every moment and every hour they spent together.

"It's such a wrench, but needs must, Micah," she sighed as she bent to pick up her travel kit. "And with this big push coming, all leave is canceled. I don't even see when I'll be able to come home again. But it's all toward the same aim – to conquer the Germans for good, and bring back peace and prosperity for us all."

"You're right, little one. And the Bosch should be terrified of you. You are a proper gunner girl. Official and so self-possessed. You're not that little mouse in your sister's shadow anymore, Maggie." He tilted her face for one last kiss.

"Your love sustained me," Maggie replied candidly. "As it will sustain both of us now."

And then she was gone. Micah sat in the station for a while, absorbing the murmurs and hum of voices as tearful goodbyes were said. American accents mingled with those of Scots, English and Welsh from across the tiny but mighty island. Everyone coming together to defeat a common foe.

Finally, he rose to his feet and retraced his steps back home to his sister and his new life back on British soil.

* * *

Maggie jostled her way through the crammed cars, trying to spot a seat. Finding none, she resigned herself to standing all the way back to Bristol. She perched on her bag in the corridor, and leaned back against the moving wall, as it shifted and heaved, rumbling to their destination.

As luck would have it, two stations later, several passengers disembarked, and she scrambled to claim an empty seat. She stowed her bag overhead, and wedged herself next to three Canadian soldiers.

Sitting back, she ignored the smoke and chatter, and lost herself in memories of the last three days. She still felt the warm glow of Micah's love enveloping her like a warm quilt on a frosty winter's day. They'd been inseparable since she got home, walking and talking for hours. They'd only made a start on getting reacquainted, but found their budding love grew more intense with each hour spent together.

Micah, Maggie, and Hannah went for a walk on the second day. Maggie could tell something was on the young girl's mind.

"Hannah, it must be somewhat overwhelming to finally see your brother again. It is for me," Maggie gave the girl a tremulous smile.

Hannah kept close to her brother's side.

"I almost can't believe it, Maggie. I fear letting him out of my sight, and discovering this will all be a dream."

Micah stopped and held both her hands in his.

"It is not a dream, dear sister. I'm here, and I will not leave you." He stole a glance at Maggie who nodded.

"And when we marry, and the war is over, we shall make a home together – all three of us."

Hannah gasped.

"Truly?" she whispered. "That is my dearest wish." She turned to Maggie. "Not that your parents haven't been more than gracious and kind. They have treated me as if I were their own daughter. And this home has been a comfort during these dark days."

"Hush, sweetheart. We won't let anything bad happen to you ever again, Hannah," Maggie soothed her.

"And I will stay with you both? Where shall we live?"

"We have many unanswered questions still, sister. It's difficult to make tangible plans until the war is over – and it will be soon, I know

221

it. But you will be part of our plans, always. Do you feel reassured now? Both Maggie and I want you to understand you are our family, and we must stay together and look after each other."

"I wasn't sure where I fit in any longer. This has steadied me no end. And I shall be no bother. I will help with cooking, cleaning, queuing, whatever you need."

"Shhh, dear sister," Maggie quietened her. "It will all come together as it should, in due time. We have learned to be patient and have developed forbearance beyond what we thought we could manage, haven't we? Just a while longer."

Hannah kissed them both, and the trio walked in contented silence.

Having wasted so much time apart, the couple agreed not to waste another moment. They planned to marry as soon as possible, in a modest ceremony. With the recent death of Micah's parents so fresh and raw, they didn't think a big wedding was appropriate in the circumstances. All the couple wanted was to be together, forever.

Maggie had never felt so completely loved – just for herself. And finally, she felt she deserved it.

The chronic lack of sleep, worsened by only a few hours of snatched rest the last couple of days, had taken their toll. Maggie closed her eyes and fell into a fitful sleep.

She and Micah had stayed up into the late hours of the night, Micah confiding in a halting voice some of the horrors he'd seen. And these images floated through Maggie's half-sleep.

He spoke of the roundup when he and his parents had been woken by loud banging, snarling dogs, and Nazis screaming at them in German. Micah understood a little of what they said – pack your things, ten minutes, one case per person. His Mama stood mute in fear, while the two men quickly gathered what clothes and valuables they could. They had no idea where they were going, but Micah signaled to his father to pack or wear a warm coat. At Nazi prodding, Mama threw some skirts and jumpers into her bag, with some jewels she had sewn into the hems. Micah told them both to wear sturdy boots. Papa had managed to collect a few books, and some food. Within minutes, Nazis waved their guns, ushering them roughly down the stairs and out the front door, which was left swinging.

Micah fleetingly wondered what would become of their little farm. Would the Nazis take it over as a base or headquarters of some sort? Would it be abandoned? Mama had softly cried as Micah couldn't help but think they would never see it again.

On the truck, the little family joined a silent group of other local Jews. Papa nodded at those he knew – it seemed the entire neighborhood had been raided. Nazis stood on guard, poking their rifle barrels at anyone who spoke. Micah could smell the fear amongst the confused people all crushed together. More people crammed into the back of the truck in the next few hours, with lengthy stops to collect more dazed prisoners. They ate a little of what they'd brought, saving as much as possible for an unimaginable later. Without water, the time passed slowly. They traveled north for hours, until the truck stopped abruptly and the travellers were ordered out, and forcefully pushed and shoved into what looked like an abandoned factory or warehouse. There, hundreds of others were gathered, sitting on the concrete floor, clutching their belongings.

The German shouting never ceased.

"Schnell, Schnell!" they screamed over and over, though Micah could not understand the urgency. Everyone just sat in silence. An overpowering stench hung in the crowded room, where an overflowing bucket in an open corner served as a latrine.

Interminable hours later, watery soup and stale bread were passed out. Everyone ate hungrily, grateful for the meager sustenance. Micah urged his parents to rest, so they lay on their belongings and tried to doze.

They waited like that for three days. They received the same meager meals twice a day, with weak tea provided from time to time. After a while, they were allowed to talk. The Goldbachs talked with families they knew from the village, endlessly speculating on where they were going and why.

Loaded onto empty cattle wagons, the train departed. Again, they were herded into dark cars with no seats or windows. They were forced to stand for hours with no food or water, huddled together in the dark, relieving themselves in another brimming soil-can. Women and children wailed while the men tried in vain to comfort them.

Micah had glossed over that wretched journey, saying that it took long hours, with frequent, unexplained stops. Mama had clung to Papa, suffocating from the stench and press of bodies.

When at last they were released from the overcrowded, stinking rail car, they realized they were near Paris. This gave them a false sense of hope that they would be liberated, which was soon shattered, as once again they were ordered into what looked like a half-finished set of flats.

More German screaming, whistle-blowing, barking hounds, and searchlights criss-crossed a central courtyard. It was a rectangle surrounded on three sides by unfinished high-rises where the new prisoners were made to stand. It was mid-day, and they'd had nothing to eat or drink in two days. Strangely, it was a beautiful October day, and the sun beat down on the group, dressed in warm winter clothing.

Men and women were split into different lines where they gave their names and addresses. Little care was taken for proper spellings, or frenzied insistence upon family members being counted together.

Micah and his father were pushed and shoved towards a small tower. They couldn't see where Mama was led, but it was to a different part of the building. Babies and small children were allowed to go with their mothers, but older ones were shuffled sobbing to other towers. All of their bags and suitcases were seized and placed into a giant pile, which Micah eyed with dismay.

Shoved up a staircase that was soiled with human excrement, the men coughed and choked as they tried to make their way up slippery steps to the third floor.

Bursting into a large open room with straw mattresses, Micah and Papa were confronted by a sea of dirty, exhausted faces. The men were welcoming in a ghostly way, and room was made for the newcomers. They learned that this place was called Drancy, and was a transit camp for points eastward. No one knew exactly where they were going, but had been told it was a Jewish repatriation camp in either Poland or Germany.

Micah tried to befriend the guards, pleading for more information, and to determine Mama's plight. He was met with nothing but cold stares and gun pokes.

At that point, in his story, Micah broke down into great, heaving sobs. Maggie could hardly make out his words, but pieced together that three days later, Mr. and Mrs. Goldbach had been deported on the same transport. The oldest people were sent first, and no matter how he tried to beg, barter or bribe – he was left behind as his parents boarded a train for an unknown destination.

Micah tried to make himself invaluable at Drancy, and was soon assigned as the record-keeper of the incoming and outgoing prisoners. He did whatever he could to exempt people from deportation based on age or infirmity, with little success. For every man he saved, another was put in his place. At its peak, a thousand Jews at a time were deported twice a week.

Conditions were appalling, with bedbugs, lice, dysentery and other diseases rampant in the overcrowded quarters. Food was scarce, tasteless and almost without nutrition, but it kept him alive. He tried to help as many inmates as possible, but they just kept coming. Making himself useful to avoid transport, he kept going from day to day – only the thought of Maggie kept him from going insane or throwing himself off the balcony, as many had done.

He and Maggie had cried together until he was spent. He promised to share more later, but was utterly drained. Maggie dried his tears and drew him close.

She woke instinctively just before her stop. The voices buzzed all around her, and the hushed talk was all of the upcoming push. She shook her head to clear the harrowing images of Micah's story.

"I heard that all of the beaches in the south of England that were still open are now closed," commented one of the Canadian soldiers.

"For the incoming troops, transport and munitions to mobilize, I understand," responded another.

Maggie wanted to remind them that *Careless Talk Costs Lives*, like all the posters plastered across London, but she listened intently, nonetheless.

"It's going to be a coordinated attack – by air and sea. We will breach French shores, and take back what doesn't belong to the Germans."

"Hey, mate. You never know who's listening. Best to keep mum" a British officer interjected crisply.

"Sorry, old chap," the Canadian soldier teased.

With a straight face, Maggie fetched her bag from the overhead compartment, and made her way to the door as the train pulled into the station. She stepped down, and made her way to the Lowery farm as dusk settled over the town.

Pip pounced on her as soon as she heard Maggie's weary steps on the stairs.

"How was it? How was Micah? Was he as dishy as you remember?" Pip peppered her friend with questions as Maggie removed her cap and slung her bag on her narrow bed.

Maggie held up a restraining hand.

"Give me a minute, please, Pip. I'm just that fatigued, and I'm still sorting it all in my mind. But I'm happier than I ever thought possible, and Micah is more handsome, kind, and wonderful than I remembered. Satisfied?" She brushed her hair in the communal mirror.

"Not by half, Mags, but that will do for now. Mrs. Lowery held supper for you. Are you hungry?"

"Always. And I adore her cooking. What are we waiting for?"

Despite her exhaustion, there was a new bounce to her step that matched her overall glow, which her friends couldn't fail to notice.

Back at base, the hive of activity was overwhelming. Trucks and other vehicles kept coming and going, and aircraft were flown in daily. The station was near bursting, with soldiers and airmen of all nationalities and branches of service flooding the small base.

"Where they be puttin 'em all?" Addy asked as another dusty truck full of soldiers rumbled down the dirt road.

"Bring 'em on is what I say," Pip grinned wickedly. "Just queue them up by height and weight, and I'll take my pick."

War service hadn't toned down Pip's spirit or appearance. Her uniforms always seemed to strain across her ample bust, and she wore lipstick whenever she could get away with it.

"What about your scouser, Albie?" Maggie asked curiously over a cup of watery tea.

Pip shrugged.

"I'm still writing to him, but he's rubbish at writing back. A girl has to have choice, doesn't she?"

Olive, the new girl snorted.

"Well, you're spoiled for choice round here, that's for sure," Olive chuckled. "I'll stick with my Giles, ta very much."

"Off to drill, girls," Maggie sighed.

They were put through their paces double time, extra drills, more inspections, extra cleaning of the equipment – all to ensure everyone was ready for the big day coming soon. The nation held their collective breath.

CHAPTER TWENTY-NINE

June 1944

The big push. Operation Overlord. D-Day. The coordinated efforts of the Allied forces joined together to reclaim France and occupied regions east.

The operation had been planned for more than two years. Heading up the massive invasion was the American General Eisenhower who had been assigned to lead the Allied invasion of Western Europe six months earlier. This followed his appointment as the commander of the American forces in Britain in June 1942. He had successfully led the Allied invasion of French North Africa, and had been involved in the initial efforts of the Italian campaign, as a partner in the Western European initiative.

Rumored in all allied countries for months, the offensive involved a complicated set of false information being leaked to make the Germans think the invasion was happening at a different time and location. Decoy tanks and airplanes were used to trick German spy planes, a false American army offensive was staged, and fake radio transmissions kept up a false drumbeat to distract the Nazis.

By early June, more than two million Americans soldiers and another 250,000 Canadian troops arrived at the island to join their British comrades in preparation for the Normandy invasion. The American military shipped seven million tons of supplies to the area, including 450,000 tons of ammunition.

It was to be the largest amphibian attack ever attempted. The Allies used over 5,000 ships and landing craft to position more than 150,000 troops on five beaches in Normandy. With code names *Gold, Juno, Omaha,*

Sword, and Utah, the Germans were fooled into thinking the target was Calais, aided by decoy operations set up along the English coast.

The original plan was for intense aerial bombing to obliterate the Nazi guns, and cut off roads and bridges to trap Germany's ability to retreat and ship up reinforcements. Paratroopers would then drop in to targeted locations in advance of British, Canadian, and American troops, who would devastate the blindsided Nazi defenses.

But it didn't quite happen that way.

First of all, the weather did not cooperate. The original invasion was planned for June 5, 1944, but was postponed by a day due to volatile weather. There were only a few ideal dates, all predicated on a full moon illuminating the landing places for gliders, and a low tide to expose German underwater defenses.

Though the weather was hardly better the next day, the order was given to invade Normandy's beaches. The aim was to breach Hitler's 2,400-mile Atlantic Wall, built over two years, armed with bunkers, landmines, and a multitude of obstacles. The Allies hoped to surprise the Germans who would not be expecting an invasion in such awful conditions.

As it happened, the day went horribly wrong in many ways. The aerial bombing did not do the required damage to Nazi bunkers. Paratroopers were blown off course, and many were killed as they hit the water. The stormy waters made the amphibious landings treacherous, and many were sunk and men lost as they failed to meet their destinations. Nazi anti-aircraft fire was fierce, causing enormous casualties.

Despite more than two thousand American troops killed, wounded or reported missing after the stormy all-day ordeal at Omaha beach, by nightfall the Allies managed to capture it. Following a horrific landing, the Canadian troops succeeded in driving the Nazis inland at Juno. They suffered an almost fifty percent casualty rate, and added to the other invasion points, over four thousand Allied soldiers lost their lives fighting for victory at Normandy.

But overall, it was a tremendous success. The Allies ultimately unloaded 2,500,000 men and hundreds of thousands of tons of supplies to continue the advance towards Germany. France was liberated.

That was a major turning point in the war.

* * *

Trevor was re-assigned to a Portsmouth base to assist with returning damaged bombers and injured fighters, and to cope with any blazes set by Nazi Luftwaffe or anti-aircraft retaliatory barrage. Working for seventy-two hours straight, he and his teammates put out blaze after blaze, and fought fire damage of the returning aircraft, limping home with burning fuselages. Again and again, the British and American flyers were sent back over the Channel after being patched up and declared fit for duty.

Exhausted, sweaty, and jubilant, he and the lads celebrated with a few pints at the local NAAFI, proud of their contributions to the Normandy invasion. Stumbling back to his tent, covered in perspiration and grime, he penned a semi-coherent letter to Tillie, declaring his undying love for her and Jamie, and vowing to return home to them as soon as humanly possible.

* * *

Speeding back from North African waters, Kenny's Royal Navy ship was one of many bombardment warships to attack the German defenses on D-Day. Returning to active duty, Kenny was witness to the devastation firsthand – to his fellow naval officers aboard, as well as seeing ships blown up, and men stranded or shot in the stormy waters. He considered himself lucky to have survived the day, and celebrated with an extra shot of rum together with his team, trying to forget those horrific images.

He thought longingly of the girl he'd met at the last port, and raked a hand through his mucky hair, grinning to himself. With any luck, he'd find another smashing blonde on his next shore leave.

* * *

Huddled next to the radio, Thomas and Shirley Fowler quietly cheered for the Allied efforts taking France back and pushing Germany further east.

Tears poured down Shirley's cheeks as she thought of her son,

Geoffrey, killed on the beaches at Dunkirk. This victory would never bring back her son, but it was a small but sweet taste of vengeance.

Thomas patted his wife's hand.

"As Prime Minister Churchill famously said: *This is not the end. This is not even the beginning of the end. But perhaps it is the end of the beginning.*" He puffed on his pipe. "This may actually be the beginning of the end. I should think we've jolly well done it, dear. This calls for a sherry."

* * *

With her radio set glued to her head, Katie Kingston took down scrambled messages on German frequencies. Coming fast and furious, she barely took a break. After a twelve-hour shift with no German U-boats to report, Katie sat back, ripped off her radio set, and beamed around the smoke-filled room, teeming with operators, decoders, and supervisors.

"Three cheers for the Allies."

* * *

Tillie picked up Jamie, grabbed Hannah by the hand, and danced around the kitchen with a big smile on her face.

"The war is ending, the war is ending," she chanted over and over again. "And Daddy's coming home. Daddy's coming home." She threw Jamie up in the air, and they all fell into giggles.

"Is it really so, Tillie?" Hannah asked with wide eyes. "Is the war over? Will Trevor and Maggie and well – everyone – be coming home soon?" Her eyes shone with excitement.

"I don't know exactly when, Hannah, but this is a major victory for the Allies. Surely, Hitler and his abominable Gestapo, SS and the entire Nazi military might will give way. They can't hold fast with so much of the world marshaled against them."

"I believe you, Tillie. It will all be over soon. Then I can have chocolate every day."

"And Jamie too," agreed Tillie. "The poor love has never had it. He won't know what to do with all the sweets we'll be feeding him."

They laughed again.

* * *

Upstairs, Micah sat in his room with Robbie in his lap. He heard the commotion below, and smiled as he rhythmically patted the chubby gray cat.

His talks with Maggie brought the couple closer, but were extraordinarily painful. He had kept the bleakest memories to himself – not because he didn't trust Maggie, because he did – it was just so raw and agonizing to relive the grim months at Drancy that he could only reveal them bit by bit.

Hearing the commotion downstairs brought back the sounds of deportees waiting for their turn to depart. Rather than laughter, it had been screams and sobbing as families were torn apart. Businessmen, lawyers, musicians, doctors, and shopkeepers were humiliated and subjected to body searches, hours of standing for roll calls, sub-human hygienic conditions, starvation, and violent treatment by gendarmes and Gestapo.

His own treatment over the months at Drancy had been scarcely better. Because of his excellent performance in managing the lists, and never complaining about the abhorrent conditions, he made himself useful whenever he could. His accommodations were in a separate part of the camp, a fraction less horrific than the deportees' were, and he received a slightly better ration, which he shared either with the children or with the frail and handicapped.

Exempted from daily roll calls, Micah was worked to the bone, from early morning to late at night. He didn't care – it was a distraction from the hopelessness and horror he and his inmates experienced day in and day out.

He thanked God every day that he had organized Hannah's escape. He was constantly grateful for the fact that she was sitting downstairs after enjoying a full and nutritious meal, with fresh clean clothes, and a safe roof over her head. If she had been with Papa and Mama, she would almost certainly have perished alongside them. This had to mean something in this chaotic and jangled world. He would protect his younger sister with his life, for the rest of his days. He was more than content that Maggie felt the same way and included Hannah in all their future plans.

He put down the cat and went downstairs to join his new family.

* * *

Walter, Alice, and Isla Drummond sat with tea, listening to King George VI.

"After nearly five years of toil and suffering, we must renew that crusading impulse on which we entered the war and met its darkest hour. We and our Allies are sure that our fight is against evil and for a world in which goodness and honor may be the foundation of the life of men in every land."

"Very moving, I must say. And His Majesty is sounding more himself with every speech." All Britons had felt the King's discomfort as he stuttered during his war speeches. "He's a fine wartime sovereign," Walter declared with satisfaction.

"I agree, Walter," Isla smiled. Although she missed her only son Trevor desperately, she was fiercely proud of the work he was doing, and had done in the four years of this terrible war. She prayed every night for his safety, and cherished every letter and short visit. And now she had young Jamie to spoil and love. Life would soon be wonderful again, wouldn't it? They could start making plans for a future without air raids, rationing, and loved ones far away. Couldn't they?

* * *

Alice wiped away a tear as her knitting needles clicked furiously. She thought of her children risking their lives to win this war, Maggie on the ack-ack guns, Kenny at sea serving with the navy, and young Katie clerking for the WRNs. She couldn't be prouder of them, though constantly worried for their lives. Tillie had more than done her bit for the ambulance, and was a marvelous mother and wife, keeping up morale at the sometimes-depressing Kingston home.

* * *

At the gun park, the squads were called out time and again. Only a few German planes soared across the channel, dropping bombs and creating havoc. Filton Airfield in Bristol contributed to the onslaught along the Normandy coast, shooting guns into the sky, pushing the enemy bombers away from England's shores.

Wheedling a lift back to their boarding house, the girls were tired but happy. Addy and Pip chattered about the high number of servicemen who had passed through their station. They had no idea of the extent of the wounded yet, but word of the Allied capture of the coast had trickled back, and was received with joy and pride. She hoped Kenny and Katie had done their part without injury. She wouldn't hear for weeks, probably. But somehow it cheered her to think they were pulling together for a common good, even if their posts and duties were completely different.

Maggie was immensely thankful that Micah was safely home in England. It was wretched enough being separated from him again. But to worry for his safety in a France under attack would have been unbearable. She scribbled him a short letter before stumbling into bed without even washing her face. Her last thought before sinking into a dreamless sleep, was that it would surely all be over in a matter of months, if not weeks. Then life could truly begin for all the Kingstons and those they loved.

* * *

And then, Germany retaliated by launching V1 rocket bombs toward London.

CHAPTER THIRTY

"Steady on, dear. Take a breath,"
Tillie pushed her hair back from her face, chest heaving from running until her heart almost burst out of her chest to reach home.

She had burst through the door, calling for Alice at the top of her lungs. Alice had come running, fear choking her.

"Mum, it was frightening. It almost hit me," she panted, still out of breath. Her eyes were wild, and her hand flew to her throat. She had a stitch in her side from running.

"There, love. Come down to the kitchen for a cup of tea, and you can tell me what's happened," she soothed calmly. But inside, Alice was shocked.

"Where's Jamie? Where's my baby?" Tillie's eyes darted around the front hallway.

"Shh, love. He's having his nap. He's just fine."

"Sorry, Mum. I'm just that shook up."

A cup of tea and two biscuits later, Tillie had quietened down.

"Mum, I was walking back from the shops. Thank heavens I wasn't standing in a queue. I heard the buzzing – it sounded almost like a motorbike. I ducked into a street shelter straightaway. They say that if you hear the V1, and then it stops – you're done for. Once you hear it, you have fifteen seconds to take cover. If it falls directly on top of you, you're dead." She shivered.

"I saw a young couple hurrying across the road. The engine cut out. I kept expecting to see them rush into the shelter. But they didn't make it, Mum. They didn't make it. And there was nothing left of them. Just gone." Tillie was shaking. "It could have been me."

"These bloody doodlebugs. Just when we were thinking we'd beaten Hitler, he devises a new way to torture us."

"Mum, to hear you swear, my goodness," Tillie raised an eyebrow and attempted a feeble smile.

"It just makes me so furious, Tils. These new revenge rockets coming across – and with no pilots. How evil to conceive such a thing," she tutted, shaking her head. "That first attack on Grove Road was such a blow. All those people killed and injured. It brought back such dreadful memories of the Blitz."

The nation had not seen it coming. The first V1 attack had come unexpectedly on June 13th – a week after D-Day. The pilotless missiles had been launched from the French and Dutch coasts. With limited range, their main target was London. The flying bomb seriously damaged many houses, and completely decimated the train line from Liverpool Street to Stratford. Six people had been killed, and forty-two injured. It had escalated the war to a new level.

Less than a week later, over 120 soldiers had been killed and a further 140 injured by a flying bomb at Guards' Chapel on Birdcage Walk – terrifyingly close to Buckingham Palace. The roof collapsed, and the smashed remains of walls had trapped dozens. It had been a tricky rescue, and a devastating loss. Truly sobering.

"But it won't bring our spirits down, will it, Mum? We can see the end now. And Hitler is afraid. We have taken back France, and it's just a matter of time until he's defeated."

Alice patted her daughter's hand.

"Naught can beat us down. We've been through so much; we will not chuck up the sponge now. But I'm so sorry you had such a fright, love. And that poor young couple. With their whole life ahead of them."

"And Mum, when I came out of the shelter, there was a hole – a crater in the middle of the road – right where they were standing."

V1 flying bombs or buzz bombs had been under German production for quite some time. Launched by a ramp or specialized aircraft, they were powered by pulse jet engines, giving them a speed of over 300 miles per hour.

Using a guidance system, they flew for a pre-determined amount of time, then the engines would stop and the bombs dropped in a steep dive toward their target.

Many did not reach their mark, but countless did, causing damage and havoc to a long-suffering capital. But it just made Londoners more determined than ever to win this war.

"You have such a brave spirit, Tillie dear. You have a buoyant ability to recover."

Tillie gave a short laugh.

"I'm not sure about that, Mum. We just have to carry on, don't we? What keeps me going is my love for Trevor and Jamie – and all of you, too," she amended. "And planning for the future. Trev and I have been talking about where we are going to live after the war." Tillie had been loath to bring up the subject, but the timing seemed right.

Alice felt a pang. Her married daughter would be aching to make a home of her own, but it was too soon. She didn't even have her whole family gathered together yet. But this was part of life.

"You realize that you, Trev and the baby are welcome to stay here as long as you like. There's no need to scurry away. I'll miss that little angel so much when you go," she bit her lip. She had gotten so used to seeing him every day. Watching Jamie grow and learn new things had been a joy for her. She mentally shook herself.

"He's hardly an angel," Tillie snorted, helping herself to another raisin crisp. "But he is a dear little love, isn't he? Thanks Mum, you and Trev's mum have been such a tremendous help since he was born. I couldn't have done it without you. It's been so hard without Trev. But it's time for us to start our life as our own little family. I long for my own space – tiny as it might be, with my own kitchen, putting up wallpaper and curtains and such. I need a place to put my own stamp on, don't I?" She shrugged. "You understand, Mum."

"Yes, love. What do you have in mind?"

"They've been talking about these new pre-fabricated homes for after the war. Trev thinks that might be a first-rate idea for us. Supposed to be fairly small, they will have an indoor bathroom and central heating."

"What luxury," Alice gushed.

"Mum, there's an exhibition at the Tate gallery, showing five different housing styles. Would you fancy having a look with me?"

"I'd love it, Tils. Then you can really tell if one of them might suit you. It sounds mad fancy." They both laughed.

The baby cried, and Tillie sprung up to tend to him, needing to inhale his soft, warm baby scent and hold him close after her near-death ordeal.

As she cuddled her son, Tillie forced her mind to think of something happy. Maggie had written her saying that on her next leave – in a fortnight's time – she and Micah were getting married. She wanted something simple at the local registry office, with just the immediate family.

Tillie was determined to make the occasion a little more festive. After all, it was her sister's wedding day, and she wanted it to be memorable, even in wartime.

Conferring with the women at home, Alice agreed with Tillie. They decided to set up a small wedding breakfast or dinner at home after the simple ceremony. Aunt Shirley and Isla had joined them for tea and planning. It was a warm June day, and the women all wore light cotton dresses, as the curtains gently blew in the humid kitchen.

"We can combine our rations to make it as lovely as possible. It will just be us. Maggie said no friends," Tillie started.

"No friends?" Aunt Shirley exclaimed. "What about her friends from the ack-ack that she has written about? Pip and Addy, and that new girl, Olive? Or her mates from the WVS, or Lyons even?" Shirley was appalled.

"She had a hard time getting leave, so it's impossible for any more of the squadron to be let off – even for the day. As for her other mates – she doesn't think it's quite right during wartime to have such a big do. And you know Maggie, she doesn't like a fuss, that's the real reason," Tillie explained.

"Too right," Hannah agreed. "Both she and Micah want to keep it small." She herself didn't want to subject her fragile brother to a big crowd having to put on a bright face and make conversation with lots of strangers.

"That's settled then," Alice declared. "So that's me and Pops, Hannah, Uncle Walter, Aunt Shirley, Isla, and Tillie – you and Jamie. What about Trevor? Will he be able to get leave?" Alice paused in her tick list.

"I rather doubt it, Mum. He's busier than ever with all these V1 rockets being blasted towards Britain. So many fires to extinguish, and the resulting destruction has the firefighters working day and night. It seems that London is a major target for Jerry, so I'm hoping against hope Trevor will be transferred here. Then, at least he'll be closer to home."

Alice nodded but said nothing. He would be nearer to bombs and danger, too.

"Neither Katie or Kenny can get home on such short notice. So that's eight altogether," Alice tallied. "Plus, Maggie and Micah, of course. Seems very modest." She was thinking of Tillie's larger wedding and party.

"That's what she wants, Mum," Tillie insisted gently. "Now as far as dress, Mags is insisting on wearing her uniform. I suggested she filch some parachute silk to make a wedding gown, but she turned me down flat. What can we do to make a fuss over her?" She handed blocks to Jamie, distracting him from pulling Robbie's tail.

"Can we get some flowers or a posy? And for certain, we can give her hair some nice curls and share whatever makeup we've got between us," Hannah offered. "I've been saving a scrap of bubble bath from before the war. She can have a nice soak with it the night before."

"That's grand, love. And I've put by a bit of lace for a handkerchief for her. She'll need something to make her feel like a bride, after all," Isla offered, as she picked up her boisterous grandson, and bounced him on her knee.

"That sounds splendid. I'll take a look in my jewel case for something she can borrow. Perhaps my diamond brooch given to me by my mother on my own wedding day," Alice suggested.

"I'm sure she'd love that, Mum. As far as what the rest of us will wear, I expect it's going to be make do and mend. We'll have a good rummage and find something we can cut down for Hannah. Something old will have to do for the rest of us. But certainly, none of these dratted utility garments. Something from before the war."

As the years had dragged on, the government had introduced lines of utility clothing that citizens could purchase with ration coupons. They were very plain, in just a few styles, and with little to no adornment, they were unpopular but necessary. It was disconcerting to see other women on the streets wearing the same dress in one of the only few available colors. But, at the same time, prices were reduced so anyone could purchase a decent cotton dress or a coat. The Kingston women had avoided them, but at the same time, they were sick to death of their pre-war dresses, or mended and worn hand-me-downs.

They all groaned in sympathy.

"It is Maggie's day, after all. We mustn't outshine her," Alice chided gently.

Tillie burst into gales of laughter.

"Chance is a fine thing, Mum. Maggie will be that beautiful, despite the horrid khaki uniform. She's finally marrying the man she loves. No one will be looking at the rest of us."

Hannah smiled as she patted Robbie, who had grown quite chubby with all the love at the Kingston house.

"And there's the Lyons cake and all. I'll chat to Alfie to sort it," Tillie put in, as she snatched her son before he toppled a vase to the ground.

The women chatted companionably about what food would make the wedding breakfast as special as possible.

"Maggie loves her sausage rolls, but with sausage now on the ration, that's out of the question. Even if they even resembled real meat. The best we can muster is Sardine Rolls," Alice moaned. "I heard the recipe on *The Kitchen Front* on the radio."

"That sounds just fine, love," Isla encouraged. "I suppose spam fritters or some type of fishcakes will have to do."

"Please no Woolton Pie," Tillie balked. "I don't think I can stomach it."

"Alright love," Alice agreed. "What else? I suppose we'll round out the table with veg – the usual sprouts, cabbage, and perhaps some early peas or runner beans?"

"I'll have a word with the butcher and see if he can put by a bit of chicken that we can stretch with some potatoes. And I'll nose around for a spot of cheese. I'm sure we'll all do our best for our Maggie."

The women smiled.

And two weeks later, all went according to plan.

"Well, Maggie, now it's your turn," Tillie said as she put the finishing touches on Maggie's golden hair. Still shorter than Tillie's, she left it loose and the blonde locks shone with fresh washing, a night of pin curls, and Tillie's brush-out. "How are you feeling?"

"I can't bear having any attention on me, so I'm relieved that it's just the family, if I'm honest. And Micah and I like things simple. He still has so much on his mind; he doesn't feel comfortable around a good deal of people. He gets proper fidgety and jumpy. To answer your question, I'm feeling marvelous. I'm finally marrying the man I've waited for all these years. He's been returned to me. I couldn't be happier," Maggie beamed.

"Are you nervy about the wedding night, darling? I can fill you in on the magic of married life."

Maggie held up a hand.

"No, darling. I've already experienced a glimpse of what it can be, and I want to discover the rest for myself."

Alice and Isla entered Maggie's small room, looking lovely in their pre-war summer dresses, carrying presents.

"Darling, you look lovely," Alice said with a catch in her voice. "I've brought you the brooch my Mum gave me. It's for your something borrowed."

Maggie was touched.

"Thank you, Mum. I always admired this brooch. I used to sneak into your room and try it on when I was little." She was delighted to see the small diamond brooch in the shape of a bow. "I'm not meant to wear it on my uniform, but no one will report me, I should think," Maggie smiled.

"And here's something new I crocheted for you, dear. It's old lace, but a new handkerchief," Isla handed it to the bride.

"How lovely. Thank you, Mrs. Drummond. I suppose my something old is this uniform," Maggie shrugged.

Hannah burst in holding a spray of bluebells.

"And here's your something blue, dear Maggie," she grinned.

Maggie felt a lump in her throat.

"You've all gone to so much bother. It's so sweet. I can't thank you enough."

"This is a special day. We don't want you to ever forget it, or how much you are loved," Tillie hugged her twin.

"And I never will," Maggie replied simply.

An hour later, a radiant bride in her ATS uniform and a handsome groom in a loose-fitting suit, exchanged simple vows at the local registry office. Though the ritual was brief, love still filled the air, and the couple kissed with the promise of much happiness to come.

Stepping out into the warm June sunshine, Mr. and Mrs. Goldbach turned to each other and smiled. Holding hands, and bursting with long-held back emotions, they stood at the top of the steps, gazing down at the waiting family, beaming in their finest, ready to throw rice on the newlyweds.

"Shall we go, little one? It's our time now."

ReadMore

Press

DISCOVERING THE NEXT BESTSELLER

Would you like a FREE WWII historical fiction audiobook?

This audiobook is valued at 14.99$ on Amazon and is exclusively free for ReadMore Press' readers!

To get your free audiobook, and to sign up for our newsletter where we send you more exclusive bonus content every month,

Scan the QR code

Readmore Press is a publisher that focuses on high-end, quality historical fiction. We love giving the world moving stories, emotional accounts, and tear-filled happy endings.

We hope to see you again in our next book!

Never stop reading, Readmore Press

ACKNOWLEDGEMENTS

Writing Maggie's experiences in World War II was fascinating for me. Of course, I wanted to continue with Tillie's love story, and to tie up loose ends with other treasured characters from *The War Twins of London*. From your correspondence, I knew you wanted more, and were eager to find out what happened to the rest of the Kingston family.

I wanted Maggie to come into her own, as the shyer twin who finds her voice and strength serving in the Auxiliary Territorial Services. After much research, I decided that the role of ack-ack girl would suit her perfectly, and give her the opportunity to shine. I also wanted to cast a spotlight on the vital work that these gunner girls performed under the worst of conditions.

It was important to explore what happened to the Jews in WWII France. As Micah and his family were stranded in the unoccupied French zone, I needed to research the terrifying history of roundups, detention camps, and transport to work camps like Auschwitz. This tragedy can never be forgotten and is an important element to the Kingston family saga.

Diving into World War II history is mesmerizing and overpowering at the same time. Deciding what to include and how to integrate it into Maggie and Tillie's stories seemed like a never-ending journey. As always, I am determined to be as factually accurate as possible, while giving you a taste for a *day in the life* of these incredible women.

I'd like to thank my two British fact-checkers. Roy Williamson and Jeremy Clinch provided rich details to enhance my story, while keeping me honest to the facts and daily London life.

Here are some of the critical sources I mined to make *A Burning London Sky* as powerfully realistic as possible:

Brown, Gordon. *Wartime Courage, Studies of Extraordinary Courage by Exceptional Men and Women in World War Two*. Bloomsbury Publishing, 2008.

Brown, Mike and Harris, Carol. *The Wartime House, Home Life in Wartime Britain 1939-1945*. The History Press, 2011.

Gray, Andrew & Timereel Studios. *London's War During WWII*. BFS, 2012. (DVD)

Christophe, Francine. *From A World Apart, A Little Girl in the Concentration Camps*. University of Nebraska Press, 2000.

Jeffreys, Alan. *London at War, 1939-1945, A Nation's Capital Survives*. Imperial War Museum, 2018.

Karlsen, Chris. *The Ack Ack Girl*. Books To Go Now, 2021.

Knight, Katherine. *Spuds, Spam and Eating for Victory, Rationing in the Second World War*. The History Press, 2011.

Nicholson, Virginia. *Millions Like Us, Women's Lives During the Second World War*. Penguin Books, 2012.

Ninepence Net. *Roof Over Britain, The Official Story of the A.A. Defenses, 1939-1942*. The Stationary Office, Ltd., 2001.

Waller, Maureen. *A Family in Wartime, How the Second World War Shaped the Lives of a Generation*. Imperial War Museum, Conway, 2012.

Wellers, Georges. *From Drancy to Auschwitz*. M. Graphics Publishing, 2011.

Wynn, Stephen. *City of London at War, 1939-1945*. Pen & Sword Military, 2020.

I'm also thankful for all the online resources, videos, first-hand accounts, podcasts, and so much more at the Imperial War Museum and BBC archives.

Made in the USA
Monee, IL
06 December 2024